MADDY MADRIGAL MYSTERIES BOOK 2

SOMEWHAT MAGIC

DEBRA CASTANEDA

SHADOW CANYON
press

ISBN: 979-8-9903956-7-1
Edited by: Lyndsey Smith, Horrorsmith Editing
Cover design by: Jacqueline Sweet

To my husband Jim, the love of my life
and Alpha Reader extraordinaire.

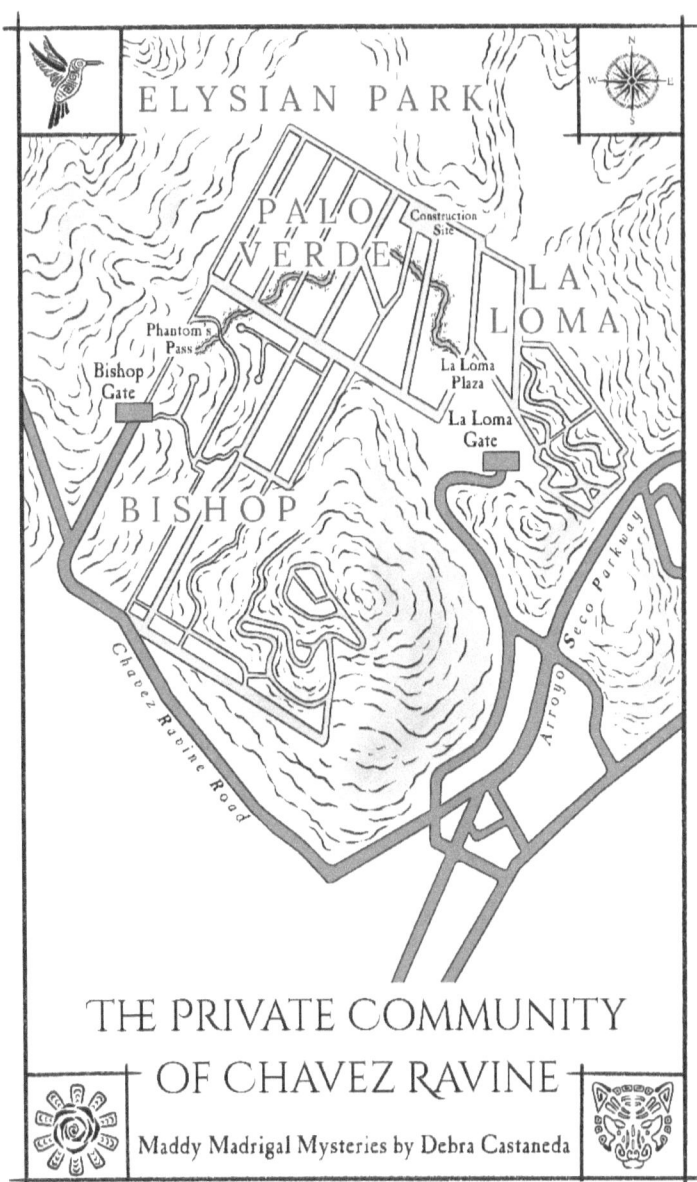

ELYSIAN PARK

N
W E
S

PALO VERDE

Construction Site

LA LOMA

Phantom's Pass

Bishop Gate

La Loma Plaza

La Loma Gate

BISHOP

Chavez Ravine Road

Arroyo Seco Parkway

THE PRIVATE COMMUNITY
OF CHAVEZ RAVINE

Maddy Madrigal Mysteries by Debra Castaneda

Chapter 1

Spending a few years with the LAPD's Occult Affairs Division teaches one to expect the worst. Wrestling with Mexican fairies, being chased by trolls, and fending off attacking nixies develops a heightened sense of danger. One finds themselves looking for things that are out of place, for slight disturbances which might indicate an entity eruption is imminent.

And often, finding them is easy.

So even though I had been out of the force for months, I immediately recognized the little indentation in the field for what it was.

And that's when a soccer game turned into a disaster. Unfortunately for Clare Wells.

When Clare invited me to her game, it seemed to signal a turning point in our relationship: Stu's daughter had finally warmed up to me. Stu and I were sitting in the bleachers, watching the sixteen-year-old play. She was good—fast, nimble, and focused.

So centered that when the small hole opened in the middle of the field and tar started bubbling out, she didn't even notice. In fact, nobody did.

Except me. Also, we were just half a mile away from a recent emergence at the La Brea Tar Pits.

So, I wasn't the least bit surprised when a small head popped out of the black ooze, followed by bony shoulders and a twisted body.

I jumped to my feet and began shouting, "Run, Clare, run!"

Which did nothing.

People yell things like that all the time at soccer games. I had to try something else.

"Clare! Get off the field! Everyone, off the field!"

That worked.

Stu caught on first and rushed down the bleacher stairs.

The game gradually stopped. The girls stared at the rapidly expanding pool of tar.

More small shapes pulled themselves out of the pit, some rolling around and wailing in distress. Others lurched to their feet, arms outstretched in a Frankenstein parody.

And that's when the girls in their blue and gold soccer uniforms began to run, except for Clare, who had the bad luck of being closest to the pit.

One of the things hopped toward her and threw its arms around her waist. Right about then, Stu reached her and started to pull the creature off his daughter. I ran too. Straight for my Jeep in the parking lot.

It didn't take long to find what I was looking for: the entity smoke bomb I kept in my glove box. With the rubber pouch in hand, I dashed back to the field, where Stu was still trying to pry bony little hands from a shrieking Clare's waist.

The rest of the crowd was yelling and rushing for the parking lot at top speed. Only Stu and Clare were left on the field, surrounded by a growing mob of sticky, knee-high figures. The thing clutching Clare wasn't making any attempt to bite her, but it wouldn't let go either.

I threw the rubber pouch onto the ground and gave it a good stomp. A purple mist rose into the air. Humans were immune to the stuff, but the scientifically derived compound nicknamed "Smoke Bomb" had an immediate effect on most entities.

The tar-covered biped attached to Clare went limp and fell to the ground.

Her reaction was interesting. One minute, Clare was panting and screaming, trying to break free, and the next moment, she was furious. Fists clenched, she ran toward the slack form on the ground, screeching words I was surprised she knew. Stu intervened just before she kicked it. He wrapped his arms around her waist and pulled her away from the field.

I didn't exactly blame her for getting pissed off. The entity hadn't hurt her, but it must have been terrifying all the same.

In the distance, sirens wailed. It wouldn't be long before Occult Affairs officers rolled up. There had been no need for me to call the LAPD's emergency number; the heatmap tracking entity arrivals must have lit up like a Christmas tree, and since Jo was working, she had sent the cavalry.

I looked at Stu standing in the shade of a tree, his arm around Clare. She was sobbing. It was best to give them some father-daughter space.

Stu and I were still in the early stages of our relationship, and I swear Clare did everything she could to make sure it stayed that way. Which, honestly, was fine by me. Two months into my job as head of security for the Chavez Ravine Homeowner's Association, I was plenty busy, and Stu had his hands full running a security firm with a growing celebrity clientele.

So, for now, neither of us needed the distraction of a relationship. Still, I looked forward to the day when Clare would allow her father to stay out past nine o'clock without text bombing him.

A few Occult Affairs officers ran over, hands on the Smoke Bomb pouches dangling from their belts.

Bailey Nixon reached me first, which was no surprise. She was an avid runner and kept herself in good shape. As always, her copper hair was pulled back, and she wore minimal makeup, except for a shimmery shadow ringing her brown eyes. Today, it was a bright blue matching the clear sky.

"Hey, Mads! Surprised to see you here. What are they?" Bailey asked.

"Well, we won't know for sure until all that tar is cleaned off, but considering their size and beards, I think we're looking at goblins."

"Goblins!" Bailey echoed. "We haven't seen those before, have we?"

"Not for a long time. Fairies, the odd brownie, and the elves that appeared in that maternity ward during the nurse's strike…But very few goblins. Until now, if I'm right."

"Lucky you were here." Bailey turned to the approaching officers. "Hey, guys, Maddy's got it under control. How about bringing some crates? The medium ones ought to do it."

Bailey was the youngest officer in Occult Affairs, and she wasn't their boss, but that didn't stop her from taking charge. I had always liked that about Bailey. She stepped up and got things done.

"How's it going back at the farm?"

Bailey sighed. "It sucks. Except for Jo. I *love* Jo. But the chief? He's such an asshole." She paused, biting her lip. "When you left, it got me rethinking my choices. I'm going to start looking around. Life is too short to put up with that jerk. So, if anything opens up where you are, I'd…be interested." Bailey's pale, freckled face turned pink. She wasn't normally the blushing type, so that must have been hard for her to say.

"I just hired some security guards," I said. "But you're way overqualified for a guard shift. But I'll tell you what: if anything better opens up, I'm calling you."

Bailey brightened. "Awesome!"

4

I walked past officers stuffing sticky, dazed entities into crates and went to find Stu and Clare. They were in the nearly empty parking lot. Most of the other families had gone, but Stu stood next to his fancy SUV with tinted windows.

Clare was leaning back in the passenger seat, hands over her face, crying softly.

Stu slid an arm around my waist. "I'm not sure what we would have done if you hadn't been here," he said into my ear.

I wasn't sure either. It was fairly rare for a new arrival to grab a civilian, so there were no protocols for that. "Is she okay?"

Stu took my elbow and steered me away from the SUV. "She'll be fine," he replied in a low voice. "But ever since her mother and I split, any little blip seems to throw her for a loop. It's like she's three again, and if you give her the pink cup instead of the purple cup, she just sort of falls apart, you know?"

My own teenage years of living with a mother who was exploring her psychic abilities and her flair for PR had caused me overwhelming embarrassment and anxiety. Stu's wife had slept with Clare's best friend's father, which, arguably, was worse than having a self-absorbed psychic for a mother. Clare had earned the right to freak out.

"Stu, this whole entity thing is a lot scarier when it happens to you. She's in shock. Take her home, get her some pizza, and watch some sappy movies."

Stu's shoulders sagged. "You make it sound so easy."

True that. I wasn't her parent and all that came with it, but there was no reason for him to expect her to bounce right back. Hell, even Occult Affairs officers got a mental health day after their first attack.

"Stu," I said firmly. "She's been traumatized, okay? A creepy-ass goblin slithered out of a tar pit and grabbed her. Take

5

her home and baby her a little. She'll be fine. Come on, don't be a jerk."

Stu's mouth opened, then closed. A moment later, he laughed. "I guess I needed to hear that. Maybe if I'm really good, she'll even allow us to spend some time alone."

Without looking back to see if his daughter was watching, Stu leaned in for a kiss. A voice called from the car.

"*Dad!*"

Chapter 2

When I caught up with her, Julia Suarez was in the middle of a hushed conversation with the woman behind the counter of the botanica in downtown Los Angeles. As usual, Julia was impossible to miss—tall and majestic, with auburn hair held back by a yellow headband matching her flowing top.

My Spanish wasn't as good as hers, but Julia was asking about Santa Muerte—or Holy Death—the folk saint personifying the afterlife. Several figurines of the skeletal woman holding a scythe stood on a shelf, one draped in gold brocade embroidered with red roses.

Julia smiled when she saw me. "You've got to buy her!"

Did I mention Julia was a little impulsive? We had come to buy crystals and herbs, not the saint of death who came with a bunch of unspoken rules.

Besides, my great-aunt Lencha Bantacorte, the famous bruja who had somehow become my magic coach, had not mentioned Santa Muerte even once in her journals. In fact, Lencha hardly mentioned any saints at all.

Warily, I eyed the Santa Muerte statuette. She exuded an aura of grim authority. I knew little about her, but she demanded respect. Definitely not for beginners like me.

"We're sticking to our list," I said firmly.

Julia sighed, then pulled out her phone and checked her notes. "Okay. I'm looking for the rocks and crystals. You're getting the herbs and candles, yeah?" She grabbed a basket and headed toward a wall of bins.

The clerk, a stern-looking woman around my age, wearing a red smock, held up a small mortar and pestle made of stone.

Nice. I would need one of those to grind my herbs.

"I'll take it. I also need red string for bracelets, some incense sticks, a bunch of sachet bags, and a deck of tarot cards."

There were several options for tarot cards. Julia wanted the deck with Santa Muerte, but I refused. We went with one inspired by colorful Mexican folk art.

The clerk held up a set of small clay bowls. "You'll need these to hold your herbs."

Julia quickly turned to face the woman. "We've already got plenty of those, but thank you." And indeed, we did. Julia had made them in her pottery studio in various sizes, and they were sitting on a shelf above the workbench in my sunroom, just waiting to be filled.

When we were done shopping, the counter was overflowing with our finds. But we had to wait to pay because the clerk had disappeared into a back room with a bow-legged man wearing a cowboy hat.

"She's a curandera—a healer," Julia whispered. "She says people come from all over to see her. Her grandmother used to own this shop, and she was a curandera too."

"Then she must know what we're up to."

Julia's eyes widened. "Oh, she does! I told her you were learning brujería. She's a big fan of your mother, and she's totally heard of your grandmother. And Lencha Bantacorte!"

Wow, okay. My new friend didn't have a lot of filters, apparently.

Julia reached up and plucked a Santa Muerte statuette from a shelf. She rocked it back and forth in front of my face. "Buy me, mija! I can't wait to sit on your workbench! I'm sure Little Lencha won't mind!" Julia pursed her lips and looked at me with a hopeful expression.

I shook my head. "Julia, no. She's lovely, but I'm not ready for Santa Muerte just yet. That's some heavy stuff."

And I had serious doubts Lencha would be okay sitting next to the saint of death.

Julia gave me a mock pout.

I took the statuette out of her hand and put it back on the shelf. "I promised to take you to lunch. Where do you want to go?"

We ended up where we always went: Philippe's for French dip sandwiches. Delicious and not fancy. Not only was Julia a good friend, but she was also as down-to-earth as they came.

After lunch, we climbed into Julia's ancient Volvo and headed home. Sick of the congested streets, the traffic, and the grit that was downtown LA, I couldn't wait to get home to the quiet, beautiful neighborhoods of Chavez Ravine. I was even thinking about taking a nap.

On the drive, I checked my messages. There was one from the HOA President, Cora Bernal. I quickly opened it, hoping it wasn't bad news. Notes from Cora often were.

Cora had sent the communication to the board and included me. It was an update on Hernan Frias, the board member who had fallen severely ill a few weeks earlier. Apparently, Hernan had recovered from his heart attack and was back home.

He had stayed in a convalescent hospital for a few weeks and had not been expected to be released for some time, so this was an unpleasant surprise.

Ever since I caught Hernan using his dark magic skills to animate clay creatures and send them out to scare certain residents of Chavez Ravine, I had struggled to figure out how to handle him. Then he suffered a heart attack while lunging at me with a knife, so that problem solved itself, at least for a while. Instead, I was able to focus on learning the basics of Mexican witchcraft.

I would need to know some magic to counteract Hernan if he decided to get up to his old tricks, but I thought I had more time.

Hernan Frias wasn't just an egomaniac; he was stubborn. As long as he was healthy, he was a threat. And he had a dark side. Hernan wanted to get rid of the newer residents of Chavez Ravine in order to bring in more descendants of the families who had lived in the old neighborhoods.

Julia patted my arm. "He's just had a heart attack. He's probably too weak to do anything, Maddy. Don't worry."

I hoped she was right. The road straightened out in the final stretch before the La Loma guardhouse and its tall, wrought iron gate.

Julia gasped and pointed. "Look!"

My heart skipped. I followed her finger with my eyes. There, beside a prickly pear cactus on the side of the road, was a large, dark shape.

With the bright sun in my eyes, it was hard to see. "Slow down so I can get a good look."

I squinted at the figure in the distance. A dog maybe. A *big* one.

It slowly rose, revealing four legs and a long tail. Did it belong to someone in the city below? Or maybe it had escaped its backyard in Chavez Ravine and somehow found itself on the other side of the gate. Dogs were smart. Maybe not as smart as my cat, Sam, but smart enough. It might be waiting for the gate to open so it could go back home.

10

"Maybe it has a tag or something."

Now a pet owner, I thought of stuff like that—a consequence of letting oneself get bossed around by a fifteen-pound cat.

Julia flung open the Volvo door. "He must be lost." She started walking toward the animal. "Look at you! You poor thing! I think he's got mange or something! We need to help him, yeah?"

For a woman who not long ago had beaten the crap out of a naked, hairy man, Julia did not seem to register the danger.

The animal lurched closer. It was no ordinary dog.

The canine was ugly as hell, with patchy fur, wrinkled, diseased-looking gray skin, large bat-shaped ears, and sharp fangs protruding from a long snout. It was unsteady on its feet, like it was just learning to walk.

"Get in the car, Julia!" I shouted.

Only visible in profile, her mouth opened, and her hands came up, palms facing the thing. She slowly backed away. "It's okay; it's okay." Julia was trying to sound calm, but the panic was evident in her voice.

She had almost reached the car door when three hulking figures emerged from behind the large, prickly cacti.

These weren't sick dogs with mange. Dogs did not have red eyes. These creatures were something far more sinister.

They were chupacabras.

Chapter 3

I used to believe the chupacabra was nothing more than a hoax, something dreamed up by farmers to explain livestock deaths. But spending a few years in Occult Affairs had taught me not to dismiss anything, no matter how crazy. And here I was, face-to-face with a pack of them.

But even while they advanced toward Julia, they acted dazed and disoriented. They were entities—no question about it. This was my second entity encounter of the day, and unfortunately, I had already used my Smoke Bomb on the goblins at the soccer game.

Worse, I had left my slingshot at home.

One would think the head of security for Chavez Ravine would be better prepared, but I just had not imagined a shopping trip with Julia could take such a dangerous turn.

I grabbed the only thing I could use as a weapon—the stone molcajete I'd bought to grind my herbs—jumped out of the car, and ran between Julia and the advancing chupacabra. With any luck, I could stun it and buy us some time to get back in the Volvo.

Up the road, a figure stepped out of the guardhouse. A moment later, Ron Mendez was running toward us, shouting and waving.

The noise startled the creatures. They swiveled their ugly heads in the direction of the sound.

"Get in the car!" he yelled, his hand reaching for his baton.

He didn't have to tell Julia twice. She scrambled back into the driver's seat, and I slammed the door shut behind her.

For a moment, the chupacabras hesitated, their red eyes locking on Ron.

One of them lunged toward him, but its movements were clumsy and sluggish. Ron took a giant step backward. The creatures, having just emerged into our world, were exhibiting the classic signs of entity confusion, and Ron could easily have outrun them. If he hadn't stumbled over his own feet and landed on the ground, baton flying.

In a series of unsteady lopes, the chupacabra in front of Ron closed the distance and sunk its fangs into his leg.

Ron screamed.

Chupacabras were bloodsuckers. The damn thing might have been disoriented, but it still had its instincts. I darted forward, picked up Ron's baton, and brought it crashing down on the ugly creature. It took a few more whacks, but it eventually unlatched and toppled to its side, panting heavily.

It didn't crumble to gray dust, so it wasn't one of Hernan Frias's magical creations. The things were real entities, and the remaining three slowly headed our way.

Ron clutched his bleeding leg and tried to stand up.

I waved the baton in front of me and inched my way toward Ron.

Behind me, Julia shouted words of encouragement, but I didn't dare turn around and look at her. All my concentration was on the chupacabras, staring them down while I edged closer to Ron to help him up.

From down the road came a thundering roar. It drowned out Julia's cries and froze the chupacabras in their tracks.

A motorcycle hurtled toward us. The rider slid to a stop between us and the menacing creatures.

Clad in black leather from head to toe, the rider, a helmet hiding their face, unclipped a pouch dangling from a low-slung belt and hurled it at the ground near the chupacabras. It released a cloud of purple smoke.

The beasts went limp and collapsed.

The rider removed the helmet, and a cascade of copper hair tumbled out. It was Bailey Nixon.

I was so relieved to see her I laughed. "Since when does Occult Affairs have motorcycles?"

"They don't. It's mine. Jo picked these things up on the heatmap, and I happened to be nearby, so I said I'd respond." Her eyes flicked to Ron, frowning. "Did you get bit?"

Julia came running toward us, holding a rag.

"Yeah, but it's just a flesh wound." Ron grunted, wincing. He pressed the cloth to his leg. "It should be fine once I get a bandage on it."

Bailey and I exchanged looks.

"You'll need to have a doctor look at it, Ron," I said. "Entity bites aren't anything to mess with."

"Some have venom," Bailey added. "You could end up with a nasty infection."

Julia gasped. "Oh, no! I've heard about that. Didn't some officer lose a leg or something?"

Ron's face drained of color. "Did that really happen?" He looked at me with pleading brown eyes.

"You'll be fine. That was an unusual case."

Bailey nodded. "*Very* unusual. Only recorded case of a basilisk bite. Could have been worse. It was a juvenile." She walked up to the closest creature and studied it. "Is this what I think it is? One of those chupa things?"

"Chupacabra," Julia said with a shudder. "Thank goodness you got here so quickly. My name's Julia." She stuck out her hand.

"Sorry. Where are my manners? Julia, meet Bailey. Thank you for coming to our rescue."

"Not a problem." Bailey swung a leg over her motorcycle and jerked her head toward Ron. "If I had a squad car, I'd take him to the doc's and save you some time. Hope it's not serious."

Bailey took off down the hill. Julia walked with me and Ron to the guard station, then drove home. I called the Bishop gate and requested a guard to take over Ron's shift. Then I found a "Gate Closed to the Public" sign and put it next to the card reader. Homeowners with access cards would be able to come in, but everyone else would have to use the Bishop gate.

I put Ron in the passenger seat of his SUV and drove down the hill to the nearest medical facility approved for entity encounters. By then, Ron was getting nervous, so I accompanied him into the exam room. As soon as the door closed behind us, a nurse bustled in, clipboard in hand.

"Mr. Mendez, can you tell me what sort of entity attacked you today?"

"Chupacabra," Ron replied.

The nurse lifted her eyebrows. "My mother lives in New Mexico. She swears she's seen them in the canyon behind her house. I never believed her, but I guess now I owe her an apology. Did it have spines along its back?"

Ron shook his head. "No. It bit me."

The nurse made a sympathetic clucking noise and handed Ron a gown. "Take off your pants and put this on. The doctor will be right with you." She stopped and stared at me. "And who are you? A relative?"

"No, he works for me on the security team at Chavez Ravine."

She glanced down at the chart. "Mr. Mendez, you have a right to privacy here. Would you like me to show this woman to the waiting room?"

With his smooth baby face and helpless expression, Ron looked like he was twelve. This was his first encounter with a real entity. He gave me a pleading look. "Do you mind staying?"

"No, of course not."

The nurse raised her eyebrows again but turned and left.

I stared out the window at the parking lot to give Ron some privacy while he changed and climbed up on the exam table.

A moment later, a cheerful young man came in and introduced himself. Dr. Timothy Chen slipped on a pair of gloves and examined the wound. Ron bit his lip and looked straight ahead at a picture of a woman doing yoga on the beach.

There were two puncture wounds, each surrounded by angry, inflamed skin.

"This might sting a bit," Dr. Chen warned. He picked up a plastic bottle and squeezed the liquid onto the area.

Ron let out a strangled cry. He looked miserable and sweaty. A dark, viscous fluid oozed out of the holes.

Dr. Chen furrowed his brow. "Well, Mr. Mendez, there does seem to be some sort of toxin at play here. Is your leg feeling numb at all?"

"Yeah, a little." Ron's voice was faint.

"Well, that's not surprising, given the nature of the chupacabra. The venom is probably intended to paralyze its prey. I'm sure it's just temporary, but I don't want to take any chances. The good news is that we have a serum for just this kind of thing, and so far, it's been one hundred percent effective across the entity spectrum. I'll be giving you an injection today, but you'll have to come back for two more doses, one week apart. Okay?"

Ron nodded, and Dr. Chen swiftly jabbed a needle into Ron's arm.

Ron winced. "Is that it, then?"

Dr. Chen glanced over at me, then shook his head. "I'm afraid not, Mr. Mendez. I'm going to give you a local anesthetic so I can clean out the tissue. Then I'm going to start you on an IV drip to get you jump-started on antibiotics. I'll send you home with a prescription for more antibiotics, and you'll need to take those for ten days. Please don't skip a dose. And avoid alcohol."

Ron's shoulders slumped.

"He can eat tacos, right?" I asked Dr. Chen.

Dr. Chen grinned. "As many as he'd like."

Ron sat quietly and gazed out the window during the drive home after making a pit stop for tacos. But when we approached the La Loma gate, he broke his silence.

"I don't get it. How did those things get so close to Chavez Ravine?"

I was wondering the same thing myself. Entities had avoided Chavez Ravine ever since they first emerged. But the chupacabras had been right outside the gate.

"I'm not sure why they were so close. Guess it was bound to happen eventually," I finally said, trying to sound nonchalant.

But I was worried. And I sure as hell hoped Hernan Frias had nothing to do with it.

Chapter 4

After the incident with the chupacabras, I called in extra security guards to patrol the perimeter around Chavez Ravine, just in case more entities showed up. One couldn't be too cautious. If nothing happened, I would reassess later.

After all that excitement, I was too wound up to relax, so I spent the rest of Saturday in the sunroom, putting away the stuff I had bought at the botanica.

Sam sat in a box for a while, but it was a bit too small to comfortably contain him—he was an exceptionally large cat—so he leapt onto the counter to watch me work. I sorted the stones and crystals into clear plastic containers on a shelf where I could easily see them. The soft, smooth ribbons were in one box and the sachet bags in another. I transferred seeds from plastic pouches into the delicate clay bowls Julia had made. Like everything she created, they were beautiful and distinctive, with intricate patterns etched into their sides.

Next to them, I added small vials of oil. I pounded a few nails into the wall above the shelves to hang the dried chili strings. The ristras added a pop of color above my workbench.

My workbench. Mine.

The bench that used to belong to my grandmother, Liliana Bantacorte, who learned her craft from her aunt, Lencha Bantacorte, who had been taught brujería on a ranch in Mexico.

Julia had sculpted a stunning figurine of Lencha and given it to me. Little Lencha sat on my workbench, observing and supervising.

I stood back and admired my work. But I was far from done. In Lencha's first notebook, she emphasized the importance of cultivating my own herbs. Unfortunately, I had never had any luck with houseplants. Each one I had ever owned eventually withered, so I decided to start small.

On Sunday morning, I checked in with Ron to see how he was feeling. His grandmother had rubbed Vicks Vapor Rub all over his chest, which was the go-to for the mothers in my family too.

> *Does it still hurt?*
> *Yeah it does. Chupacabras suck.*
> *Maybe rub some Vicks on it.*
> *You're trying to kill me, boss.*
> *Seriously, I hope you feel better. Take off as much time as you need.*
> *I've been having trouble sleeping, but I'm sure I'll be fine tomorrow, boss.*

A few minutes later, my phone chimed again.

> *Hey boss, Bailey on the bike? Do you think she'd be okay with it if you gave me her number?*

I had no clue, but I wasn't going to involve myself in workplace matchmaking.

> *You can ask Bailey yourself if you see her again.*
> *Oh. OK. Got it boss.*

I made a shopping list based on Lencha's notes and drove to a nursery in Pasadena. There, I picked up herbs: rue, sage, rosemary, and oregano.

Back home, I planted the herbs in large clay pots and set them on top of the retaining wall, where they would get plenty of sun. Sam watched intently while I watered the plants and asked them politely not to die.

I made myself a cup of coffee and sat on the couch in the sunroom, pondering my next steps. Stocking my workbench was one thing. Learning how to use my new supplies was another.

It seemed overwhelming and a bit pointless. Nobody was asking for folk remedies like they did back in Lencha's day. There was no line of mothers and their sniffly children or old men with their aches and pains outside the sunroom.

I chased those thoughts away. After all, I had to start somewhere.

I needed a guinea pig.

Ron had said he was having trouble sleeping. Which sounded exactly like what Lencha described after people had a "susto," a serious fright. And Stu had said his daughter, Clare, was listless and cranky since the goblin incident. Also symptoms of a susto.

A susto remedy seemed like a good starter project.

One option involved placing herbs in the form of a cross under the pillow of the susto victim. Ron might be okay with that—his family had probably visited one of my ancestors back in the day—but I couldn't imagine asking Stu if I could bring magic herbs into his house. And besides, there was no way I was going to tell him the spirit of my great aunt had visited me or that I had decided to embrace my magical destiny. It was way too early for all of that. I would send him running for the hills.

The next best thing was a protection sachet. Perhaps I could get away with bringing Clare a little get well present, explaining it was an item from my culture, a little something to cheer her up.

Using my freshly consecrated iron scissors, I cut a string for the white brocade sachet bag. I had chosen white for protection, balance, and harmony. It sounded like Clare could use all three.

I dropped seeds, herbs, and a small alum stone into the bag, along with a little tin medal of El Santo Nino de Atocha, the folk saint with a sweet face.

At first, Lencha's instructions had filled me with anxiety because many of her cures and spells involved prayers, and I wasn't the praying type. But neither was Lencha, as it turned out. Several pages in, she made it clear one could change the wording or make up one's own incantations. Brujería was not dependent upon the church and its priests. Her magic was its own thing.

So, I said a few words I hoped would empower the items in the bag to protect its owner. It made me feel even sillier than when I talked to the cat, and that was saying a lot.

When I was done, I put the sachet on the workbench. I didn't know what I expected—a mysterious gust of wind, maybe, or Lencha glowing like a jack-o'-lantern—but nothing happened. With no idea if anything I had done had worked, I closed the bag and tied it off with the string. I messaged Stu, explaining I had a little something for Clare. He seemed happy and said they would be home all afternoon.

I put the sachet into my purse and a few other items into the back of the Jeep. Minutes later, I had parked in Stu's driveway in Palo Verde and was ringing the bell.

It was the first time I had seen his house. Since Clare had moved in, we had decided it was best for me to steer clear. Which just added one more layer of awkwardness. We were still in that weird zone between being more than friends but not yet an official couple.

Stu's house was a large, two-story Craftsman painted gray with white trim. He came out wearing shorts and a T-shirt. Suddenly shy about going in, I made an excuse about needing to be somewhere.

"Come in just for a minute. Say hi to Clare." He glanced over his shoulder, then leaned over and kissed me. "My chaperone is still in her funk. She even says she's too scared to go to school. The company might do her good."

She didn't need to worry. After the first big earthquakes, entities had emerged outside schools, mostly in hilly areas with a lot of foliage. The schools had dealt with the problem by paving over their grounds. Ugly but effective.

Our lips met, the softness of Stu's skin against mine. My fingers tangled in his silky hair. Would we ever have a chance to spend more than a few hours together?

Behind Stu, a figure appeared in the entryway.

"Clare," I whispered.

Stu stepped back like I was suddenly radioactive and gave me a sheepish grin. I smiled back to show I understood.

"I've got a little something for you." I waved Clare over.

She scanned the front yard like she expected a goblin to leap out from behind a tree. Clare slowly stepped out onto the porch. "Hi, Maddy. What's up?"

"Not much. Just wanted to come by and give you this." I handed her the sachet bag.

Clare frowned. "What is it?" She sounded suspicious.

"It's a protection sachet. It's something the women in my family make to keep people safe from scary things. Just keep it close to you, like in your pocket or something."

Clare titled her head and examined the bag. "Will it work against entities?"

I shrugged. "With any luck it will." No use overselling it. Who really knew?

After a few moments, Clare looked at me with a small smile. "Thank you. For thinking of me." She paused and glanced over at her father. "We were just going to watch a movie. Want to watch it with us?"

I smiled back, genuinely touched. But I shook my head. "I can't, sorry. There's someplace I gotta be. Another time?"

She nodded, clutching the little sack to her chest. "Can I wear this around my neck?"

"I don't see why not."

"I've got the perfect chain for it." Clare turned on her heel and ran into the house. In the foyer, she stopped and turned around. "Thanks, Maddy! See you!"

Stu stared after her, mouth slightly open. "She smiled. How the hell did you do that? What's in that thing you just gave her?"

"Magic, apparently." I grinned.

Another kiss, this one longer, and then I was on my way to Ron's house. He lived in Bishop, across the street from Cora Bernal and Hernan Frias.

I drove past the old brujo's gloomy place. He had been gone for weeks, but his garden looked as lush and beautiful as ever. The next second, I could see why—master landscaper Ben Tomas was there, tending to the colorful bushes. Before he could spot me, I made a U-turn and hung a right into Ron's long driveway.

The Mendez property was a multi-generational family compound consisting of three large buildings. Ron lived in a small cottage at the back.

I got out of the Jeep, pulled some supplies from the rear, and walked up the path. The front door was open, so I knocked on the doorframe and went in, a basket hanging from the crook of my arm and a broom in my hand.

Ron, wearing shorts, was stretched out on a couch in the living room, the television tuned to a soccer game. His right leg was wrapped in a bandage and propped up on a pillow. The room smelled strongly of menthol, eucalyptus, and camphor.

"Hi, boss. Are those tacos, by any chance?"

"Sorry, no. But considering the whole chupacabra thing and the big scare you had, I thought you would be willing to let me do a little…ritual…that might help you." I winced when I said "ritual."

Ron rubbed his forehead. "Are you planning to hit me with that broom?"

"Of course not." I cleared my throat. "Ron, I know this is a little weird, but I'm not here as your boss."

Ron's eyebrows shot up.

Crap. That wasn't what I had meant.

I quickly continued. "You know about my family, right? Cora told you about my great-aunt Lencha?"

"Oh, yeah. I've heard all about her. Cora says, one of these days, you're going to be as big a deal as bruja Lencha. Is that what this is about? You want to do a spell on me or something?"

"No…Well, not exactly. Just a little something to help you recover from your scare with the chupacabra yesterday."

Ron raised his chin slightly. "Who said I was scared?"

"No one, no one." I put the basket down on a table by the door. "But come on. You were bitten by a bloodsucker, and that's got to be a bit traumatizing, right?"

Ron sighed. "I've been feeling weird since it happened. Sort of wobbly and dizzy. My grandma says I've got something called susto." He rolled his eyes.

I held up the broom. "That's what this is for. To sweep it away. To be honest, this is the first time I've tried it, but if you're willing, we can give it a shot. Only if you're okay with it."

So much for that line I had drawn. Matchmaker, bad. Curandera, good. At some point, I needed to think this through.

Ron sat up. "I'm okay with it. Why not? Anything to feel better, you know?"

I took a clean sheet from the basket and unfolded it, told Ron to lie down, and covered him with it.

"Really? My face too?" The sheet puffed up near his mouth.

"Your face too."

Now that I had started, I felt silly, like I was playacting. I needed to get it over with.

"Don't move," I instructed, then swept the broom over him a few times.

Ron giggled. "That tickles."

It was better than complaining. I followed up by rubbing a raw egg against the sheet over his face, neck, arms, and legs before brushing a bundle of rosemary across him.

When that was done, I took a note card out of my pocket.

"Are we done?" Ron asked, his voice muffled by the sheet.

"Not quite."

I read an incantation from the card and asked Ron to repeat it with me. He did, with such enthusiasm that I couldn't help but smile.

"Now, we're done." I yanked off the sheet and stuffed it into the basket.

Ron sat up and looked around, appearing slightly dazed. "This is so weird, but I actually feel better."

"Ron…" I said in a warning tone. Though I might have been his boss, he didn't need to suck up to me like that.

"No! I'm serious. I was feeling kind of nauseous, and now I'm not. And I'm not dizzy anymore."

He swung his legs over the side of the couch and stood, grinning.

"You're a real deal bruja. Wait till I tell my grandma. I'm going over to her place now and see if she'll make me a quesadilla."

I pointed the broom at him. "Telling your grandmother is one thing, but do *not* say anything to the staff about this whole bruja thing."

"Sure. Whatever." Ron gave an unconcerned shrug.

"Are you really going to ask your grandmother to make you a quesadilla?"

Ron opened his eyes wide. "I can't make them like she does."

I couldn't help but laugh while he practically skipped toward the main house.

Was it Lencha's—or rather, *my*—spell, or was it just the power of suggestion? I didn't know, but it also probably didn't matter.

———›·—›· |||||| ·‹—·‹———

That evening, while I was making myself a chicken quesadilla, Stu called.

"That thing you gave Clare?" he said in a low voice. "It turned her around. She's telling all her friends about it, and she can't wait to show them at school tomorrow. Thank you for being so thoughtful!"

Minutes later, my phone chimed with a message from Ron.

Grandma says she owes you one for helping me feel better. I'll see you in the morning.

My first attempts with Lencha's spell book had been pretty successful. They left me determined to learn more.

Why had I put off exploring that side of myself for so long? Childish rebellion against my family's history, probably. And the feeling that magic was somehow an old-fashioned concept— something practiced by my long-dead relatives, but not by a modern, practical woman like me.

My experiences with Ron and Clare were proof one could be modern and practical and magical at the same time.

When I finally crawled into bed, I was so tired I immediately began drifting off to sleep.

I was barely aware of Sam jumping up on the bed until he howled.

A terrible dread gripped me.

Something was coming.

Chapter 5

It was a rough way to wake up. The cat jumped off the bed and darted into my home office, with me following. He leapt onto my desk, rose on his hind legs, and howled again.

That was very creepy behavior. Still, I might have been able to ignore it and go back to bed except for a horrible feeling of dread making me cold all over. There would be no more sleeping for a while.

I went to the kitchen, grabbed a flashlight, and swung the beam around the front yard.

Nothing.

The only creature Hernan Frias had created that was currently unaccounted for was Dog Face Bride. I had given her a good beating when I found her in my backyard. She had run away whimpering but hadn't disintegrated like the others.

Maybe she was back, but I didn't think so. I wasn't exactly sure how Hernan's dark magic worked, but he most likely needed to be well enough to keep it active, and Hernan had been very sick for weeks.

Sam paused the feline drama and stared at me as if to say, "What are you doing about this, human?"

The cat turned his head and looked north. He pivoted back to meet my gaze and again swiveled his head toward the same direction.

"Okay, I get it, big guy. There's something going on to the north of us."

Sam jumped off the desk and walked into the living room.

My house was at the bottom of the street running up to the boundary of Elysian Park. At the top of the hill was a construction site, one run by a developer and former cat owner named Rory. The border with Elysian Park and the construction site were both to the north.

I called the guard at the Bishop gate and asked for an update on the patrols.

"Nothing so far," he said.

I had asked the guards to periodically check the roads leading to Chavez Ravine and the perimeter too, but I hadn't said anything about walking through the construction site. And since Sam was acting strangely, I figured it might be a good idea for someone to scope out the border with Elysian Park. We were replacing a wooden fence along the property line with a stone wall, but the project was just getting started, and there were large gaps. Security cameras might keep out human troublemakers, but *anything* could waltz into the community that way.

"Can you please send a guard to pick me up at my place?" I asked. "There's something I want to check out."

"Just one guard?"

"For now. If I need backup, I'll let you know."

I threw on jeans, a sweatshirt, and sturdy boots, then grabbed my slingshot and a small box of ammo and stuffed them into a front pack. From my Jeep, I retrieved my baton and two entity pouches. I stuck the baton in my belt.

When the SUV pulled up, I was relieved it was Brandon. He was fast on his feet and, most importantly, hadn't panicked in the face of some really scary monsters. I climbed in and set a Smoke Bomb down between us on the middle console.

Brandon's eyebrows lifted. "You're kidding. You think we're gonna need that?"

"It might be nothing. Drive up the hill, keep the lights off, and park across from the construction site. And when we get out, bring that pouch with you."

The night air was heavy with an ominous energy. Was it my imagination or could Brandon feel it too? His shoulders were up around his neck, like he was expecting something to jump out at us.

The construction site wasn't completely dark. A few weak lights illuminated the portable office and a couple of storage containers. In the distance, the rickety fence cast eerie shadows in the moonlight.

I hadn't been up to the site in a few weeks, and I was surprised by how much progress the crew had made. Wooden frames now stood tall, some even sporting roofs. The area was starting to look like a real neighborhood. But anything could be hiding in those structures. A chain link fence surrounded the perimeter. In case of an emergency, the guards had the code to open the gate.

Brandon punched in some numbers. "What are we looking for?"

"Not sure yet," I replied. "Just keep your eyes open."

"They're open all right." His boots crunched over the gravel. "This place is creeping me out."

Same. But I wasn't about to admit it.

We walked down a dirt street. The beams of our flashlights cut through the darkness, sweeping across the skeletal frames of the half-built structures. It seemed to take forever to go through every building, but it had to be done.

When we were finally finished, I said, "We need to check up near the fence."

A small eucalyptus grove and a wide path separated the construction site from the fence bordering Elysian Park. During the day, the path was a popular route for hardcore runners. At night, it separated two worlds: manicured Chavez Ravine on one side and entity-plagued Los Angeles on the other.

We exited the construction site and walked up the middle of the path. Eucalyptus trees on the Elysian Park side towered above us. My sense of foreboding grew as we approached the fence.

A noise broke the silence—a strange, low rumbling.

"What's that?" Brandon hissed.

I pressed a finger against my lips and shook my head. Brandon nodded.

We crept closer. Eventually, the fence would be replaced by a stone wall with electrified wire running across the top.

The knot in my stomach tightened with every step. The rumbling grew louder and more ominous. Whatever it was, it was on the other side. I ignored Brandon's whispered offer of assistance, wedged my foot between two slats, and pushed myself up.

My flashlight swung across trees and brush but illuminated nothing. The noise seemed to be coming from just a few yards away, like the earth itself was moving. It intensified, and the fence began to vibrate.

Behind me, Brandon gasped. "What the hell is that? Are we having another earthquake?"

I found the spot with my flashlight. A hole was beginning to form in the earth, dirt pushing up around it. I knew exactly what I was looking at: an entity eruption in progress. Something was about to come through.

"Get up here," I said to Brandon. "And get ready to use that Smoke Bomb, but not until I say so."

Even experienced officers could get a little pouch-happy and throw them too early. To be effective, the entity had to be fully engulfed in the purple cloud.

Brandon scrambled up the fence. We both dropped down on the other side, our backs pressed against the wooden boards to give us as much space as possible from whatever was about to surface.

"Don't freak out," I said in a low voice. "We'll be fine if you do as I say."

In the clearing, dirt flew into the air and a head popped up, followed by the rest of its body. Tall. Humanoid. Dressed in a tattered shroud. Its face was white, and its mouth was open, revealing two rows of sharp teeth. It wobbled and fell, lunging forward on all fours, sniffing while it began to crawl toward us.

"What the hell is that?" Brandon's voice quavered.

Bad news. That's what it was. I had hoped for something a little more familiar, like a gnome. Even a troll would have been okay. But this thing? Whatever it was, it was nasty.

The creature's eyes were glassy, but they were fixated on Brandon. And then, the terrifying monster got blurry all over. The next moment, we were staring at a curvaceous woman with boobs spilling out of a tight bodice. Brandon yelped in surprise.

Well, that isn't good. A ghoul. I had never encountered one myself, but there were a few in the entity database. From the look of its teeth, it had a taste for human flesh. We had one advantage on our side. The entity was a fresh one, so it was slow and uncoordinated.

"When I give the signal, throw your pouch at its head."

He nodded. The ghoul started moving toward us.

When it was about six feet away, I turned to Brandon. "Now!"

He threw the rubber pouch and smacked it right in the face. Purple smoke filled the air, and the entity went down like it was made of lead.

"Nice shot."

32

Brandon beamed.

I got out my phone and called the Occult Affairs command center. The heatmap had alerted the night crew, but I let them know we had subdued the entity so they could just send a cleanup team.

"What is that thing?" Brandon asked when my call was over.

I sighed. "A shapeshifting ghoul, I think. Which is bad news anywhere, but it's *really* bad news this close to Chavez Ravine."

Chapter 6

After sending my report on the Elysian Park incident to the board, I slept for a few fitful hours before my phone rang. It was Jo at Occult Affairs command center. Straight off, there was panic in her voice.

"Mads, is there anything I should know?"

I sat on the edge of the bed and flung open the curtains. Another dramatic dawn—streaks of pink and gold painted the sky.

"You mean besides twelve goblins at a soccer game and a ghoul next door at Elysian Park? I'd say that pretty much sums it up," I replied groggily.

Sam stretched, rested his big head on my lap, and stared up at me.

"Not them. The heatmap is blowing up. It's showing entity eruptions on the roads to both your gates, at the movie studio near Bishop, and Elysian Park. Plus the neighborhoods just to your south."

I bolted up in bed. Sam jumped and glared.

"What the hell's going on?" I put Jo on speaker and pulled on the jeans I had worn the night before.

"I was hoping you'd tell me. Is your mother visiting?"

Fair question. Malena Bantacorte had a one-of-a-kind connection to entities. She also attracted them.

"No! Of course not!" My thoughts spun in different directions, finding nothing to land on. "Is the heatmap showing entities *inside* Chavez Ravine?"

"Not yet." Jo paused. "Shit. I've never seen anything like this before. Chavez Ravine is surrounded, and more just keep appearing. If they emerge inside, you're not going to be able to handle them alone with your staff, Mads. You're going to need help. Are you going to let us in so we can get in front of this?"

Another reasonable question but one I couldn't answer alone. "I've got to talk to the board first."

"Mads," Jo said sternly. "You're head of security up there. You don't need permission."

I sighed. "Trust me, I do."

Chavez Ravine operated as a private organization. Residents forked over big fees to cover all the costs of running the three neighborhoods, from the fire department to the landscaping crew. Since the community had a troubled history with the city and police, the HOA had a strict rule keeping both out of Chavez Ravine. I might have been in charge of security, but letting in Occult Affairs was a decision only the board could make. If I went rogue, I would surely lose my job.

The department was dying to get inside Chavez Ravine, to figure out how it had managed to avoid entities while no other place in all of Los Angeles County had been spared. And Jo wouldn't *just* send in officers to help. She would dispatch those pesky researchers too. The nerds' projects never ended, so once inside, it would be tough getting them out.

"You're just going to have to sit tight. I gotta go deal with this. Until I get an answer, can I send some of my people to you to stock up on Smoke Bomb refills? We'll pay, of course."

"Yeah, all right," Jo snapped. "Call me as soon as you know something. I'll put some officers on standby."

I alerted the guard gates about what was happening, sent someone to the Occult Affairs Maintenance Yard to pick up as many boxes of fast-acting entity control powder as they would let him have, plus extra rubber pouches, then dispatched security cars to monitor the perimeter of Chavez Ravine. Within minutes, I had reports of disoriented ghosts floating around in Elysian Park, a troll peering over the fence from the movie studio property, and more chupacabras staggering along the road leading to the Bishop gate.

I called the board president. Cora picked up immediately. There was no time for small talk, so I quickly explained the situation.

"I don't know why this is happening, but it doesn't look good. I've got my entire staff on duty, but if entities begin popping up, our people will be overwhelmed. Cora, I know how you feel about the police, but you're going to have trust me on this one. I could really use their help."

A long silence followed. I could hear her breathing and her husband asking questions in the background. She shushed him.

"I understand your request, Madeline. But the answer is no."

I wasn't sure what shocked me more: how quickly she had said no or the uncharacteristic sharpness in her tone.

"Please. This is serious. I know what I'm talking about here, and I'm very concerned that if we're not prepared, things will get bad very quickly. *Please*."

"I'm sorry, but that's something I can't allow." Cora didn't sound the least bit sorry.

"Isn't this something the board should vote on or something? In an emergency session?"

As soon as the words were out of my mouth, I had the feeling I had gone too far.

Cora gave a little gasp, like she couldn't believe I had challenged her.

I could hardly believe it myself.

She had recruited me, defended me, and made it possible to inherit the house I lived in. I owed her. But as I saw it, I owed it to all the people who lived in Chavez Ravine—not just Cora—to keep them safe.

"I'm sorry, I didn't mean—"

"No, I suppose you're right," Cora said stiffly. "These *are* unusual circumstances. Please be available for a video call if anyone has any questions."

After we hung up, I finished getting dressed and headed to the Bishop gate in my Jeep. I wasn't too concerned about the ghosts or the troll, but the chupacabras troubled me.

There was no need for worry. Occult Affairs officers were on the scene, collecting the limp bodies of the bloodsucking creatures and loading them into crates to take to the Dump—a not-so-nice name for the calming entity processing center downtown.

I didn't recognize any faces—apparently, the division's officer retention problem persisted—but I thanked them for responding so quickly. Some residents were already lined up just inside the Bishop gate, waiting to get to their jobs in the city.

There were no entities outside the La Loma gate, but traffic still crawled, with drivers keeping their eyes out for entities.

I was getting into my Jeep to head to the office when a familiar SUV with tinted windows pulled over. It was Stu with his daughter Clare in the passenger seat. I assumed they were on their way to Clare's fancy private high school on the west side of town, which would mean she was feeling better.

Stu got out of the vehicle and leaned against the door. "I heard about your request."

Oh, for crying out loud. That news was only minutes old. I was in awe of Stu's information-gathering skills but also a little peeved.

"How did you—"

He held up a hand. "Eileen called me. She just wanted my opinion about letting the PD in."

Eileen Simpson was the board member and real estate agent who had made my life hell when I first got the job. She had calmed down a bit, but I still didn't trust her. Or her entitled brat of a son.

"And what did you say?"

Stu leaned forward and gave me a little hug. He was wearing a white shirt and skinny black tie, a combo which made him look like a Secret Service agent. A very *hot* one.

Clare smiled at me from the passenger seat and held up the sachet I had given her. She had attached it to a chain, and it was hanging around her neck. I gave her a smile and a thumbs-up.

"I told her I didn't know what the issue was," he replied in a low voice. "But considering you were advocating for it, I said to let them in."

Stu was choosing his words carefully so as not to alarm Clare, but she was busy scrolling through her phone. He continued.

"One of these days, the board's anti-city, anti-police attitude is going to bite them in the ass." He placed a hand on my shoulder. "You look tired. I hope you catch a break today and can get some rest."

That was one of the things I liked about Stu. He owned a security firm and understood the demands of the job, and they were substantial.

Even Occult Affairs had left little time for a personal life. The few men I had dated over the past few years thought I was a workaholic and either pouted or issued me-or-the-job ultimatums. Neither was very attractive, so out they went.

Stu gave me a quick kiss and drove off with Clare, who gave another friendly wave. She had certainly thawed since we first met. Maybe that protection sachet had worked more than one miracle.

On my way to the office, Jo called again. "We've just had a second wave of goblins up at Elysian Park and a couple of cowboy ghosts at the movie studio, which is crazy because they used to make Westerns there in the old days. You heard anything yet from the board?"

"No. Because it's been like two minutes since we last talked, Jo. Seriously, I'm on your side here, but if this doesn't go our way, it's out of my hands. Okay?"

"Okay," Jo replied grudgingly.

A half hour later, Cora called. "I'm sorry, Madeline. The board voted. Two for letting Occult Affairs in, three against."

The significance took a moment to process. "Three against? So, Hernan's back? He was able to vote?"

"He's back home and well enough to vote remotely," Cora said, tone softening. "We need to talk about him, but we can do that another time."

Cora didn't need to explain how the vote broke down. The two people who had voted for Occult Affairs were Eileen and Dan Berman, a former music label executive. The three who had voted against it were Cora, Charlie Perez, a real estate investor, and Hernan Frias, a retired professor of mystical studies and a brujo.

Cora, Charlie, and Hernan all had one thing in common: they were legacy stakeholders. They had had family living in the old neighborhoods of Chavez Ravine back when the city tried to evict the residents. Some legacy people never forgot the rough treatment of their grandparents at the hands of law enforcement.

I got it. After all, I was legacy too. But it wasn't the 1950s anymore, and we weren't dealing with a racist city council.

We were dealing with a massive entity eruption.

And we were surrounded.

Chapter 7

Being raised by a difficult mother and moving around a lot as a child had been a mixed blessing. I was resilient and independent, and it took a lot to get under my skin. But I could also be stubborn and proud. So, it took a while to admit I needed help.

That was why the board's refusal to let me have it felt like such a blow.

"Cora, if that's the decision, that's the decision. I respect that. But that leaves us with two choices: build the technology and the staff to handle a large-scale entity invasion on our own or hope for the best. I'm pretty sure hope isn't going to get us anywhere, so I'm going to my office, and I'm putting together a proposal. Please don't be shocked when you see it. And I'll need a quick decision from the board. As in, hours. We need to be ready, and there's a lot to do before we can be anywhere *near* ready."

A long silence followed. I was having too many stern conversations with Cora. At some point, I would need to lighten things up.

Finally, Cora sighed. "Of course. I'll put everyone on standby for an emergency budget session. Please message me when you've sent your proposal."

I hurried to my office. The place was spotless and smelled of lavender. The cleaning crew was top-notch, and they always went for premium products. I hoped that would bode well for my proposal.

After making myself a cappuccino with the fancy coffee maker that had come with my fancy office in fancy Palo Verde Plaza, I sat at my computer, where I could monitor the incoming updates.

It didn't take long to assemble my wish list, but it made me nervous. I was worried about accidentally leaving something out and didn't want to have to keep going back to the board with my hand out.

My mind was still fuzzy from lack of sleep, so the list started off as a hodgepodge of the things that had first come into my head:

Command center with communications network - $$$$

Heatmap with service contract - $$$$$

Six more full-time guards for patrols and rapid response to simultaneous events

24/7 command center staff: 6 full-timers

Entity sedation and containment system, including crates and smoke bombs

Contract with Occult Affairs Dump for processing of contained entities

Professional slingshots and ammunition plus training

When I was finally done, even I was surprised by the length of the list. The costs were mostly educated guesses. They were close, but there was no time for proper estimates.

The heatmap was going to cost a fortune, but at least it was possible to buy the technology. Occult Affairs had originally funded the research to create it, then prohibited anyone else from buying it. Lucky for us, that restriction had just expired, and the company that made the heatmap had announced it was open for business. I made a quick call, talked to the sales manager, and was given a quote that took my breath away. Within minutes, I had a written estimate in my inbox.

Handling emerging entities was like playing whack-a-mole, even with the heatmap. Without it, we would have complete chaos. I was already beginning to line up my argument: the heatmap would allow us to arrive where we needed to be within minutes, neutralizing and capturing entities before they bothered residents or became entrenched. In other words, with the heatmap, it would feel like Chavez Ravine didn't have much of an entity problem.

Without it, we would be another Hollywood Hills wasteland.

I went over my proposal again, added a few items, then attached the heatmap quote and hit send before I could change my mind.

While I waited for Cora's response, I monitored the updates closely. The reports were increasingly concerning—more entities were appearing at an alarming rate outside the perimeter of Chavez Ravine.

I was really proud of my team. Not long ago, being a guard in Chavez Ravine meant chasing down the occasional vandal and keeping solicitors out. But with the outbreak, I was asking them to become the face of the association, to calm nervous residents when they went through the gates and reassure everyone the board was on top of things. That took confidence and maturity, and they were doing a great job.

My phone started chiming loudly. Leo, the lawyer who lived next door:

Driving down to the city today was a freak show. Is it G and T time yet?

His husband, Toby the chef:

There goes the neighborhood!

Then a bright spot: Julia invited me for dinner.

I'm making tacos al pastor!

Well, that cheered me right up. Tacos always had that effect on me. I suspected she knew they would because Julia was a very considerate friend.

Then a message from Cora brought my sense of dread right back. She had something to tell me, but she wanted to do it in person. Never a good sign.

We agreed to meet at Muertos Café.

As usual, the air in Muertos was filled with the enticing aroma of freshly baked pan dulce, making my mouth water and my stomach grumble. The place was crowded and buzzing with news about entities appearing outside the gates.

Cora and I brought our pastries and coffee to a table in a corner ,where we could talk without being overheard.

The board president was wearing white pants and a turquoise blouse that showed off her silver hair. Her brown skin was remarkably unlined for a woman in her seventies. One of these days, I would get up the nerve to ask about her beauty routine.

"Congratulations. You got what you asked for," she said without preamble.

"Everything? The heatmap too?" My voice squeaked with surprise.

"*Everything.* I was a little surprised at the vote myself. It was unanimous. Apparently, Stu Wells told Eileen, who told Dan, that if we ended up with a major entity problem up here, the city could require us to let Occult Affairs respond. Something about protecting the rest of the city from entities that emerge here. But you know how long it can take them when there are a lot of appearances, and right now, we have a *lot* of appearances awfully close to home. We'd be in a world of hurt." She paused. "We will find the money. Charlie even pointed out that having the heatmap will be good for property values…if the unthinkable happens."

She gave a little shudder.

"This is great news. I'll move as quickly as I can to fill the new positions and order the equipment…"

A random thought popped into my head, and I changed the subject.

"Remember when I visited Hernan in the hospital and he said we needed him to keep the community safe?"

Cora nibbled her pan dulce and lowered her eyebrows. "Of course."

"I think he was saying he's been keeping entities away from Chavez Ravine. I think he'd been trying to duplicate Lencha's old magic to keep them away."

"Hernan?" Cora scoffed. "I seriously doubt that."

It was a rare Cora Bernal blind spot. She was convinced Hernan was just a wannabe witch. I needed her to reconsider.

"I really think he may be more powerful than we know," I insisted. "He's called into the latest board meetings, right? How did he seem to you?"

Cora set down her coffee cup. It clinked against the saucer. "Not so great. Before everyone else arrived today, Hernan and I had a chance to catch up a bit. It's always awkward with him. You know how he is. But he did say he thought he might have had another little stroke last night. He said he was done with hospitals, so he didn't tell anyone. I told him he was crazy, but he said if he was going to die, he wanted to die at home."

The news hit me like a two-by-four across the head.

Hernan went into the hospital, and for the first time, entities started appearing near Chavez Ravine. Then he had a stroke, and boom, entities appeared right outside our fence with Elysian Park and, by morning, all along our perimeter.

When his health declined, entities got closer. It couldn't have been a coincidence.

"I believe Hernan created some sort of protection spell, but it's falling apart now that his health is failing."

Cora still wasn't buying it. "We know Hernan made creatures to frighten off some of our residents. Why do you now think he is protecting the community? You can't have it both ways."

"Maybe those are two different things. He wants the non-legacy people out, so he sent his creatures out to scare *them* and make room for more legacy owners. But something's been keeping entities away from Chavez Ravine. I think Hernan is doing the same thing Lencha did—or at least trying to. He's cast a spell protecting the community, but he needs to be healthy to keep it going."

"If Hernan did something like that, we'd never hear the end of it. He'd be bragging to everyone in Chavez Ravine."

I shook the pastry crumbs from my lap. "Maybe. It's one thing for Hernan to give talks about brujería; it's another to go public saying he was responsible for making Chavez Ravine entity-free. If entities *did* start appearing, they'd blame him. And also, people would think he was nuts."

"True. And I would have been one of them." Cora sipped her coffee, her frown deepening. "But what are we going to do about it?"

"Well, thanks to the board, we will soon be equipped to handle whatever comes our way."

Cora looked at me expectantly. "Is there anything else you're doing to protect the community?"

I hesitated, knowing what she wanted me to say, but I wasn't sure I was ready to admit it. Making a sachet to treat Clare's susto was a long way from casting a protection spell over an entire community. And yet, I *had* taken that first step.

"Well, yes, I am doing something else. I've begun to develop my skills. It won't be an immediate solution, but eventually, I hope to do what I believe Hernan has been doing."

Cora smiled. "I'm glad you've made that decision. It's the right thing for the association, but more importantly, it's the right thing for you."

I nodded. While I had known that news would make her happy, I expected more of a reaction.

Cora took a small bite of her pastry. "And in the meantime?"

Cora was tough. One didn't build a tamale empire or manage a difficult HOA board by being a softie. But I had never seen that side of her before. It wasn't enough that I was creating an entire entity detection and containment system from scratch or that I was swallowing my pride and learning magic. She wanted more.

Cora was right, of course. We needed a plan to handle our immediate problem.

"Okay. I'll pay a visit to Hernan. See what I can find out about his spell and ask him to help me recreate it."

"Yes. And?"

I took a deep breath and let it out slowly. "And my mother. I'm going to ask for my mother's advice."

Chapter 8

My meeting with Cora had been short, but when it was over, my to-do list was long. I had to prioritize, and seeing my mother would have to wait. Number one on the list? Place the order for the heatmap. Next, hire guards with entity experience. I knew just where to start.

Bailey picked up right away.

"You still want a job up here?" I asked. Neither of us was into small talk.

"You're kidding?" Bailey sounded out of breath. Running, I guessed.

"I'm not. You've probably heard by now that we've got a bunch of entities showing up around Chavez Ravine. We're taking it seriously and staffing up. Just in case. I can use someone with your skills."

"I'm so there. I don't even care how much it pays, as long as I don't have to have to deal with that asshole chief anymore. When do I start?"

Bailey was young, and I didn't know much about her personal life, but it sounded like she could use some parental guidance. And I wasn't about to take advantage of someone I valued.

"Bailey," I said sternly. "This is business, okay? I know you want out, but you've still got to do this the right way. Ask me how much it pays. And while you're at it, ask about the benefits."

"Okay, how much does it pay?" Bailey was ballsy in the field but suddenly sounded embarrassed. Maybe it was a woman thing.

Some females had a hard time negotiating a salary, even though it could make such a big difference in the quality of one's life.

I told her the salary, and she gasped. When I described the generous health benefits and the other perks of working for the Chavez Ravine Association, she gasped again. When I informed her she would receive a below-market-rate one-bedroom condo in La Loma that would be cheaper than anything down in the city, she whooped.

"Do you mind if I put you on hold for a moment? I just need to run in and quit right now."

I laughed. Bailey sounded positively ecstatic. Which exactly how I had felt when I handed in my notice.

But lesson time wasn't over. "Do you have a written offer in hand yet?"

"No," she admitted sheepishly. "Will you send me one?"

"Yes. You should have it in less than an hour. Sign and date it, send it back, and we've got a deal. Then you can give your notice."

Bailey cleared her throat. "I will. And I've got a bunch of comp time coming to me since we're so short-staffed and I haven't been able to take a vacation in more than a year. So two weeks of that will cover my notice period, and today can be my last day."

Smart girl. The chief had made his bad-boss bed and would have to live with the consequences.

"Any chance you can start Monday?"

"I'll start tomorrow if you want," Bailey replied without hesitation.

"Monday's fine. Unless entities show up here. And Bailey, I'm going to need a few more people, so if you think of anyone, please let me know. They'll have to interview, of course, but I'd love to talk to people you think would be good."

"I can think of a few names off the top of my head."

"Great, thank you. Give me their names, and I'll reach out to them."

Within a few hours, I had talked with two more disgruntled Occult Affairs officers. I set up interviews, and they both acted like they had won the lottery. The generous pay and housing made recruiting a breeze.

Liam Hansen was in his mid-twenties and single. Justin Torres was in his mid-thirties and lived in a crappy studio apartment in North Hollywood with his wife and new baby. He couldn't wait to get off the phone and share the good news with his wife.

I felt like the fairy godmother.

Which lasted all of a minute because my phone rang.

It was Rory, the developer working on the project up the hill. Sam's former owner. *What the hell does he want?* I punched the answer button.

"Maddy Madrigal." I made my voice sound as pleasant as possible.

Rory didn't bother with niceties. "We have a big fucking problem up here. It's entity central on the other side of the fence, and my guys are beginning to freak out. I've got a tour of prospective buyers coming this afternoon. How the hell am I supposed to sell homes with that shit happening in our backyard? What's taking so long with that fence? I want something done about it immediately."

I was in no mood to deal with an entitled, arrogant real estate developer, but at that moment, part of my job was to provide reassurance to a nervous community, including the people who did business in it.

After taking a deep breath to calm myself, I replied in my best soothing tone. "Are you at the site now? I can be there in a few minutes, and we can chat in person."

"Where else would I be?"

Charming. Did this guy really think that when he treated people like crap, they worked extra hard to help him out? He needed to learn a lesson, but I wasn't going to be his teacher. Not this time, anyway.

"I'm in Palo Verde," I said. "I'll be there in a few."

With a resigned sigh, I grabbed my tote bag and headed out for La Loma.

Sometimes, I would have rather faced entities than people.

Chapter 9

Since Rory's construction site was just up the street from my house, I thought about stopping to let Sam out for a potty break but decided against it. I needed to calm Rory down as soon as possible.

And Sam had a litter box. A spotless, unused litter box.

I parked on the street opposite the site. The air smelled of fresh-cut wood and dust. I made my way through construction workers and piles of building materials, a maze of half-finished homes behind them. Despite all the activity, everything was surprisingly tidy.

Rory's office trailer was next to some large metal storage containers. He must have been watching from a window. When I walked up, the door swung open. Bushy eyebrows dominated the top half of his beet-red face.

"Nice to see you, Rory," I lied.

"I'd say the same under better circumstances." His rather high voice contrasted oddly with his thuggish looks.

We were yelling over the sounds of hammers and saws, so I nodded meaningfully at his trailer. "Shall we talk inside?"

He shrugged. "Might as well."

Rory had turned the trailer into a man cave. A sign tacked up opposite the door read: *"Warning: Enter at Your Own Risk."* The walls were covered in team pennants, and a shelf displayed a row of bobbleheads. There was even a giant TV and a mini fridge below a sign reading: *"Hydrate with Beer."*

Rory was a big fan of the Van Nuys baseball team, judging by the amount of memorabilia he had collected. It all looked like clutter to me.

Rory sat behind his desk and gestured at the empty chair across from him. As I edged toward it, I spotted a cat tree next to a window at the far end of the trailer. I could easily imagine Sam squeezing through the opening to escape.

Rory brought his bushy eyebrows crashing down. "I haven't forgotten you stole my cat, in case you're wondering."

My hands balled into fists. I lowered myself into the chair. "I *wasn't* wondering, and I did not steal your cat. He ran away. And came to me."

"You probably lured him with treats." Rory folded his arms across his chest.

"It's impossible to lure that cat with anything. And in case you've forgotten, you took him home and he ran away. Again. To me. It's unfortunate, Rory, but I did offer to pay you—"

"It's not about the money," he interrupted. "It's about my cat living in your house."

Rory really, really didn't like losing.

"I thought I was here to talk about the entities in Elysian Park."

He raised his hands in the air. "That too. We can walk and chew gum at the same time."

If I had known Rory was going to rehash his grievances over the cat, I wouldn't have bothered coming.

Time to set some boundaries. "Rory, I've got a lot on my agenda today, and the cat isn't one of them. Regarding the entities, I understand your concerns, but I have no control of what's ̄ppening in Elysian Park and—"

 ̄ ̄ing to do nothing?" he interrupted again.

"I don't have many options. Have you thought about rescheduling the tour until the situation is under control?"

Rory huffed. "Why the hell should I do that?" He jabbed a finger at a calendar on the wall. "I have a timetable. I need to stick to it."

The tiny trailer felt smaller while the tension rose.

"If you're worried about buyers seeing entities in Elysian Park, then you might want to consider putting up a temporary fence. That should do the trick."

Unless the entities could fly, which was rare but not impossible.

Rory's face got redder. "I'm already going to pay for half that damn stone wall you're building. Just ask Charlie Perez. And now you're telling me I should spend *more* of my resources to put up a temporary fence? That's some nerve."

I shrugged. "It's not nerve; it's practical. You've got materials and a crew right here. Even if I could justify spending money on a fence that doesn't benefit any of my owners, it would take me days to get something like that approved by the board, then even more time to get bids. If I were you, I'd just postpone the tour until everything settles down. Why take a chance? Treat it like a rainstorm or any other natural phenomenon, which is what it is."

Rory's eyes narrowed. "Do I really need to explain this to you? Do you have any idea how much money is at stake here? And what are you saying? That the entities are a natural occurrence and might come over here? That's never happened. Except for that nonsense that went on a few months back, but we were all assured that was different and it's over now."

"Anything is possible. Look, I'm about to spend a fortune on a state-of-the-art entity detection and suppression system, in case we do end up with issues. It will be the first of its kind outside the LAPD, and just having it will boost the value of all the properties in Chavez Ravine, including these homes."

He sat back in his chair, thinking for a few moments. "A fence might not be a bad idea. All right. We'll put up a fence."

That was easier than it should have been. But I wasn't going to argue.

He stared at me for what felt like an eternity. "The cat is not my only issue with you."

I clenched my jaw. "This doesn't have anything to do with my property, does it?"

Rory cursed under his breath. The guy had a very foul mouth.

"Well?" I pressed.

"It has *everything* to do with it. Do you realize you are the only legacy stakeholder on this street? If it weren't for you, I'd be able to buy out all those rinky-dink properties and expand my project."

In Chavez Ravine, being a legacy stakeholder had its perks, including a guarantee that one never had to deal with outside pressure to sell their property. Rory knew that.

"That's my family home you're talking about," I snapped. "Say that one more time, I'll file a grievance with the board and ask to have your company pulled from the project."

Rory pumped his hands in the air. "All right, all right. No need to get all politically correct and sensitive. You people get all the breaks, don't you?"

"I'm sorry. What did you say? *You people*?" My voice rose. "Care to elaborate?"

He had the decency to pale.

"That came out wrong," Rory said hurriedly. "I apologize. What I meant to say was, it can be a little frustrating for the rest of us—who pay big money for the privilege of living here—to see legacy stakeholders get special treatment because of stuff that happened forever ago. Come on. You guys pay a fraction of the HOA fees we do! And then there are all the special funds for landscaping and whatnot. It's ridiculous!"

The man just couldn't help himself. I got to my feet.

"I didn't know I came all the way over here to relitigate decisions made long before I arrived." I was very pleased I was maintaining my professionalism.

Rory groaned and scraped a hand across his bald head. "I'm just so frustrated, that's all. First the cat, then the damn wall, and then thinking about how many more of these awesome homes we could build if only you'd see reason and consider an offer. With what I'm willing to pay, you could buy something a hell of a lot nicer in Palo Verde or Bishop than the dump you're in."

My body temperature rose. "That's my grandmother's house you're talking about, and I happen to love it. Not everything is about money, but maybe that's something only *us people* understand."

I stomped across the trailer. The floor vibrated beneath my boots.

When I flung open the door, I said, "I believe you just pressured a legacy homeowner to sell her property, in direct violation of HOA rules. Whoops. And about the cat? Let. It. Go."

So much for professionalism.

I half expected Rory to chase after me with another one of his sorry-not-sorry apologies, but when I turned around, he was standing on the top step of his trailer, staring after me, hands shoved in his pockets.

The guy was such a jerk, and even though I usually hated it when I lost my cool, I felt really good.

I marched toward the gate, trying to calm down, and rounded a corner.

Someone screamed, "Watch out!"

I looked up just in time for a massive wooden plank to plummet from above. Instinct kicked in, and I dove to the side. It hit the ground with a deafening thud, sending up a cloud of dust which made me cough. The thing must have been twelve feet long. It had missed me, but not by much.

Strong hands pulled me to my feet. They belonged to a tall man around my age with a cap of curly dark hair, a mustache, and a goatee. His skin was very pale.

He began brushing off my yellow trench coat. "You should be wearing a hard hat, miss."

The "miss" thing was a bit much, considering my age, but he was right. Everyone on the site was wearing one. Not that it would have helped much, but it was the principle of the thing.

The man's gaze traveled up the framed structure the plank had fallen from. No one was up there. There was no obvious explanation for what had caused it to come tumbling down. He frowned and shook his head, clearly troubled but keeping his cool.

The man turned back to me. "You all right? Are you lost or something?"

I shrugged. "I'm fine. I'm Maddy Madrigal. Head of security for Chavez Ravine. I was just having a chat with Rory."

"I'm Rory's cousin, Paul. It's his company, but I manage the project. If I'd seen you come in without a helmet, I'd have stopped you and asked you to put one on." Paul talked with a distinct Irish accent.

"I'll check in with you next time," I said. "Nice to meet you."

My entire body had begun to tremble from the shock of the near miss. All I wanted was to go home and take care of Sam. I craved a cup of hot mint tea to calm my nerves before getting back to work.

When I was about to drive off, a knock next to my head made me jump. It was Paul. I rolled down the window.

"Can I get your number?" he asked.

"You mean, for an accident report or something?"

He shook his head. "No. So I can call you."

Well, well, well. Paul and Rory might have been cousins who didn't look anything alike, but both had big balls. And Paul was handsome. But I was taken. Probably.

"I'm kind of seeing someone." That didn't come out the way I intended. My voice held a hint of regret.

Paul winked. "When you're not kind of seeing someone anymore, I hope you reconsider." He slapped the side of the Jeep and gave me a jaunty wave.

My hands were shaking while I drove down the hill, thinking how odd it was a beam came out of nowhere and nearly killed me. Just minutes after Rory complained I was in his way.

Chapter 10

What does one bring to a man who tried to stab them? For that matter, what does one give to a man caught creating monsters to terrorize his neighbors? And who thought they caused his heart attack? Which they probably did, but not in the way he thinks.

After some consideration, I decided pan dulce would do the trick. That it would come from a place called Muertos Café was deliciously ironic.

I was first in line when the doors opened and bought two sugar skull conchas and a few semitas, then drove to Palo Verde. By the time I arrived at Hernan Frias's gloomy house—a big Craftsman painted black with a glossy red front door—my intestines seemed tied in knots. I had to sit in my Jeep for a while, trying to collect my scattered thoughts.

My mission was simple: find out about the spell he had cast over Chavez Ravine to protect it from entities. But there was nothing simple about Hernan. He was self-important and insufferable, and he had a big chip on his shoulder about my magical lineage. Plus, Hernan really didn't like me.

Otherwise, I was sure we would have a super fun chat.

If I stayed in the Jeep any longer, I would have started eating the conchas all by myself, so I took a deep breath, marched past Hernan's beloved rose bushes, and rang the doorbell.

The door opened. It was Marta, whom I had met the day I busted in on Hernan and destroyed his rodent creations. And gave him a heart attack.

"Hi, Marta." I held out the pink box of pan dulce. "I was hoping to see Hernan for a few minutes, if he's up to it."

Marta was a petite woman of around fifty with freckles across her nose. She wore a sleeveless floral top and loose skirt. "I'm not sure he wants to see you," she whispered.

I sighed. "No, probably not. But it's important. I'm head of security for Chavez Ravine, and there's an urgent matter I need to discuss with him." Which was generally true. When her eyebrows came together and she bit her lip, I added, "I'll keep it short, I promise, and I'll do my best to try and not upset him."

Marta glanced over her shoulder. "I don't think this is a good idea. You know how he is. He'll blame me for letting you inside, and I could lose my job."

Her fear was not unfounded. Hernan was a very difficult man.

I thought for a moment. Keeping my voice low, I said, "How about this? Unlock the back door and I'll go in that way. I'll say I sneaked in. That way he can't blame you."

Marta stared down at her feet, pinching her bottom lip, considering.

"Okay. I'll go open the door. Wait a few minutes, then go around the side of the house. His bedroom is in the back, at the end of the hall." She eyed the pink box. "Is that from Muertos Café?"

Not above a little bribery, I lifted the lid and held it out. "Please, help yourself."

Marta peered into the box and selected a semita. *Good choice.* They were excellent with coffee.

Several minutes later, I was tiptoeing down the hallway toward Hernan's bedroom. The walls were lined with wainscoting in a dark wood, which seemed to suck up the light. All the doors looked custom-made—inset with carved panels. I wondered where he had gotten them. Something like that would look nice in my place.

I knocked on the door.

"Que queres?" Hernan barked from the other side.

Nice. So that's how he spoke to Marta. *What do you want?* The poor woman. She had a hard job.

I hesitated, summoning my courage, then went inside. Hernan was propped up in a four-poster bed fit for a king, a white coverlet neatly folded down. His eyes were closed, his head resting against a mountain of pillows. There was an open book on his lap.

The living room had been dark and filled with furniture, but the bedroom was a surprise. Natural light streamed in from windows overlooking the backyard. The room was comfortable and uncluttered, with just a dresser, nightstand, and a leather easy chair. One of those hospital-style tables was pulled over the bed. It was covered in pill bottles and a plate with bread crusts.

My toes curled. Of course, Hernan refused to eat the yummiest part of toast.

Hernan looked better. His skin was no longer a disturbing gray color. It wasn't exactly rosy but was getting back to its normal shade of brown. For a man his age, he had an enviable head of hair—thick and black and streaked with silver. It was longer than I had ever seen it and looked freshly washed. The smell of lemon-scented furniture polish was losing a battle against camphor and menthol.

Now for the fun part. I cleared my throat. "Good morning, Hernan."

His eyes snapped open. "What the hell are *you* doing here?"

"Just here for a quick chat." I closed the door behind me. "Marta's out front, watering your roses, so I came in through the back door."

He glowered. "Are you here to try to kill me again?"

Good question. It was tempting. "I could ask you the same thing." I scanned the room for sharp objects. Nothing. "No, I want to talk about that protection spell you've put up around Chavez Ravine."

"Not that again." He rolled his eyes.

"Yes, that again," I said firmly. "I'll remind you that it's my job to keep this community safe. As much as it pains me to say it, you've done a very good job keeping the entities away with whatever spell you cooked up. But you've got leukemia, and now you've had a heart attack, so you can see why I might be a little concerned your spell might not be doing so well. You've heard about the entities that have been showing up outside the gates. That makes me think something is going wrong. What do you think?"

Hernan pointed at the door. "I think you should leave."

"We need to work together, Hernan."

"The Friases and the Bantacortes have never, in the history of Chavez Ravine, worked together. And that's because your great-aunt looked down on us. Why the hell should I help you?"

"You're not helping me. You're helping the community you profess to love so much. Can you please, please, for one second, think of la gente." The reference to *the people* was a nice little touch.

"La gente." Hernan gave a derisive snort. "You don't know the first thing about *la gente*." He picked at a thread on the coverlet. "My magic might have become a little weaker while I was sick. But I've been feeling much better. When was the last time you had an entity eruption nearby?"

"Three days."

"There you go." Hernan shrugged. "Everything is back to normal now. No need to worry. Goodbye."

The man was unbelievable.

"Señor Frias, how old are you?"

"Seventy-seven. Not that it's any of your business."

"Aren't you concerned about what might happen to Chavez Ravine if you got sick again?" That was the nice way of putting it.

Another shrug. "You got your heatmap, didn't you? You can use that. Once I'm gone, my responsibility to Chavez Ravine ends, and I can rest in peace."

"No," I said with more patience than I felt. "There's another option. You can teach me what you did. And your responsibility becomes a legacy."

Hernan folded his arms across his stomach and snorted.

I could hardly believe I was suggesting we work together either, but yet, there we were. "I'm serious, Hernan. *This* is serious. You are a member of the board. We are required to work together for the good of our community."

He just stared at me from his cushy bedding. The look on his face made me want to pick up a pillow and smother him.

Instead, I added, "You really should get over yourself."

Not as satisfying, but less murdery.

His mouth opened, then closed. "You're not even a real bruja. You were just faking. Trying to trick me. Even if I told you what I did, you wouldn't understand." He raised his arms and wriggled his hands in the air. "It's way, way over your head, little Madeline *Bantacorte*." He said my surname like a curse. "You're a nobody. A nothing."

My eyelid twitched. For all my mother's faults, she had given me a stiff backbone and a strong sense of self. It would take more than this brujo's empty words to take me down.

I lifted my chin. "Try me."

Hernan flapped a hand at me. "I wouldn't waste my time." He paused, noticing the pink box for the first time. "Is that from Muertos Café?"

I had forgotten I was still holding it. "Yes, it is. Because I'm a polite person who never shows up empty-handed, even when visiting someone who calls her a nobody." I smiled.

"Thank you," he said stiffly. "I love their pan dulce. Did you get one of the special conchas?"

I rolled my eyes and placed the box on the tray. "I did. Although, after all of that, I really don't think you deserve it."

Hernan reached for the sugar skull concha and took a huge bite. His eyes closed while he chewed, and he began to smile. I knew that feeling well.

"Okay. Let's try this again, one more time. Will you help me learn that spell?"

If he got crumbs all over the bed, Marta would have her work cut out for her. I laid a couple of sections of paper towel across his chest.

He took another bite, his eyes rolling back in his head. "Now this…*this* is magic."

I gave him a moment to savor the concha, then stamped my foot. "Hernan. Are you going to help me or not."

Hernan chewed thoughtfully. "No," he finally said. "But feel free to stop by anytime with pan dulce. Who knows? I might change my mind."

"You are unbelievable. I'm giving you a chance to do right by the community. And if you won't teach me, I'll figure it out on my own. But let's be clear about this: if anything happens to Chavez Ravine because you refused to help, it'll be on *your* conscience. If you have one." I turned on my heel and banged out the door.

In the hallway, I could hear him laughing.

the idea of surveillance cameras to keep them safe but weren't so crazy about it when the video captured them.

Dan Berman came in next, followed by Charlie Perez wearing a bright yellow polo shirt and dark slacks. He shot a quick glance at Eileen and, when he noticed she wasn't looking, rolled his eyes. My office was a battleground of scents—Charlie's woody aftershave clashing with Eileen's floral perfume. My eyes watered, and I sneezed.

Cora was next, appearing anxious. Hernan Frias was probably not feeling well enough to come. Which was fine by me. The last time he was in my office, he had left a hex bag taped to the underside of my chair.

I flashed my brightest smile. "To what do I owe this honor?" Whatever it was, I hoped it wouldn't take long. I wanted to hit the road to my mother's place in Beverly Hills before I wimped out.

Eileen whirled around. She was wearing her blond hair in a new style. The severe bob had been replaced by a shaggy 'do with wispy bangs. As much as I hated to admit it, it suited her. Made her look less like the uptight real estate agent I knew her to be.

"When is the heatmap going to be installed?" she demanded. "We have to tell the residents *something*. People are beginning to panic. I'm getting calls from people who bought their houses from me. What am I supposed to tell them?"

Charlie snorted loudly. "The truth would make for a nice change."

Eileen shot him one of the nastiest looks I had ever seen.

"The board just approved the purchase, you'll recall. I put a rush on it, but it'll take at least another few days."

"And if entities appear in Chavez Ravine while we're waiting?"

"We're as ready as we can be. We've stocked up on Smoke Bombs, and we'll respond as soon as we hear about any incidents." Best to keep it vague.

Eileen groaned.

Dan Berman wasn't happy with that answer. "But that means there's a good chance residents will encounter the entities first."

Clearly, Eileen and Dan were beginning to panic.

"That's right," I said calmly. "But please remember, people who live here frequently deal with entities outside the gates. They know the drill. What you need to do is let people know, if they see an entity beginning to emerge, they should call the security hotline immediately, and we'll respond. But you don't need me to tell you that. It's kind of obvious, isn't it?"

Eileen and Dan exchanged looks.

Cora said, "That's what we wanted to discuss with you. We think that note would be better coming from you."

"As head of security," Charlie added.

I shot him a dark look. The board had never had a problem sending notes to the owners before. They had not hesitated to blast out an update as soon as they put me on a performance improvement plan, so I wondered what had changed. Though, it wasn't necessarily a bad idea. A security update from the head of security wasn't unreasonable.

Still, I had my suspicions. If they associated themselves too closely with an entity outbreak, residents might take it out on the board and punish them in the next round of elections.

I, on the other hand, could only be fired by the board. They just wanted to put a little distance between them and the very real possibility of entities arriving in Chavez Ravine.

And for me, storing a little goodwill in the bank was never a bad idea.

"Sure. I'd be happy to."

Cora and Charlie looked relieved. Eileen and Dan appeared surprised but pleased.

"Excellent," Dan said.

Eileen nodded. "Just be sure to add plenty of specifics to your instructions so people know exactly what to do and under what circumstances."

Like that had never occurred to me. I took a deep breath. "Absolutely. How about I write it up and send it to Cora for everyone's approval before it goes out?"

Eileen clapped her hands. "That would just be terrific, Madeline."

Everyone except Cora trooped out. She hovered near the door, her eyes never leaving mine. I gave my computer a longing glance, hoping she would get the hint, but Cora was not so easily deterred.

"All of these precautions are very well and fine, but you know what would be even better?"

"Me being a bit more magical?"

Cora smiled. "Exactly! How are things going in that department?"

"Oh, they're…going." I shot the computer another wistful look.

Cora hadn't built a tamale empire by playing softball. "In which direction?" she said briskly. "Up, down? Sideways?" She paused. "You are, I hope, being proactive?"

What, exactly, did proactive bruja training look like? "I'm doing everything I can," I replied, matching her brisk tone.

"That's very good to hear." Cora smiled again, this time more genuinely. "The closer you can get to your potential, the safer we will all be. I'll let you get back to work."

69

When she left, a tension headache was beginning to come on. I wasn't sure whether it was because of the conversation with Cora or because I needed to go see my mother.

Chapter 12

My mother's house wasn't the biggest or the fanciest on the block, but it was easily the most charming. It was done in the Spanish Colonial style, with a red tile roof and a turret. The front yard was picture-perfect, with an expanse of emerald lawn, palms, and towering cypress trees separating it from its neighbors.

It was also the busiest house on the block. Several Occult Affairs vehicles were parked out front, and two officers were carrying a large crate between them. My mother stood on the threshold, wearing a long, striped caftan in the traditional colors of a Mexican serape.

"Please be gentle with him!" she called after the officers.

Behind her, I could just make out a large camera—the kind filmmakers used. That's when I noticed the gray van parked at the end of the driveway. It looked like I had walked into a film shoot.

I got out of the Jeep. A wave of exhaustion hit me. It had been a long couple of days, and I really wasn't prepared for this, but I had to do it.

"Madeline!" A colorful blur of motion came rushing down the red tile path toward me, a cameraman on her heels.

My mother threw her arms around me as if she hadn't seen me for two years.

Oh, that's right. She hadn't.

If I had known the cameras were going to be there, I would have touched up my makeup. At least I was presentably dressed, in a blue top and pants and one of the trench coats that had become my uniform. Today's choice: lavender.

"Hi, Mom."

We stared at each other for a moment. My mother's dark eyes begged me to play along. I nodded and forced a smile to my lips. Neither of us wanted to make our personal relationship part of whatever project my mother was involved in.

My mother turned to the camera. "This is my daughter, Madeline. She used to work for Occult Affairs. Didn't you, sweetheart?"

Her voice sounded strained. The lines around her mouth seemed deeper, more pronounced. Whatever procedure she'd had to smooth her forehead hadn't extended to the bottom half of her face. Except for her lips. Those were fuller than I remembered.

I smiled at the camera. "I did! So, what's going on? Have a little entity action here?"

My mother's hand fluttered up to her head. "Oh, you know how it is. Where I go, they follow."

That was no exaggeration. Jo at the command center joked my mother needed her own dedicated response unit.

Malena motioned for the cameraman to stop filming. When he had turned it off, she said, "We were almost done for the day when that ghoul showed up, weren't we, Felix? How fortunate we were!"

Felix had a long thin face, intelligent eyes, and stringy, mousy brown hair. He grinned. "The ghoul was a bonus. Thank you for letting us stay longer to catch all the excitement. I'll tell the crew to start breaking down." He hurried away toward the open front door and disappeared inside.

"Another documentary about you?"

My mother slid her eyes past me toward the Occult Affairs truck. "It's a one-hour special. It's going to run before my next tour."

That was news to me. My mother hadn't been on tour for several years. Then again, how would I have known?

"Let's go to the backyard where we can have a little privacy until the crew is gone," she said.

I followed her around the side of the house. The landscaping was just as nice there, with a small deck leading into an all-white kitchen. The French doors were open. A man and a woman were folding up light stands.

My mother had just pushed through a gate when two gnomes came rushing to greet her. I wasn't used to seeing entities so alert, so alive. The gnomes which had avoided Occult Affairs and infiltrated Beverly Hills usually acted squirrely, but not these.

"Can they talk?" I kept my voice low, just in case.

My mother shook her head. "I'm afraid not. But *I* can understand them perfectly, of course."

Of course. That was Malena B's claim to fame: her psychic connection to entities and her ability to not only calm them down, but also to tame them.

My mother always said she had no idea why she was the sole person with this particular gift. She had also been the only one to learn about entities based on thousands of "conversations" with them in the desert refuge.

According to my mother, the entities remembered little about their previous lives, didn't know how they had appeared in our world, and most importantly, didn't know how to get back. Whatever portal, gateway, or passage that had brought them to us was gone.

The gnomes—small humanoids with grayish-green skin and bright red ears—showed no interest in me. They hurried to the covered patio, plumped up some cushions on the chairs, then crossed the lawn to a tree-shaded area near the back fence and worked on some kind of gardening project.

"I wanted something simple, like ferns, but they insisted on camellias. Gnomes are very partial to color." My mother paused, frowning. "They tell me that, despite what Occult Affairs calls them, they're not gnomes, but the word they use for themselves doesn't translate to anything. I suppose it doesn't matter. They're here and not where they want to be. Poracitos."

I fell into the closest chair and looked around. The patio had a small outdoor kitchen. My mother fetched two cans of sparkling water from a mini fridge and handed one to me. I gulped it down.

"You scored with this place," I said.

My mother nodded. "With the gnome problem, it went cheap. My neighbors are very happy I moved in. I organized the gnomes so they're more equally distributed and not overrunning the houses with the biggest gardens." She sighed. "They won't tolerate dogs, so that's still a problem, but we're working on it." My mother glanced over her shoulder, noticed the camera crew still inside, then turned back to me, brow furrowed.

Whatever my mother had to say—and I was sure it was plenty—would have to wait until we were alone. She obviously wasn't about to risk having it captured on video.

"What's this about you going on tour?" I asked. "I thought you were done with all that."

I had assumed her star was dimming. Her last tour hadn't been as popular as earlier shows, and her autobiography hadn't sold as well as her publishers had hoped either.

My mother shrugged. "Money, of course. I never held a regular job with a pension. I need to sock away as much as I can, while I can. Since it's unlikely my only child will help me in my dotage, I'll have to hire people, and that's going to take money. And just so you know, I have no plans on going into assisted living. I bought this place because it's one story and all the doors are wide enough for a wheelchair, should I ever need one." She sighed again. "But the point is, I plan on aging in place. Just remember that."

I wasn't about to point out that at seventy, she was well into the aging process. But I had to admit, she looked pretty damn good. "Please tell me this conversation isn't about to get morbid."

"It's important you know these things, Madeline," she said sharply. "It's not morbid. It's reality. It's planning ahead." She leaned toward me, eyes narrowing. "Whether you like it or not, you're on my advanced healthcare directive. If you hadn't cut me off, you'd already know that."

As if on cue, Felix appeared in the doorway leading to the patio. "We're all packed up and heading out. See you tomorrow, Malena. Nine o'clock still work?"

My mother turned and gave a jaunty thumbs-up. "I'll have the coffee ready."

Felix grinned, waved goodbye, and left. My mother glanced down at her gold watch. Unlike most regular people, she never consulted her phone for the time.

"You must be hungry," she said briskly. "I'm starving. Let's go in the kitchen and get something to eat."

I was alone with my mother for the first time in two years.

While I followed her inside, I looked around, curious about her new home. It was lovely, with arched doorways, exposed wooden beams, a cozy fireplace in the living room surrounded by Spanish tiles, and lots of windows allowing natural light to flood in.

It was warm, although not stuffy. I spotted a thermostat on a wall. A place this nice had to have air conditioning, but my mother's internal temperature ran cold, so she rarely used it, even when she had lived in the desert.

All the walls were freshly painted white, adding to the airiness of the place.

"I haven't gotten around to unpacking my artwork yet." She pointed at a row of boxes stacked up against the far wall of the living room. "It would be nice to have a little help later."

Message received loud and clear.

The kitchen was well-designed with a wooden island. Gleaming copper pots hung from hooks in the ceiling. Something was simmering on the stove: spicy, familiar, and delicious.

"Steak guisado?" I asked hopefully.

"I thought you might be coming."

I ignored this. It seemed unlikely my mother had sensed I would be visiting in time to make a big pot of spicy beef stew with green beans, peppers, and potatoes. During a video shoot. Still, I wasn't about to complain.

My mother opened a cupboard, brought out two bowls, and set them on the built-in table under a large window. The marble top looked new, but the turquoise vinyl upholstery seating seemed vintage.

"Is this table original to the house?" I asked, curious.

Malena spooned the guisado into two bowls. "It is. The real estate agent actually suggested I rip it out, but I love it."

"I do too."

My mother rewarded me with a tight smile.

I didn't want to open the refrigerator and start poking around for a club soda, but I really wanted one. That or a glass of cold white wine.

My mother, the psychic, set out both on the table.

I drank down the club soda and chased it with a sip of crisp wine, then hungrily dug into the stew. My mother had a lot of faults, but the woman knew how to cook. She might have ignored my emotional needs for most of my life, but never my stomach.

My mother barely seemed to taste her stew. While I savored every spicy bite, she watched me. Each time I glanced at her, her nostrils were flaring, and there was a tightness around her eyes. She was just waiting for me to finish before having her say.

When I set my fork aside, stomach full, she began. "So why are you here? I'm assuming it's not just because you've missed me."

"Mom," I said in a warning tone.

Malena crumpled up a napkin and flicked it into her empty bowl. "Do not *mom* me. Not after what you've pulled. You owe me an explanation."

"I do? After what *you* did?"

Malena jutted out her lower lip and gave a little shrug.

My entire body trembled with rage after a lifetime of being constantly overlooked, dismissed, and undervalued.

My mother scoffed. "That's not how I remember it at all." Her reaction was typical, forever denying any wrongdoing on her part.

"Of course not." I slammed my hand down on the table so hard it shook. "Because you are incapable of seeing things from anyone else's perspective." I let out a bitter snort. "Unless that someone else is an entity. Maybe that's what I should have been, to get even an ounce of attention from you. An entity!"

My mother gasped. She appeared genuinely shocked. "Madeline Bantacorte! I have always, *always* had your best interests at heart. My life was far from easy, but I did the best I could, considering what a misery your father made of my life."

"My life too, remember?" I nearly shouted. "You act like he only happened to you, but I got it just as bad as you did." I had a few scars still visible on my skin to serve as a constant reminder.

My mother lifted her chin in defiance. "We escaped, didn't we?"

"He fell," I said. "And died."

"Yes, of course he did," she replied coolly. "But we were free."

My mother looked proud of herself, which struck me as odd. I had often wondered if she had pushed him off that balcony. Not that I would have blamed her. The police had never done anything to protect us, despite her repeated calls for help. And we never talked about the day he died. Some things were better left unsaid.

Unbelievable. My mother had almost succeeded in distracting me with that reference to my father.

"That trip was such an eye-opener for me. I saw clearly for the first time how little I mattered to you."

My mother's hand fluttered to her chest. "How can you say such a horrible thing? After everything I've done for you! Didn't I help pay the bills while you went through the police academy? Didn't I pay the deposit for your apartment? And what about the time you didn't have enough money to fix that rattletrap Jeep of yours? Didn't I help you?"

My frustration was boiling over while my mother continued to bring up financial help as a defense for her behavior.

The truth was, I would never have accepted her help if I hadn't been desperate. Those times had been very, very tight.

"Money, money, money. Is that all you think matters? I'm talking about *emotional* support, not dollars and cents. And you didn't just give me the money; you've held it over my head ever since. Luckily, I'm finally in a position to pay you back."

My mother gave a dismissive sniff. "Don't be silly. I don't need to be paid back. It wasn't that much money to begin with."

Hah. To have heard her talk over the years, she had handed over thousands of dollars. I picked up my phone, opened an app, and sent her a nice round figure to take care of the problem.

"There. We're even. The money I owe you is in your bank account. Now back to what we were talking about. I needed a break from our relationship because it was toxic, and no matter how many times I tried to set some boundaries, you ignored them."

"I'm your *mother*," she said sternly. "We're familia. There are rough patches, but we do not take breaks."

I laughed grimly. "There have been plenty of rough patches, Mom. But after that time in Mexico, I needed a time-out. For my mental health. Because you…you make me crazy!"

My mother gasped again. "I make *you* crazy? How do you think I've felt, watching you throw your life away, ignoring the gift you were born with?"

"So, what? I didn't want you to parade me around on stage like a trained dog? Whatever small gift I was born with was mine. It wasn't yours to turn into a revenue stream!"

My mother stiffened. "Your grandmother felt your gift too. She told me so, many times. But you were so stubborn. She tried to teach you, but you didn't want any part of it."

I rolled my eyes. "I was, like, six when she died. I probably thought she was just playing games or something."

"You were always a willful child," my mother said hotly. "When I was dealing with your father and I tried to talk to you about the emotional toll it was taking on me, what did you do? Leave to hang out with your friends. What kind of daughter does that?"

A parentified daughter, according to my therapist.

"I was a kid, not your bestie." I squeezed my eyes shut and silently counted to ten, struggling to regain the calm I had lost. "Okay. You asked why I cut things off. I don't expect or need an apology. What happened, happened. And it'll probably happen again. But you're right. There are only the two of us. So how about we hit the reset button? Can we do that?"

My mother stared at me for a long time.

"I'd like that," she finally said with a sniff.

Her eyes filled with tears. She reached across the table, her fingers curling tightly around mine. The delicate bones moved beneath her cool, dry skin.

"It's been so lonely without you, mija. I'm glad you came today to get this all settled because I'll be going on the road soon. So, tell me, what did you want to talk about?"

My mother's display of emotion caught me off guard. I had expected her to argue or deflect some more, but instead, she seemed genuinely relieved and eager to move forward. How about that?

Chapter 13

It was finally my turn. I needed answers to immediate questions, but if my mother was going to help, she needed to know everything that was going on in Chavez Ravine.

But first things first. "Can I have another glass of wine?"

She shrugged. "You're a big girl. Do whatever you want."

Lovely. Those tears had dried up pretty fast. I poured myself another glass and held up the bottle.

"How about you?"

My mother covered her glass and shook her head. "Oh my, no. Not for me. I can't handle more than a glass these days. It ruins my sleep."

She had said that in Mexico too, when we were alone. But as soon as fans showed up, she had become the life of the party.

Staring at my wine glass, I told my story. I started with Hernan Frias, giving her the condensed version, and ending with me taking out his clay rodent army before he could unleash them on the people he wanted out of Chavez Ravine. Her eyes were wide when I was done.

"And you think he was able to cast a protection spell around Chavez Ravine to keep entities away? It's a big area. My mother used to say that Lencha had done something like that to keep out El Cucuy after he showed up, but Lencha was very powerful."

"You never told me that."

My mother sniffed. "There are a lot of things I've not told you because you never showed any interest."

81

My face was getting hot. How was I supposed to show interest in something I didn't know existed?

Deep breaths. I had to avoid taking the bait and focus on what I needed. "Can you please, please set aside your grudge long enough to help me? It's important."

She sniffed again and stared down at her hands. "All right. What I'm asking is, do you believe this Fran Hernas character has the skills to create a protection circle? *And* maintain it?"

"It's Hernan Frias," I corrected automatically. "I think he might. The board president, Cora, has known him forever, and they don't exactly get along. She called his grandfather a sad, wannabe brujo and pretty much said the same thing about Hernan. But he's got a lot more going on than she gives him credit for.

"So yes, I do think he's been keeping entities out of Chavez Ravine, and now that he's sick, he can't maintain it. That is how it works, right? Spells cast while someone is alive will lose power when they're sick?"

My mother shook her head. "I have no idea. Your grandmother never talked about that kind of thing. After she left Chavez Ravine, it's like she allowed that part of herself to die. She didn't keep up with her curanderia when she moved to Salinas, and whatever she learned from Lencha about witchcraft died with her."

I picked up the dishes, set them in the sink, and looked through the window. A gnome scurried by, carrying an armful of greenery. He stopped abruptly and slowly turned toward me. His eyes were small, round, and black. I wasn't used to entities with such focus.

"Mom, has anyone ever come out to study the gnomes? You know, because they're so different?"

"Many times," my mother replied. "Researchers from Occult Affairs have tried over and over, but the gnomes just won't have it. They immediately disappear into the ground. One second they're here; the next they're gone."

"Have you tried asking them? Do they realize they're different from other entities?"

"They don't know anything about the others. None of them do. Honestly, the more I learn, the less I seem to actually know."

I turned and stared at her. "I guess you're not going to say *that* on tour."

"Of course not." My mother ran a hand through her hair. It was caramel-colored like mine but had a lot more highlights these days to hide the silver. She wore it longer than most women her age, but it suited her. I couldn't imagine her with short hair.

"The people are coming for a show. To see new entities up close while they're safely under my command." She reached across the table for my wine glass and took a healthy swig. "I'm a one-woman circus."

Something had changed since the last time we had spoken. My mother had always been endlessly fascinated with entities and had genuine compassion for their plight. But sitting in her kitchen, she sounded tired and jaded.

"Are you sure this tour is such a good idea?" I filled her wine glass.

She sipped it absently, her eyebrows furrowed in thought. "Probably not. But my accountant says I need to do it. The sponsor made an offer I couldn't refuse, and this time, it will get some proper advertising and marketing, unlike the last tour. The tickets are almost sold out, and they're talking about adding some dates. I have my new publicist to thank for all of this. It's the same gal who handles Bad Pete."

Bad Pete was a British pop star who lived in Chavez Ravine. I had used my slingshot to rescue him from some giant birds Hernan Frias had created and sent his way. Pete Drury was one of the world's wealthiest celebrities, so if my mother shared his publicist, she was in good hands.

"Sounds amazing," I said.

"She and her team think of absolutely everything. They coordinated with someone at Occult Affairs to get me close to entity eruptions—the ones in scenic settings, of course—and then they hired the film crew to shoot me welcoming the entities into our world. They're using the vignettes to make a documentary and create some ads. Have you seen them?"

My mouth opened and closed like a fish. Jo had to have been in on this, and she had not said a word, probably knowing how much the information would annoy me. I understood why Occult Affairs would agree to it—the agency was always looking for ways to improve its public image—but Malena B was my mom, for crying out loud. I would have expected a phone call.

"How long has this been going on?" I asked.

"Several weeks. There's been so much rushing around."

Something my mother had said made my skin itch. *Scenic settings.* Like the photogenic entrances to Chavez Ravine.

I folded my arms in front of my chest. "Any chance you were outside Chavez Ravine?"

Malena tilted her head from side to side. "The bottom of the road that goes up to La Loma. But don't worry. We were far, far from the gate. The guard couldn't even see us down there. Well, that's not exactly right because one came to see what we were up to, but the camera crew had a film permit, so everything was all right. And the young man was very grateful we were dealing with the situation.

"And Maddy, it was a *bad* one. A dog with the feet of a monkey and a human hand growing out of its tail. I knew what it was as soon as I saw it. They're called ahuitzol. They're flesh-eaters. From Mexico. It was not only very confused, but it was also in bad shape—coming up in all that dirt and with it being so hot outside. They live in the water, so something must have gone very wrong. Occult Affairs had to bring a water tank for it."

The entity was from Mexico, and it happened to appear close to Chavez Ravine, where most residents were of Mexican descent. Coincidence? Let's just say I had questions.

I started a pot of coffee and cleared my throat. "There's something I've always wanted to know."

Malena's eyebrows shot up. "And what is that?"

"Can you…summon them?" When she continued to stare at me blankly, I added, "Make them appear on command at specific locations?"

Like, all around Chavez Ravine? To get the film crew there in advance so they didn't miss anything.

My mother shook her head. "That's not how it works. I can't summon them. I'm not an entity conjurer. I wouldn't begin to know how to do such a thing. But for whatever reason, once they're here, they're attracted to me, and if they're reasonably nearby, they gravitate to me. Most times, Occult Affairs gets to them before they can get to me.

"That was part of the problem with my previous tour. Occult Affairs would swoop in and remove the entities in the area before they could join me on stage. This time, the tour sponsor and my publicist made a deal with the agency to not respond while the show is going on. It will still be hit or miss, of course, but we should at least get one or two entities. And the stage will be built next to areas where entities are more likely to emerge."

The amount of planning that was going into the tour was astonishing.

"It's important you're straight with me, Mom. You're saying you've not had anything to do with the entities surrounding Chavez Ravine?"

My mother gasped. "Are you interrogating me? Questioning your own mother? Like I'm a…suspect!"

"It's my job." I poured myself a mug of coffee, then one for my mother. "You didn't happen to visit Elysian Park the other night, did you?"

"No! Why would I go all the way over there? I have much nicer parks around here."

She got up, grabbed a carton of cream from the refrigerator, and poured some into her mug.

"So, here's a question for *you*, dear daughter. I sensed something different about you the minute you arrived. I think you've been trying some magic, haven't you?" She held up a hand. "It's what I've wanted all along, and if that's what's happening, more power to you. But has it occurred to you that *you* might be the one attracting entities?"

"Me?"

"Yes, you. If I can do it, you probably can too. And if you're becoming a bruja, well, maybe that's what's pulling them to Chavez Ravine. Except they can't get in because of that protection spell Herman Frye cast."

"Herna…Oh, never mind." Her theory was ridiculous.

I had worked in Occult Affairs for years, and I had never experienced even a hint of a psychic connection with an entity. Sympathy, yes. But I had never been able to read their sad, muddled thoughts. And I was only at the very beginning of learning Mexican witchcraft. My efforts had been pathetically basic. And yet, the little spells I had done for Ron and Clare seemed to have been successful.

"That's ridiculous," I said faintly.

Two black eyes appeared in the window, and I nearly screamed. It was the gnome again. He was staring straight at me, head cocked.

My mother came to stand by my side. She nudged me, none too gently. "Look at that. I think he likes you."

A chill ran down my spine.

Chapter 14

Out of the blue, entities stopped appearing around Chavez Ravine. I had no idea why, but it gave me the break I needed to tackle my to-do list.

And get back to Lencha's notebooks.

I had gone to my mother to ask her advice, and she had given it. But I desperately hoped she was wrong. The notion I was attracting entities to Chavez Ravine while being paid to keep them away made me crazy. Had my simple attempts at magic inadvertently summoned entities and brought them as close as Hernan's protection spell allowed?

I pushed these thoughts firmly aside and checked my list.

First up: talk to Charlie about space for the heatmap and my new staff members.

We met in my office. He had already come up with a solution.

"We're taking over the library annex. There's nothing much in there except some old books and boxes. It's perfect for what you're looking for."

"The library has an annex?" That was news to me, and I had spent a lot of time in the library.

"It does, but it's not actually attached to the library. It's a separate building. Come on, I'll show you."

Charlie led me across Palo Verde Plaza to a small, standalone building located near the pool, with stucco walls and a tile roof. "This was originally built as a teen center, but since we've never had enough teens to justify it, the library uses it for overflow. It was Hernan's idea. He's talked about turning it into a reading lounge or something, but that's never happened."

"Wow, this is perfect." The annex had one large space ideal for a command center and two smaller rooms in the back. While I walked around, I could already envision the giant heatmap on the wall and a long desk to hold the monitors. There was also a compact parking lot nearby.

I thanked Charlie profusely for his help. Next, I called Ron and offered him a job in the command center.

"Hell yes, boss. Anything to get out of the guardhouse."

I sighed. "Ron. Try that again. This time, think about your response before you say anything."

A long silence followed. "This is great. Thank you, boss. I appreciate the opportunity."

"Much better. Now, ask me if you can expect a salary increase."

Ron cleared his throat. "Does this job pay more than I'm making now?"

I named a figure, and it was followed by a swift intake of breath.

"Are my hours the same?"

He was catching on.

"I'm working on a shift schedule," I explained. "But for tomorrow, why don't you come in at eight thirty to help me get set up."

"Okay. But, boss?"

"Yes?"

"I didn't accept yet."

I had created a monster. "Ron, do you accept the position of Command Center Dispatcher?"

"I accept. I thought you'd never ask."

I made two more calls. One to Brandon at the Bishop gate, offering him the overnight shift. He was the newest hire and didn't seem to mind the hours. It helped that overnights came with a five percent shift differential.

—⟶‧⟶‧⫴⫴‧⟵‧⟵—

The next morning, I drove to La Loma Plaza and was at Muertos Café just before it opened. Nothing like welcoming new hires with pastries and strong coffee.

As usual, the bakery smelled amazing. My mouth watered while I approached the counter. The barista recommended the fresh buñuelos, so I bought a large stack of the fried flatbread and a to-go carton of coffee.

Charlie had already delivered chairs and a long, heavy wooden desk to our new command center by the time I let myself in. I had just finished tapping out a message to thank him when the installation crew arrived with the heatmap.

While the technology was sophisticated, the setup was easy. Just a matter of hanging the giant screen on a wall, then connecting the console. Learning how to operate it would be the hard part, and I had arranged for several days of training for the entire security staff, beginning in the afternoon.

Ron was the first to arrive. When he came through the door, I did a double take. He had shaved his head in a buzz cut and wore camo pants and a black T-shirt.

"Do you plan on joining the military this morning, Ron?"

Ron scanned the room, blinking. "I thought I didn't have to wear a uniform anymore if I was going to be in here."

"You don't," I said, suppressing a smile.

Bailey Nixon showed up next, wearing denim overalls, electric-blue eyeshadow, and a backward baseball cap.

She took one look at Ron and snorted. "What's with the pants?"

"What's with the overalls?" he retorted. "Are we planting crops today?"

Bailey rolled her eyes.

More staff trickled in, and the command center buzzed with energy and excitement. Within minutes, the golden-brown discs of crispy dough dusted in cinnamon and sugar were gone. I introduced the group to our newest hires: Bailey Nixon, Liam Hansen, and Justin Torres.

The former Occult Affairs officers stood out from the rest of the team: harder around the edges, exuding a quiet strength earned from battles fought and won against entities. Bailey's long copper hair and striking eye makeup made her look like a fierce warrior. Justin Torres had the lean and mean build of a middleweight boxer, complete with a bump on his chiseled nose. Of the three, Liam was the most physically imposing—broad shoulders, big-boned, with rugged features and a wide mouth.

The veterans on the security staff seemed a little leery of the former Occult Affairs officers. I would have to be careful not to give the impression of favoritism either way.

Everyone was eager to learn how to operate the heatmap, and I gave them a quick overview, demonstrating how to begin monitoring the three neighborhoods for entity activity. That much I knew from my time at Occult Affairs. Since there weren't any entities in Chavez Ravine—yet—I pulled up the data for the surrounding area.

It was a slow morning. Nothing in Elysian Park and just one incident in nearby Solano Canyon. There was no predicting when or where entities might emerge. Sometimes, entire days would pass without any struggling out of the earth. Other times, more than a dozen would pop up in a single day.

"So, like, there's no pattern to it?" Brandon asked.

I shook my head. "Doesn't seem to be, and Occult Affairs has tried hard to make sense of it. You name it, they've probably looked at it: seismic activity, insect activity, weather, the gravitational pull of the moon, soil type. They're stumped."

Bailey brushed buñuelo crumbs from her overalls. "I'm just curious. Does your mother have premonitions or something before they arrive?"

"Ooo, Malena B!" Ron said. "My grandmother got us tickets to see her."

A roomful of eyes stared at me expectantly.

"No," I said firmly. "If that were the case, she'd be a one-woman advanced warning system. Occult Affairs would have put her on the payroll by now."

And she would be even more full of herself.

I handed out training manuals and told the staff to start reading. Three guards left to relieve those still on duty at the Bishop and La Loma gates, and when those guards arrived, I ran through my talk one more time.

When everyone went out to grab lunch, I stayed behind to sort out the boxes of library books which had been stored in the annex. I wanted to make sure they didn't hold anything interesting.

One box contained several copies of a book published in 1949. It had photos of Chavez Ravine before the whole eviction drama started. They looked like collector's items to me, so I made a mental note to tell Charlie about them. There were also boxes of family photos which had been donated to the Chavez Ravine Historical Society. Somebody would need to go through them and decide if they should be added to the library's collection.

The last box had more books, mostly older history resources about Los Angeles and California. I flipped through those idly, mostly looking at the pictures.

One of those had a faded blue cover with gold embossed lettering that read: "*Shadows of the City: A Chronicle of Los Angeles Politics.*" Intrigued, I thumbed through the pages. I scanned accounts of mayoral elections, corruption scandals, rumors, and power struggles.

A chapter called "Psychics and Spiritualists" caught my attention. It was about a period in the late 1940s when Los Angeles was undergoing significant urban development. Around the same time, there were rumors of supernatural influences in city government. One of the strangest accounts involved a city council member said to have mystical powers.

The book suggested he was somehow behind a plot to scare the residents of Chavez Ravine into moving out. The city had targeted the area for development and planned to evict the residents to make room for a housing project. Of course, that had ended in protests and expensive reparations for the families affected.

There was a photo of the city councilman. He was very tall, with hollow cheeks and dark, sunken eyes.

The man must have been the guy Cora had mentioned. She had called him a witch, not a mystic, but the story was the same. This was confirmation he actually existed. And he had a name. Spencer Tuck.

I had seen the name recently but couldn't remember where.

When I stepped back into the command center, the technicians were putting away their tools. Small monitors at each of the workstations showed the feeds from the security cameras.

At the front of the room, the giant heatmap screen displayed an aerial view of Chavez Ravine. I walked over to get a closer look. The image was incredibly detailed. Every street, building, and tree was clearly visible. I found my house and followed the road up the hill, past the construction site, to the border with Elysian Park.

The construction site.

That's where I had seen the name.

The builder, Rory's company, was called Tuck Family Construction.

Chapter 15

Between the new command center, training my staff, and doing all the other things the board agreed to pay for, I didn't have much time for a social life. And neither did Stu. His business was growing, and he had volunteered to coach Clare's basketball team, so the best we could manage was Taco Tuesday at Olga's Cantina.

Over margaritas and chips, Stu proved that, despite his workload, he was still able to keep up with the community rumor mill.

"I heard Pete wanted to hire you for his tour." The crinkles around Stu's blue eyes seemed more pronounced, and he appeared tired.

I suddenly felt the strong urge to kiss him.

Instead, I took his hand and squeezed it, running a finger across his wrists. He had very sexy wrists.

"It's crazy, but he did. After I took out those giant birds attacking his SUV, he decided I should run his security team. It was flattering, but I told him I knew absolutely nothing about celebrity security and that he'd be better off with an expert like you."

Stu laughed. "Thanks for sending him my way. I'm not exactly sure why he decided to switch security firms, but I'm not complaining. And for such a big name, he's been very easy to work with. He's even recommended us to some of his friends."

He sipped his margarita and eyed me over the salted rim of his glass.

"Clare's got a sleepover coming up next weekend. At a friend's house. She's not wanted to spend the night away since the divorce. I credit the sachet you made."

"Oh yeah?"

"Yeah. And I've heard grownups have sleepovers too. Interested?"

My thoughts went a million directions: imagining being with Stu, wondering if I should try waxing instead of shaving, trying to remember when I had last had my period and if that was something I would have to worry about. It had been so long since I had actually been with a man. What if all the important bits had dried up and no longer worked?

I cleared my throat. "I'm definitely interested."

"Great!" Stu grinned. But the smile faded, and he sighed. "I feel like we shouldn't need to schedule it like a doctor's appointment. I love having Clare live with me, but I didn't account for how clingy she'd be. The therapist said it's perfectly normal, with all the emotional turmoil and fear of abandonment, but still."

"This too shall pass," I said lightly.

Stu reached under the table and squeezed my leg. "Let's just hope it passes sooner rather than later. I'm not getting any younger. We wait any longer and I'll need those little blue pills."

I had just taken a sip of wine. The liquid shot up my nose, and I snorted loudly.

The next morning, I woke up to an email saying my Smoke Bomb order was ready, but I needed to arrange to pick them up, so I sent Liam and Justin downtown. The professional slingshots had arrived, but I hadn't had time to open the boxes.

The combination of Smoke Bombs and slingshots was a potent one. In a residential area, firearms were a bad idea, and the board had prohibited security guards from carrying them anyway. But Smoke Bombs worked on most entities, with the exception of water-based creatures. They could hide underwater in swimming pools and ponds and avoid the chemical cloud. But when they came up, we could stun them with a slingshot and crate them up.

The staff would still need to learn how to use the new slingshots and practice.

The trouble was, I had neither the time nor the expertise to do that training. I needed to outsource it. But to whom?

The two idiots I had met at the axe bar in North Hollywood immediately came to mind. Chad and Tanner. They ran a company called The Slingshot Academy. I had watched a bunch of their videos online. They were excellent and, judging by the videos, solid teachers. But they were obnoxious, and if I brought them on, I would need to lay down some serious rules.

I found their website and messaged their phone number. Chad called immediately.

"Oh, I remember you," he said when I introduced myself.

Before he got the wrong idea, I explained what I was after.

"Oh." Chad sounded like he didn't know whether to be happy he was getting the work or sad it wasn't something else. "We can definitely help you out. We train people all the time."

"Like who?"

"Well, to be honest, it's mostly groups of people at parties," he admitted. "But we developed a program for hunters to help them level up. It's pretty popular. The new pro slingshots can be kinda tricky to learn."

It wasn't like Los Angeles was teeming with slingshot trainers, so I decided to hire them. Next problem: where to do the training.

"Do you think it's possible the axe bar might let us rent their space in the mornings before they open?"

"Oh, that's not a problem. They do that sort of thing all the time for private events and stuff. I know one of the guys there. Want me to call him? And when do you want to start?"

"As soon as possible. As in, tomorrow morning. And thanks. I really appreciate you and Tanner being available on such short notice."

The funny thing was, I meant it. Chad had forgotten to be a flirty jerk and seemed genuinely enthusiastic about the opportunity. But I needed to make one thing clear.

"One more thing. I have young women on staff. I need you to keep things strictly professional. If I hear otherwise, you'll be hearing from me."

A pause followed. "I understand. It won't be a problem."

When Liam and Justin returned, they stacked the boxes of Smoke Bombs in the back room of our new command center. I asked them both to meet me in my office and messaged Bailey to join us.

After all three were seated, I said, "Jo's agreed to let us do some ride-alongs. The idea is for each of you to take a guard out into the field and train them how to use Smoke Bombs so they're ready if entities ever show up here."

Justin and Liam nodded. "We can do that. Easy."

"Does the chief know?" Bailey asked. For someone so young, she certainly was savvy.

"Good question. He does not. And Jo and I would prefer it to stay that way. You know how he can get."

Bailey grimaced. "What if someone says something to him?"

"Won't happen." Justin shook his head. "Everyone hates him. Plus, he shoots the messenger. Even the suck-ups will keep their mouths shut."

"Especially because most of them hope they'll get hired here," Liam added.

Bailey was nodding, but it was clear she was still thinking about something. "What if entities never show up here? You won't need us anymore, right? Will we lose our jobs?"

Justin and Liam exchanged glances. Bailey bit her lip, waiting for my response. It was a good question and deserved an honest answer, but the truth was, I didn't know.

But the heatmap and the security staff running it weren't just deterrents. They were selling points. Chavez Ravine was the only neighborhood to have the technology and the know-how.

"I don't think that's something we need to worry about," I said.

My mind was already moving on. I needed to find out more about a certain cat-loving construction company owner who might have tried to kill me.

Chapter 16

When I got home, I changed into track pants and a tank top. Might as well get some exercise in while I did a little investigating.

It was hot out, too hot for a run, so I walked backward up the hill to work out my glutes. When I neared the construction site, I stuck to the far side of the wide street to avoid anyone's notice.

There was the sign bolted to the fence, just as I remembered.

Tuck Family Construction

Quality Builders for Discriminating Homeowners

Beyond it, Rory's trailer and some storage containers. And just up the hill, the fence Rory had agreed to build. I trotted up the dirt track separating the site from Elysian Park. Rory hadn't messed around. The fence was almost as tall as some of the trees. It not only blocked the view into Elysian Park and whatever entities might be lurking there, but it also prevented the cameras from seeing the construction site.

Maybe that was a coincidence. The fence had been my idea, so I couldn't exactly accuse Rory of building it to block the cameras. But he *had* agreed to it without much of a fight. Definitely not his style.

I passed the tall, majestic trees in the eucalyptus grove and jogged the length of the Elysian Park border with Chavez Ravine. None of the security cameras had a clear shot into the site.

My throat was parched, and my tank top stuck to my sweaty skin. Some water would have been nice, but of course, I hadn't brought any.

I turned around and jogged back to the street. All this exercise in the heat of the day was wearing me out. I felt sorry for the men working in the heat while wearing safety vests and helmets.

A white truck roared up the street, Rory Tuck at the wheel. He glared in my direction. It would have been very satisfying to flip him off, but there was no sense antagonizing the man, so I gave a nonchalant wave and kept moving.

When I reached the intersection where the track met the road, I turned right and walked toward the eucalyptus grove outside the construction site. A warm gust whipped up my hair and rustled the leaves in the trees. The breeze carried with it a strong, earthy scent.

From somewhere above me came a sharp crack. A huge eucalyptus limb was heading straight for me. There was no time to run. I leapt to my right, hoping I had chosen the right direction, and fell face-first to the ground. Then, a rush of air, a tremendous thud, a stabbing pain in my leg, and leaves and dust everywhere.

There was no further sound, no motion. I had been hurt, but I couldn't tell how badly. Though I struggled to breathe, I didn't know if it was because the limb had punctured something or if it was pinning me down.

It was neither.

I was choking on dust and dirt and the minty forest scent of eucalyptus. Gradually, I became aware of my surroundings. Sound returned, and I heard men yelling. I coughed and spit, but at least I could fill my lungs. There was a heaviness on my left leg, but I could move my other and my arms. I slowly tilted my head from side to side. No problem there.

Hands clasped on my shoulders. "Miss, are you all right?"

I tried to answer, but all I could do was cough. My breath came in short, rapid spasms, which only made the wheezing worse, and I began to panic.

"I'll take that as a yes. Look, we're going to have to lift this thing off you, so I'll stay with you until the dozer gets here."

I recognized Paul Tuck's voice, and my panic subsided. People were there to help, and I was alive. I took control over my respiration, slowing and deepening each breath.

The rumble of a bulldozer grew closer, and the ground vibrated. Chains rattled and men shouted instructions. After several minutes, the engine roared and shrieked as the bulldozer removed the massive limb.

The pain subsided immediately when the pressure lifted. Someone asked if I could feel my legs, and I nodded. The men gently pulled me to my feet, and Paul handed me a towel. I wiped my face and mouth and rubbed it over my neck.

"You're a lucky woman. That limb was huge—at least a foot across. Those eucalyptus trees are famous for dropping limbs like that, especially in this heat. What are you doing up here anyway?"

I sat up and checked my leg. It was going to bruise, but otherwise, it was okay. "I was just running. And I heard this sound from above."

"You run in the heat? I run first thing in the morning."

I had nearly been crushed alive and this clown was criticizing my exercise routine.

"I run when I can."

"I've never seen you running up here before." His eyes narrowed while he studied me. He was clearly not buying my story.

I got to my feet and shoved my shaking hands into my pockets. "People do. Look, sorry about the disruption. I really need to get cleaned up and get back to work." The words tumbled out in a rush.

Paul smiled. "Have you changed your mind yet?"

"About what?"

"About having a drink with me." Paul had the nerve to smirk. When I didn't say anything, he frowned. "Well?"

"It's a bad time right now. And like I said before, I'm seeing someone."

"Lucky him." Paul pretended to pout, an expression that looked especially ridiculous on a man with a goatee.

I couldn't help but laugh. "What's wrong with you? Five minutes ago, I nearly died, and now you're hitting on me? Are you always so pushy?"

"Usually not," he said flatly. "But usually, I'm not so interested."

Wow. The guy really knew how to lay it on thick. "I'm honestly very, very grateful, so how about I make you and my rescuers burritos for lunch tomorrow?"

Paul made a big show of licking his lips. "Homemade?"

"Yes, homemade. Carne asada burritos. I'll drop them off at noon, unless entities decide to show up. Then, I'll reschedule. And please thank your crew for me."

Paul grinned. "I love burritos. Not as much as I love drinks with attractive women, but I'll take what I can get. I look forward to it."

Whatever. What I really wanted, more than anything in the world at that moment, was to get in the shower and rinse off the muck coating my skin.

Then, I would try to figure out why I'd had two near-fatal accidents at the construction site.

I gave a quick wave and headed down the hill before Paul could say another word, wincing from the ache of the bruise on my leg.

Chapter 17

That day ended and another began, all without any entity eruptions near Chavez Ravine.

At work, everything was going according to plan. Slingshot and heatmap training sessions were underway. The ride-alongs with Occult Affairs had been set up. And everyone was where they were supposed to be.

The team members seemed to be getting along, and morale was good.

And most important of all: the HOA board was quiet. No entity eruptions meant nothing for Eileen Simpson to complain about.

At eleven, I got ready to hurry home to make the burritos I had promised Paul, but I had mixed feelings about the arrangement. I resented the time it would take from the middle of my day, but it did give me a great excuse to snoop around the construction site.

Before I left, I checked on Ron Mendez in the command center. He was in his element, sitting behind the big desk, wearing a black and gray camo shirt.

"If they show up, I'm ready for 'em boss," he said.

Ron might have been ready, but the rest of the team wasn't.

"Any sign of them nearby?" I asked, then held my breath.

"Nope. Another slow morning. There's a nixie out at Malibu Creek. She's a good swimmer, but it looks like they're close to catching her. Bailey and Brandon are over there, and that's what they're saying." He paused. "I've been checking in with the people in the field. I hope that's okay."

"More than okay! Communication is the most important part of the whole process."

I was pleased Ron was showing initiative. He seemed to have an instinct for what we needed to do. Everybody understood to contact me directly if something urgent came up, but we would need solid lines of communication before we were ready for an outbreak.

"Nice work, Ron. I'm heading out for a while. Call me if you need anything."

Ron saluted. "Will do, boss."

I hurried home, let the cat out for a potty break, then took out containers of beans, rice, and strips of steak. All I needed to do was chop some vegetables, heat things up, and assemble the burritos.

I had just finished slicing the cabbage when the doorbell rang. An unfamiliar SUV was parked in the driveway.

I really hated it when people just showed up without an invitation or at least a call. Wiping off my hands and grumbling, I went to the door and opened it.

It was Clare Wells wearing her school uniform, the protection sachet hanging around her neck.

"Clare!" I gave her a quick hug.

Her eyes were wide, and she was biting her bottom lip. "Uh, sorry for just showing up like this, but…" Her voice trailed off.

"Is everything okay?"

She shrugged. "It's all right. I…I…"

I pulled her inside and closed the door. Sam came running up and meowed loudly.

Clare's eyes widened. "Oh, is this Sam? My dad said he was big, but he's huge! And he's so beautiful! He looks like a little tiger!"

Sam seemed to understand what she was saying, and he strutted around the entryway, circling Clare.

I rolled my eyes. "Get over yourself, Sam. She's here to see me, not you."

Clare laughed and seemed to relax a little. She sniffed. "Oh my god, it smells amazing in here. Are you cooking something?"

Stu had admitted his cooking skills were limited to grilling meat and microwaving vegetables, so there was a lot of take-out going on at his place.

"Are you hungry?" I asked.

"Actually, I'm starving. I was going to pick something up after this."

I motioned for Clare to follow me into the kitchen and pointed at a chair. "I don't have any soft drinks, but I can get you a mineral water."

She sat and looked around. "That sounds good. It's so hot outside. I love your house. It's so colorful. Our house is so…blah."

I poured Mexican sparkling water into two glasses and added a squirt of lime. The only protein I had was beef, but I had plenty of it. Or I could easily make her a bean, rice, and cheese burrito. I had lived off those when I was her age.

"Do you eat steak? I made some carne asada. It's not too spicy."

"I *love* steak! I've never had that before. It sounds good, thank you." She grimaced. "I'm sorry. This is kind of embarrassing, me just showing up like this and you having to feed me."

"Clare," I said sternly. "It's my pleasure. I'm glad you're here. And I was getting hungry too, so I'll join you."

Sam jumped on the counter and was staring intently at our guest.

"And I'm very glad that my cat has decided not to inflict violence upon a member of the Wells family, for once. I'm sure your dad told you about Sam going after him."

Clare laughed. "He did. I wonder if Sam is jealous." Her cheeks turned bright red.

"Sam definitely likes being the alpha male in this house," I replied breezily, turning to the stove to fix her plate.

Had Clare come to visit to discuss my relationship with her father? If so, I wasn't ready for it, whatever she had to say. Teenagers today seemed a lot more sophisticated than when I was her age. I wouldn't have a clue what to tell her.

"Shouldn't you be at school?" I asked.

"We had early release because the teachers have safety training or something stupid." Clare rolled her eyes.

Instead of making a burrito, I spooned out strips of steak, rice, and beans onto two plates and served them along with flour tortillas. "Cheese? Sour cream?"

She nodded eagerly. "Ooo, both, please."

I put the plates on the table along with two forks. "Okay, here's what I do. I rip off pieces of tortilla and use them to scoop up the food. It's a little old-school, but it works."

"Nice!" Clare went for it, a little self-consciously at first, then with real gusto.

The kid was starving. Whatever she had to say could wait until she had finished her meal.

"This is so delicious. Thank you!" she said between bites.

When I offered her seconds, she held out her plate. The girl was easy to please. I assembled several burritos while she finished

108

her meal, then stuck them in the air fryer to keep them warm. At this rate, Paul would have to wait a little longer for his lunch, but I didn't want to rush Clare, not when she had made the effort to see me in person.

When she was done, I pulled a piece of pan dulce from the bread box, placed it on a plate, and pushed it across the table toward her.

"What's this?" Clare stared down at the pastry covered in pink sugary crumbles.

"It's pan dulce, which basically means 'sweet bread.' This kind is called a concha. You've never had one before?"

She shook her head. "No. My mom's always going on about carbs and sugar. My dad doesn't really care, but she's made such a big deal about it that it's kind of in my head. So, I avoid all that good stuff, like cake and donuts and muffins."

We had just entered dangerous territory. I did not believe in vilifying entire food groups, especially for teenage girls, but I didn't want Clare to think I was bad-mouthing her mother.

So, I just nodded. "I grew up with pan dulce, and even if you don't like it, it's nice to try new things once in a while."

Clare tore off a small piece and popped it into her mouth. Her eyes flicked back in her head. "Oh my god, it's so good." She polished off the pan dulce surprisingly fast for such a dainty girl. Clare sat back and groaned. "I feel like such a pig. I ate so much."

I whisked the plates away and set them in the sink. "Clare. You were hungry. I didn't even give you that much food. You needed fuel."

Clare dipped her head. "My mom would definitely not approve of how much I just ate. Plus, rice and beans. Double carbs."

The ex-Mrs. Wells was starting to get on my nerves.

Clare got up, washed her hands at the sink, then perched at the edge of her chair, knees together.

And here we go. I braced myself.

She fingered the little white brocade pouch hanging from her neck. "I'm not sure what's in this, but it really, really worked. It might just be in my head, you know, but I've felt a lot calmer since you gave it to me. My therapist said it might just be the power of suggestion, but I think it's something more. So, I wanted to say thank you, and…"

She shifted her eyes away from me, seemingly gathering up the nerve to continue.

"And my teammates all wanted to know what it was, and I told them. The ones who live in Chavez Ravine don't feel safe after what happened at the game. With everything going on—the entities and all—they're freaking out. Like, suddenly, they don't feel okay in their own neighborhood.

"So, I was wondering if you'd make sachets for them too. My dad told me not to ask you. He doesn't even know I'm here. He said you're way too busy and that it would be disrespectful of your time…or whatever. But I thought…You seem like you'd understand. And I'd be willing to help you. Put them together, I mean."

Well, that's not what I expected. Not even close.

Clare hadn't come to warn me off her dad or tell me how I had crossed some boundary I hadn't known existed. Or even to share how she felt about me dating her newly divorced father.

She wanted my magic. Which was a relief and a surprise. And to be honest, I was also pleased the charm had worked. Maybe I was somewhat magical after all.

I was about to say yes when I remembered what my mother had said. That I might have psychic abilities, and by practicing magic—as basic as my attempts were—I might have attracted entities close to Chavez Ravine.

It seemed a little farfetched, but what if she was right? What if, by making more sachets for Clare's friends, I would be summoning the things they most feared?

Clare was staring at me with hope in her eyes.

I took a deep breath, weighing the risks. It hadn't been easy for Clare to make that request. I couldn't just turn her away. She would be humiliated, which was the last thing I wanted.

My mother's notion sounded crazy. I had never had even the tiniest inkling that I might have psychic abilities. As much time as I spent with entities at Occult Affairs, they had always treated me like any other Occult Affairs officer. Rudely. Not like those weird deferential gnomes at my mother's house.

There was also the community to consider. I had given my word to Cora to do my best to protect Chavez Ravine, and that meant learning everything I could from Lencha's notebooks. Just because my mother had spent thirty seconds thinking about my problems and had come up with a crazy idea wasn't a good enough reason to break that promise.

"All right," I said. "I'll get started on them tonight after work. How many do you need?"

"Ten," she replied without hesitation.

I walked Clare to the door, Sam on my heels. She made it over the threshold and turned around, rushed back, and threw her arms around me.

"Thank you for everything, Maddy!"

I watched her go back to her SUV. She seemed buoyant and confident, just like a sixteen-year-old girl should. When she had driven off, I returned to the kitchen to pack up the burritos. The day was half over, but my to-do list just kept getting longer.

Chapter 18

The world was full of many things I would have rather done with my lunch hour than watch Paul Tuck wolf down a burrito, but these were the sacrifices I made for my job.

My plan had been to drop off the burritos and get back to the office, but when Paul offered to give me a tour of the construction site, I decided to play nice. We sat in his trailer, which was half the size of his cousin Rory's. It couldn't have been more different than that gross man cave.

The only decoration in Paul's trailer was a yellow and blue surfboard hanging on the wall.

When he caught me looking at it, he said between bites, "I collect vintage longboards."

"You surf?" I didn't know why that surprised me, but it did.

"I do. Whenever I get the chance. I used to live near the beach up in Santa Cruz, before Rory said he needed my help down here."

I forced a smile to my lips. "Are you and Rory close?"

Paul shrugged. "The guy's an asshole, but I've known him since I was a kid. We get along, work wise. But I'll tell you what's really great about him."

"Oh?" I lifted my eyebrows.

Paul must have heard the disbelief in my voice because he laughed. "I heard about the cat." He crumbled up the foil from the burrito and tossed it into a trash can, then wiped down his desk with a disinfecting wipe. "That was the best burrito I've ever had. Thank you."

I liked him better when he wasn't flirting so hard. "You were about to say what's so great about Rory."

Paul grabbed a framed photo from his desk and turned it toward me. "Them. The nephews. I don't have kids of my own, but those two are really awesome."

I stared at the photo. It showed two sturdy, red-cheeked boys, one maybe five or six, the other around ten. Both wore soccer uniforms.

"They're a handful," Paul said. "But they're great kids. That's the real reason I moved down here. So I could be closer to them. I'm teaching them how to surf, and I coach Mason's soccer team. He's the older one."

"Lucky kids." And I meant it. Paul might have been full of himself when it came to the ladies, but he was obviously a very engaged uncle.

Paul shook his head. "I'm the lucky one. I get to have all the fun. They're a blast."

The man was full of surprises.

I jerked my head toward the door. "I should get back to work. Can I still get that tour?"

"You're an interesting one." He lifted his eyebrows. "You nearly got yourself killed yesterday, and here you are, acting as if nothing happened."

"Nearly got *myself* killed? I'm pretty sure I didn't bring that limb down." I could actually feel my nostrils flaring.

"I'm not suggesting you did," he replied mildly. He plucked a hard hat hanging from a rack and held it in front of me. "This time, let's make sure your noggin is protected."

He didn't have to tell me twice. I put it on without a word of protest and immediately wondered how people could work in them all day. It would have driven me crazy.

Paul led me out of the trailer and down the middle of a wide dirt path with houses going up on both sides.

"I'm hoping I can afford to buy one of these myself," he said. "They're nice. Not too big, not too small. Just the right size for someone like me. A single man. Unless I can get someone special to take me seriously one of these days."

When I glanced over at him to see if he was joking, he laughed.

"It's too easy to rile you up. Just relax. You made yourself perfectly clear. You're not interested. I get it."

I stopped and stared at him. "Just relax? Wow. Has telling someone to 'just relax' ever worked for you?"

"Actually, no." Paul grimaced. "My ex-girlfriend said I am totally incapable of picking up on social cues. She said I didn't have enough filters, so there's that. Sorry."

"Your ex-girlfriend sounds smart."

"Smarter than me, that's for sure. She's a psychologist." Paul stopped in front of a framed house on the edge of the development and pointed at some activity behind it. A half dozen men were trimming the eucalyptus trees. "We don't want any other heat-loving joggers to get hurt, now do we?"

When we reached the end of the road, Paul stepped onto a narrow, winding path leading to a cul-de-sac. The framed structures here were smaller than the others in the area. They were far from done, but it looked like they would be quite charming when they were finished.

"These are my personal favorites," Paul said. "Fourteen hundred square feet. Two stories. Open floor plan. Indoor-outdoor living. What's not to like?"

"The price? The HOA fees?"

Paul shoved his hands in his pockets and rocked back on his heels, studying me. "You could have one of these, you know.

Rory told me he's made you an offer on your current place. It's down the street, right? The old houses down there aren't much to look at, if you don't mind me saying so. I don't know if you've talked real money yet, but I can tell you one thing. Rory's serious. You can ask him pretty much whatever you want, and he'll pay it."

Of course, he would. I was the only legacy stakeholder on the stretch of land Rory wanted for his project, and I was protected. Rory wasn't even allowed to approach me with an offer, but he had already blown that.

"Not interested," I said.

"Really?" Paul sounded genuinely baffled. "Come on. Why not?"

I sighed. Though I didn't owe Paul an explanation, I wanted him to understand. "It was my grandmother's house. There's history there. And I happen to like it. A lot. It suits me."

Paul shrugged. "Okay. If you say so."

We continued the tour in awkward silence. Every once in a while, Paul would glance over at me, and I would look straight ahead, discouraging idle conversation. When we neared Rory's trailer, I decided it was time to get what I came for.

"So the project is going well? It's on schedule and all that?"

"So far so good."

"So, who's the family in Tuck Family Construction?"

"Well, Rory, of course. His wife does the books. And there's me too."

"I was reading an old LA history book and came across your family name. Any chance you're related to the city councilman back in the '40s and '50s? He was a Tuck, if I'm not mistaken."

Paul's breath hitched in his throat, and he turned away. He pretended to be watching a group of men carrying a heavy beam across the dusty road. Finally, he barked out a laugh. "No, you're not mistaken. Good ole Spencer. The black sheep in the family."

"Oh?"

"If you've read about him, you've heard the stories," Paul said flatly. "Spencer was supposed to be some kind of warlock or sorcerer." He wriggled his fingers in the air. "But I'll tell you what I really think. Spencer came to this country at a time when there was discrimination against the Irish. He'd immigrated to Boston but eventually found his way to Los Angeles and stayed. He ended up learning accounting and started his own business, then ran for public office. Not everyone was crazy about seeing an Irish man succeed, so some people started spreading stories."

"If they weren't true, why do you call him the 'black sheep in the family?'"

"Because he was a temperamental bastard who beat his wife and children. At least, that's what my da said."

I had known another man like that. My father.

"Some people believe Spencer Tuck came from a long line of hereditary witches."

Paul tilted his head. "What's that?" He was either acting— and very good at it—or he honestly didn't know.

"You know. Where witchcraft is part of your family heritage."

Paul shook his head. "Well, if that was the case, I would certainly have heard about it." He paused. "Do you happen to remember the name of that book you were reading? Now you've got me curious."

I did, and I also knew exactly where it was. At my house, hidden in a box in a closet. "No, sorry. I don't."

Paul took my arm and steered me behind a large truck offloading supplies. "Rory just pulled up. Let's just wait a few here until he's in his trailer." He looked down at me with a sly smile.

"Unless you'd like to say hi. Maybe give him an update on how Hugo is doing."

"No, thank you."

Paul chuckled and released my arm. He peered around a corner. "It's all clear. He's in his trailer."

My phone buzzed in my pocket. I glanced down at the screen and read the flurry of arriving messages with a sinking heart. All from Ron Mendez in our new command center.

Entity emergence in Elysian Park.

Entities.

On the other side of Rory Tuck's fence.

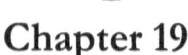

Chapter 19

I wanted to leave quickly, graciously, and without raising suspicion. But I was in no mood to pretend. "Paul, I need to go. Something's come up. Thank you for the tour, and I'll see you around."

I pulled off my hard hat, tossed it to Paul, and headed for the gate. While keeping an eye out for falling beams and tree limbs, of course.

On the way to my car, I called Ron. "I'm at the construction site, but I want to see this outbreak from the Elysian Park side. Can you have someone meet me at the La Loma gate?"

Ron was already on it. "Bailey's on standby, so I'll send her. She'll have a couple of Smoke Bombs with her. Do you have your slingshot?"

I loved how he was checking up on me. Though I could see how that might get old. "Yes, and I have a couple of pouches too. I'll meet her there, and we can take her security car."

Minutes later, Bailey and I were on our way to Elysian Park.

I buckled my seatbelt while the SUV sped through the La Loma gate. The guard waved at us, then returned to the guardhouse. After the chupacabra incident, most of them preferred to hang out indoors, even when the weather was nice.

"Any idea what they are?" I asked.

"No. But there are a lot of them, according to the heatmap."

Heatmap technology was limited. It flagged the arrival of entities into our world but didn't detect their type or even the size.

It could give us a good idea of the number, but not even that was always accurate.

I sighed. "A lot as in half a dozen? A dozen?"

"Thirteen." Glittery pink shadow ringed Bailey's eyes. Whatever she was using seemed to stay put all day.

Elysian Park was just to the north of Chavez Ravine, but it had been years since I had driven through it, and I had forgotten how big it was. It was one of Los Angeles's oldest parks, with hiking trails, picnic areas, and views of downtown Los Angeles.

It was also an entity favorite.

At this time of day, during the middle of the week, there weren't many people around. Well-publicized entity eruptions might have had something to do with that too. Not that I blamed anyone. Why risk the inconvenience of their day off getting ruined by entities?

We sped past several empty playing fields and a horseshoe pit. Bailey seemed to know exactly where she was going.

"You been here before?" I asked.

She nodded. "Yeah. After you told us about the ghoul, I decided to come check it out. So if any more entities showed up, I'd know where to go."

I looked over at her in surprise. "You're kidding?"

"No! Justin and Liam came too. And I guess it paid off 'cause here we are."

"I'm impressed," I said. And I meant it.

"Well, our new places are all near the border with the park. They're just starting to replace the fence there, so it feels a little exposed. Justin's wife stays home with the baby, and she was a little nervous moving so close to the park, so we decided to do a little field trip."

Justin hadn't said anything to me. Then again, he wouldn't want to seem like a complainer.

Bailey pulled over and parked by a grove of tall trees. It looked shady and cool. Also dark.

We grabbed our purple pouches and batons. I felt for my slingshot in my front pack, but in my haste, I had left it in the car. Ron would not approve, but I wasn't worried. I had responded to hundreds of entity emergences without one. As long as we had Smoke Bombs, we would be fine.

Long hair was a known hazard in entity management, but Bailey and I both refused to part with our locks. Before heading into the grove, I tied back my hair, and she stuffed her copper mane under a baseball cap.

Batons in front of us, we stepped into the grove, looking around warily. Except for birds chirping in the trees and squirrels rustling in the brush, all was quiet. I much preferred my entities to appear in the middle of a field or even by a lake, where I could see them. Dark places with lots of vegetation made me nervous.

"There!" Bailey whispered, pointing at a patch of ground just ahead.

The trees on either side of the trail bowed together, forming a canopy blocking out the sun. Classic eruption site. A hole surrounded by a pile of dirt. A *tall* pile.

Correction. Three holes, several yards apart.

Great.

"Where are they?" I asked, looking around.

Bailey bit her lip. She peered down into one hole, then the others. "These are deep." She sounded perplexed.

"They can't have gone far."

Bailey nodded, and we both began looking under bushes, anywhere a disoriented entity might hide. We started close to the eruption sites and began working our way outward.

I was moving toward what appeared to be a shallow cave in a short cliff when Bailey screamed. My heart leaped into my mouth.

A small figure was wrapped around Bailey's head. She had dropped her baton and was spinning around, blind, arms flailing. All I could make out was its gray, wrinkled backside, but I knew exactly what it was. A chaneque. I had encountered them on Olvera Street in downtown LA.

A rustling overhead made me look up. More chaneques were hanging from branches high in the trees. One stared down at me, leering. That was another thing about Mexican fairies. They couldn't fly, but with a spring-loaded tail, they could really jump.

I leapt to the side so they didn't land straight on me, then pinched the chaneque grabbing Bailey on the back of its meaty thigh as hard as I could.

That did it. Its arms went limp. It dropped to the ground, shrieking.

In one swift move, Bailey slammed her pouch next to its small head, and purple smoke exploded into the air. Two chaneques fell out of the tree. The others scrambled into higher branches.

"I am so not in the mood for this," I said.

"Little fuckers." Bailey rubbed her face. It was covered in scratches from the chaneque's sharp nails.

At the sound of footsteps pounding on the dirt path, we exchanged looks of relief. Backup had arrived. A small group of Occult Affairs officers hurried toward us, purple pouches dangling from their belts.

Behind them was a two-man film crew, camera rolling.

Bailey scowled. "What the hell is all this, Marcus?"

Marcus was a powerfully built man in his thirties, with long, twisted hair. "Thanks for getting this party started for us, Bailey."

He had a deep rumble of a voice. "All right, everyone, stand back. We need to wait a few minutes, but it won't be long. They're just behind us."

Marcus had started working for Occult Affairs just before I left, so I had only met him once, and that was brief. I cleared my throat.

"I'm head of security at Chavez Ravine. Formerly with OA. What exactly are we supposed to be waiting for?"

The film crew ignored us, too busy focusing on the chaneques still in the tree.

"Malena B." Marcus clasped his hands behind his back, in the manner of a soldier awaiting orders.

The skin on my face felt weirdly tight.

Bailey leaned toward me. "Isn't that your mom?"

"Yes," I managed to say through gritted teeth. "It certainly is."

Bailey gave a little shrug. "Cool. I've always wanted to meet her."

I shot Bailey a stern look, then turned to Marcus. "There are ten very bad-tempered Mexican fairies capable of jumping long distances up in that tree. Chavez Ravine is just that way." I pointed. "We can't risk them jumping onto our property. If you don't hit them with Smoke Bombs, I will."

Marcus shook his head. "No, ma'am. That won't be happening. We will all wait patiently until Malena B gets here."

The other officers avoided my gaze. Frustration bubbled up inside me. Just over the fence in Chavez Ravine, I had full authority. Here, I was just another civilian.

Before I could consider my annoyingly limited options, a familiar voice called out from behind the officers.

"Here I am!" my mother said in a sing-song voice. "Oh, Madeline! Mija! What are you doing here?"

As if my mother had forgotten I worked right next door. *Classic.*

She was wearing an outfit more suited for the stage than the woods: a long purple caftan with gold embellishments and strappy gold sandals. Her makeup was over the top too. Heavy on the smoky eyeshadow and red lipstick.

My mother clasped her hands together, looking all around. "And where are the poor things?"

I pointed. "The chaneques are above your head, Mother."

"Oh, there you are." She turned to the cameras. "Chaneques date back to the time of the Aztecs and are wonderful guardians of nature." She held out her hands to the creatures squatting in the trees. "Come down. There's nothing to fear."

Unless you're afraid of an entity preserve in the desert.

"They can be a bit feisty, Mother." The chaneques on Olvera Street had grabbed my hair and dragged me across the cobblestones.

My mother pursed her lips and shook her head. "I don't think they'll be feisty with me." She beckoned at them again. "Come now. Hablame."

"I seriously doubt they speak Spanish," I said. One of the Aztec languages was more like it.

My mother shot me a dark, warning look that said, "Back off." "We don't need a spoken language."

Message received. Besides, as satisfying as it was to challenge my mother publicly, I was probably dragging things out.

The chaneques clambered down the branches, then dropped to the ground in front of my mother, swaying as if they were about to topple over.

Beside me, Bailey whispered, "This is amazing."

The man holding the camera crept closer.

There was nothing cute or whimsical about their appearance—gray, wrinkled skin, wizened faces set in permanent frowns. I gave my mother credit. She didn't appear the tiniest bit nervous. I had seen her deal with entities a few times before, and no matter how big or intimidating, she was never rattled.

The chaneques wobbled closer and clung to her skirt, like children who had just found their mother.

Malena motioned to a small young woman with shaggy blonde hair standing behind her. The woman—presumably a production assistant—darted forward with a large floor pillow, then helped my mother lower herself onto it. For one moment, I assumed the creatures would climb into her lap, but instead, they sat crossed-legged in front of her.

She closed her eyes and held her hands out. The ugly things' eyes fluttered shut, and their faces scrunched up, as if listening. My mother was nodding. The cameraman darted around for a better angle. The production assistant appeared transfixed by the unfolding scene.

Malena might have been a difficult mother, but she was good TV.

The chaneques listed to the side, then toppled over, one by one, until they were all lying on the ground at my mother's feet.

She opened her eyes and smiled beatifically. "They're so exhausted after their journey. They say the last thing they remember, they were guarding a stream from some outsiders, and then they were here. I told them they're not the only ones and they'll be looked after, but like all the others, they just want to go home. That's the one thing all entities have in common. They can't explain how they came to be in our world, and they don't know how to get back."

When I glanced over at Bailey, she had tears in her eyes. The scene was interrupted by the arrival of a news crew. It wasn't one of our local stations, but a crew from a national network.

The production assistant rushed over to help my mother to her feet. And then my mother was giving an interview to a pretty, busty reporter with a gap in her teeth. Obviously, this had all been arranged in advance.

Malena had always known how to work the media, and she hadn't lost her edge. The cameras rolled while the reporter bombarded her with questions. There wasn't anything left for Bailey and me to do. When the cameras were put away, Occult Affairs would crate up the chaneques, and everything would go back to normal until the next outbreak.

Bailey was watching the interview intently. I tapped her on the shoulder and jerked my head in the direction of the car.

We had just reached the trail when my mother said, "I don't know why entities have never appeared in Chavez Ravine. But it's always been a very special place. Maybe you should ask the new head of security what *she* thinks."

It was a good thing I didn't have my slingshot.

Pretending not to hear, I hurried to the car, with Bailey close on my heels. I had no desire to be a trained monkey in my mother's media circus.

After I buckled my seatbelt, Bailey said, "What your mom did back there was amazing. Are you sure you can't do that? Because that would come in very handy."

That was a serious understatement.

"I'm sure," I said firmly. A muscle in my jaw twitched.

Chapter 20

We stopped by a small clinic in Palo Verde Plaza and had Bailey patched up. When I arrived back at my office, the guard at the La Loma gate called. A TV reporter wanted to interview me. It would take five minutes, she promised.

Thanks, Mom.

"Tell her I'm in a meeting and to call Cora Bernal for a statement." I hung up and punched in Cora's number.

The HOA president was used to dealing with the media, but she was surprised to learn my mother had sent them. "I wonder why she would do that?"

I sighed. If she'd had a few hours, I could have tried to explain it to her.

I took care of some paperwork and several emails, stopped by the command center to give Ron a public pat on the back for handling our first entity alert so smoothly, and headed home. All I wanted to do was take a hot bath, but I still had to make the protection sachets I had promised Clare.

My thoughts kept returning to the eucalyptus limb. Paul had made it sound like I was just in the wrong place at the wrong time, but two near-fatal accidents at the construction site? And with one common denominator: Rory Tuck, who happened to really, really dislike me and was related to Spencer Tuck, a reputed hereditary witch. Maybe Rory had inherited something more than just the councilman's bad temper. Those didn't feel like random mishaps.

Filling the little brocade bags with herbs and seeds was therapeutic, and eventually, I fell into a soothing rhythm, packing the sachets, tying them off, and saying a few words. When I was done, I felt relaxed and very satisfied, like I had accomplished something important.

I was standing at my workbench, savoring the moment, when the front door burst open.

It was Julia holding a bottle of wine. Apparently, there was something to celebrate, which was often the case with her.

"The board approved my plan for a festival!"

I didn't even have to move. Julia went into the kitchen, poured the wine, and flopped on the wicker couch in the sunroom. It was her favorite area in the house.

I sat next to her and pulled up my knees. "What festival?"

"The cactus festival! Remember?"

It was coming back to me. Somewhere between me getting nowhere with Hernan Frias and getting no further with my mother, Julia had mentioned a festival of some sort. Clearly, I had been distracted.

"Give me the highlights?"

Julia was wearing black flowy pants and a white halter top that showed off her golden-brown skin to its best advantage. Her auburn hair had been swept up into a bun. She was one of those rare women who didn't seem to know they were beautiful.

Sam sat on her lap while she stroked his neck. He blinked innocently at me with his green eyes. The cat lived in my house rent-free, and yet he denied me petting privileges while bestowing them freely on Julia and my next-door neighbor.

"Well, you know how we have all this amazing cactus that Ben Tomas planted forever ago? And I started using the cactus as a motif in my pottery, and some shops are selling all these cute pillows and throws and artwork with cactus on them. And now the restaurants have started serving up nopales dishes. So, I thought, what could we do to celebrate all the beautiful cactus we have here? You know how some neighborhoods have cute street festivals? Why not have one here? We can let the public in for a special one-day event that celebrates Chavez Ravine. It sounds amazing, yeah?

"And the board agreed?" I was stunned.

Julia nodded. "I know. I was a little surprised they went for it too. But Charlie said the board had been looking for something to take the focus off the negative headlines."

"No one asked my opinion," I said.

"Is there a problem?" Julia studied me, head tilted to the side.

"For one thing, I'm head of security, and no one bothered to ask how we'd keep our residents and visitors safe. For another, what if we have an entity incident? We'll have no way of containing the story if it's recorded on a thousand phones in the hands of strangers. It just sounds more than a little risky to me."

Julia shrugged. "Entities are popping up all the time, everywhere. It's not like the old days, when we all shut ourselves inside our houses and never went anywhere. We just go on with our lives, you know?"

She had a point, but still. I was miffed I hadn't even received a phone call before the board made its decision.

"When's this festival?" I sounded grumpy.

"Last Sunday of the month."

"But that's, like, two weekends from now!" Barely enough time to get an event security company lined up.

"We're trying to tag-team onto the street fair they're having down in the Solano neighborhood. That was Eileen's idea. She knows the woman who runs it. And the board didn't want to give too much advance notice because they don't want to be overwhelmed. I think they're doing this as kind of a test run to see how it goes."

"I take it Eileen is going to organize the festival?"

Julia laughed. "Of course. You know how she is. But she wants me to help her. I'll be doing the artwork for the posters."

The doorbell rang.

It was Clare. I handed her a paper bag with the sachets inside, hoping to get her back on her way, but it was not to be. Julia immediately noticed the little white brocade bag hanging around Clare's neck.

"Oh! Look at that! Did Maddy make you a protection sachet?"

The next thing I knew, Clare had joined us in the sunroom and was telling the whole story to an enraptured Julia.

"You know, her great-aunt Lencha Bantacorte was the most famous bruja ever to live in Chavez Ravine?" Julia said breathlessly. "And she lived right here in La Loma. It's amazing, yeah?"

Clare blinked. "What's a bruja?"

"A Mexican witch," Julia replied. Noticing Clare's eyes widen, she added, "A good kind of witch. One who helps keep her community healthy and safe. Maddy keeps saying she didn't inherit any of her great-aunt's magic, but I don't think she's telling us the whole truth."

She winked in my direction, oblivious to my discomfort.

"Every time I visit this house, I can feel it. Her grandmother, Liliana Bantacorte, used to live here. Did Maddy tell you? See that workbench? That's where her grandmother used to make her cures. She was a curandera. A healer. But who knows, maybe she was a witch too. And then there's Malena B! She's Maddy's mother. You knew that, yeah?"

Clare's mouth was opening and closing while she tried to keep up with the flood of information.

"I thought your last name was Madrigal?" The poor girl sounded very confused.

"It is," I said. "My name used to be Bantacorte, but I changed it when I started working at Occult Affairs." I gave a helpless shrug. "You know, fewer questions about my mother and all that."

"But your mom is…famous." Clare's voice held a hint of reproach. As if I had been keeping a secret from her.

I sighed. "Yes, and sometimes, that can be a problem if you're trying to live an ordinary life."

Clare nodded slowly. "Oh. Okay." Her eyes widened. "My dad's going on tour with your mother. They just signed the deal. He's leaving the day after tomorrow or something crazy."

Now it was my turn to stare. "What do you mean 'going on tour?'"

"He's doing the security for her show." Clare sighed.

"He is?" My voice rose.

Stu hadn't said a thing about it. Then again, we hadn't talked in person for a few days. Some couple we were.

"You didn't know?" Clare frowned.

Julia sat back on the couch, watching us like she was at a tennis match.

"No." Annoyance—or something stronger—bubbled up inside me. "I'm sure he will. Eventually."

He should have said something. And why hadn't my mother mentioned it? Would Stu have told her about us? If so, had they conspired to keep it from me?

Julia jumped to her feet. "It's getting late, and poor Maddy looks exhausted, doesn't she, Clare? Why don't we clear out and let her get to bed, yeah?"

With that, Julia swept Clare out the front door, and in a few moments, I was alone with the cat and my growing anger.

I snatched my phone from the side table and tapped out a message to my mother. If I called her, I would lose it for sure.

Is Stu Wells handling your security?

Typing bubbles appeared, and words followed a moment later.

Yes. Such a wonderful man. And muy guapo. He told me you were dating, but to keep it a secret. And you didn't even tell your own mother. Tsk tsk.

Why is Stu going in person?

Because I've received death threats, and the sponsors asked him.

Death threats?

That was news to me.

Yes. VERY upsetting.

At that point, I should have picked up the phone, but I was in a bad mood.

Death threats from who?

The phone rang. It was my mother, sounding peevish. "I mean, really, mija. I tell you I'm getting death threats, and you don't even have the courtesy to call?"

I pushed my finger between my eyes. *Will this day ever end?*

"We're talking now, Mom."

"Only because *I* called *you*," she snapped.

"Okay. I'm sorry. You're right. I should have called. Are we good now? Who's sending you death threats?"

The tea kettle whistled in the background. "I have no idea who. Whoever it is says I'm consorting with demons and that I'm a demon lover and that I need to die."

"A demon lover?" I echoed.

"Yes. And the drawings they've sent are absolutely filthy. The pendejos behind the notes seem to think I'm actually having relations with the entities!"

"That's not the first time idiots have said stupid stuff like that."

"No," my mother conceded. "But it's the first time anyone's threatened to cut my head off and put it on a stake. And sent pictures of a machete."

"You're kidding?"

"I am not. They said they were going to do it live on stage so the whole world could watch."

"Well, Stu's the best in the business. You don't have anything to worry about. He'll keep you safe."

"I hope so." My mother sounded uncertain and, for once, vulnerable.

I felt the faintest flutter of fear.

By the time we hung up, the sun had gone down. I grabbed a club soda from the fridge and went out on the patio, staring up at the emerging stars and wondering when Stu was going to let me know he wouldn't be around for our special night together.

Yes, I was being unreasonable, but it still felt like a betrayal.

Chapter 21

The moment I closed my eyes, my mind went back to the eucalyptus limb pinning me to the ground, complete with sound effects. And when I had replayed that horrifying scene dozens of times, I started to catastrophize the situation with Stu.

He hadn't called to let me know he would be accompanying my mother on her tour, and I was left to read a lot into his silence. Every possibility played out in my head.

He was afraid to tell me because he knew I had a difficult relationship with my mother. Which made him a chickenshit.

He was afraid I was going to be dramatic. Which made him avoidant.

He had forgotten about us planning to spend our first night together. Which meant it had never been a big deal to him anyway.

And then, while I continued to toss and turn, earning an angry meow and paw swipe from Sam: Stu decided to leave town because he changed his mind about me and jumped at the first excuse to leave.

When the alarm went off in the morning, a perfectly reasonable explanation presented itself: The deal had just closed, and he planned to tell me today. If only I had started there, I'd have slept a lot better. Still, I wasn't about to contact him. I was going to let Stu stew.

When my phone chimed while I was making coffee, my heart did a weird little skip, and I tripped over Sam trying to get to the phone. It was Cora. My heart sank like a stone.

"Good morning." I hadn't meant to sound so glum.

"Everything all right?" Cora asked.

I sighed. "Nothing a good night's sleep won't cure."

"Just wait until you're my age." Cora chuckled. "Do you have a moment? You've been on my to-do list for several days now, Maddy. I've been taking care of both my grandsons, and that's thrown me way off schedule."

Positions on the Chavez Ravine Association board were voluntary but took up a lot of time. Cora also had a hand in her tamale restaurant empire, although most of the day-to-day operations had passed on to her adult kids.

"How's the command center going along?" she asked.

"Good." I quickly scanned the last message from the Bishop guardhouse. "Everything's going fine. We responded to the eruption in Elysian Park since it was a bit too close to home, and everything went very smoothly. And no new eruptions around our perimeter since then."

Which was a big relief because I had done some basic magic—making the sachet bags for Clare—but I hadn't told Cora about my mom's suspicion that my attempts at brujería were somehow attracting entities closer to our borders.

The cat glared at me from the door, obviously outraged at the delay in his morning meal service.

"I saw your mother on the news," Cora said. "After getting that call from the reporter, I was curious, of course. She's really quite something. My son-in-law said he tried to get tickets to her show, but they were all sold out."

Good news for my mother's financial portfolio. "So, how's everything on your end?" I asked, hoping to get the conversation back on track.

"Well, if it's not one thing, it's another. Julia Suarez proposed a cactus festival in Palo Verde. I have to admit, I was dead set against the idea when I first heard about it. We've never had a public event like that before. But, of course, it came up for a vote, and everyone else seemed to think it was a wonderful idea."

"Yes, I heard. I have some concerns about letting so many people in with no vetting. And my staff is far too small to handle that kind of crowd, so I'm looking for a contract security firm to help us out."

A long silence followed. I hoped Cora was realizing the board had voted without considering the event's security and all its costs.

If she was, she decided not to say anything. "Hernan is making a very good recovery. I stopped by his place to drop off some tamales and was surprised to see him looking so good. If he doesn't have a relapse, I think whatever he's done to protect us will last a little longer."

Well, that is mixed news. Good because I hadn't yet been able to figure out how he had pulled that off. Bad because when Hernan was well enough, he had tried to stab me when I stopped him from sending rodent monsters to scare non-legacy homeowners.

"Let's hope that's the case," I said. "Especially with that cactus festival coming up."

We'd had the same conversation many times, but we were at an impasse with Hernan. Cora couldn't publicly accuse the man of using dark magic to further his goals for Chavez Ravine because she would sound crazy. And neither of us could convince him to do the right thing and help me to take over the spell.

"Let's see what the next few days bring," Cora said briskly. Then, after a pause, "My apologies for not letting you know sooner about the festival. I've just emailed you all the details. The board thinks the community could use a little image boost, all things considered. We may have moved a little too quickly, but what's done is done. Even Hernan voted for it."

Well, that isn't suspicious at all. Why would Hernan, who considered himself Chavez Ravine royalty, want a bunch of riffraff from Los Angeles stomping around his exclusive neighborhood?

"Did he say why?"

Cora cleared her throat. "He liked the notion of a festival celebrating the prickly pear cactus because it's so connected to our heritage."

In the city, life and events did not stop because of worries entities might or might not appear. Amusement parks still operated, and so did outdoor concerts, theater performances, and farmers markets. Entity appearances sometimes happened, and it was Occult Affairs's job to deal with them. It would be left to me and my team to do the same if entities appeared at the cactus festival.

When we hung up, I opened the document Cora had sent and read through the plans for the event.

It looked like there would be something for everyone. Cooking demos for the foodies, arts and crafts activities for the kids, music, and lots of vendors selling everything from churros and gift items to art and jewelry and, of course, Julia's pottery. There would even be a stand with prickly pear lemonade and margaritas and special event tickets for restaurants offering tasting menus.

I was relieved that most of the festival would be confined to Palo Verde. Though, once inside the gates, visitors would be able to travel freely within the community.

The festival looked like it would be fun for attendees but a headache for me. I needed to make sure it was as secure as any public event could be. After starting a list of everything we needed to do to get ready, I called Jo at the command center to put her in the loop.

"Just because we're opening the gates doesn't mean you get to sneak in the nerds," I said.

Jo gasped. "I would never!"

"Liar. But you and Holly are more than welcome. The festival doesn't start until eleven. If you can get here early, you can park at my place and take a shuttle into Palo Verde. I'll even make you breakfast."

"Only if you make chilaquiles."

If Jo only knew how easy they are to make. "Red sauce or green?"

"Red, please."

I was still concerned. Jo was one of my best friends, but all of Occult Affairs was obsessed with Chavez Ravine. The pressure to figure out why we had not had an entity eruption would be intense.

Well, if an entity expert or two came to enjoy our cactus festival, the board would just have to live with it. And maybe the next time they had a big decision to make, they would consult the expert they had at their disposal.

Namely, me.

Chapter 22

After I drained my second cup of coffee, I decided to work out. Hard. I pulled on my earphones, blasted some music, and sweated my way through a forty-five-minute shoulders-and-glutes weight session while Sam batted around a toy mouse Julia had given him.

When I tried taking a picture to send to Julia, he stopped abruptly and glared at me.

"What? Come on. It's cute."

He swatted the mouse and sent it skidding across the floor, then stalked out of the room, tail high in the air. Maybe my bad mood was catching. Or maybe I just had a weird cat.

"Can't you just be normal for once?" I called after him.

That made me laugh out loud.

It was pretty much all I wanted from life. Normalcy. A mother who listened to me occasionally. A boyfriend who didn't ditch me for my mother. A cat who showed me a little affection.

"Is that too much to ask?" I shouted into the hallway.

Sam meowed loudly. A door slammed.

I was in a yelling match with a fifteen-pound cat who could slam doors. Not normal at all.

The day was already heating up, but there was still enough time to get in a nice, brisk walk. If I hurried, I could even make it to Muertos Café for a piece of pan dulce. Between the calories burned by my workout and the Stu-induced anxiety, I deserved a treat.

I grabbed my keys and a water and headed out, still wearing shorts and a tank top. My next-door neighbor, Leo, waved while he got into his car. His husband, Toby, was watering the flowers, wearing a bathrobe.

"We haven't seen you in forever!" Leo called. "Can you come over for G and Ts soon?"

Leo was all dressed up in a slick blue suit, his silver-streaked dark hair slicked back.

I gave him a thumbs-up. "Are you going to court?"

"Yup. I'm saving Los Angeles, one scum bucket at a time." Leo grinned. He honked his horn and drove down the street.

I was halfway to La Loma Plaza when I heard another car honk. This time, it was Becca Tey, the actress who had been a target of Hernan's supernatural attacks.

She slowed and rolled her window down. "Hey, Maddy! Long time no see! Need a ride?"

"No, thanks. I need my steps."

I glanced into the window. She had full makeup on and was wearing a low-cut white top, which showed off her tan cleavage.

"You're looking sexy for so early in the morning."

Becca waved a hand at me. "I've got an audition. The part is a sixty-year-old woman, which means I need to look forty and show the girls off." She grimaced.

"Only in Hollywood." I laughed.

"Every time I put myself out there, I wonder why the hell I do it. You've got to be some kind of masochist to put up with the shit I've dealt with since hitting thirty-five."

I wished her good luck, and she roared off. Moments later, I was back to thinking about Stu. To make it stop, I sprinted the rest of the way.

The hill was steep, with a staircase running down to the lot below.

At the top of the staircase, above the La Loma Plaza, I paused. Among the cars parked along the street, a figure was leaning against a familiar white truck. Rory Tuck. For one awful moment, I thought he was going to lecture me about something, but instead, he climbed into his truck and began scrolling through his phone.

When I reached the bottom of the staircase and started to cross the parking lot, my phone chimed. My first thought was, of course, Stu, which sent my heart racing. I reached into my shorts to grab my phone, but an alarming noise behind me caused me to turn and look.

An SUV was barreling down the bumpy hill, headed straight for me.

I leapt aside. The vehicle shot past in a rush of air. My foot came down at a funny angle. My ankle rolled, and a pain shot up my leg when I slammed to the ground.

The SUV crashed into a light pole with a sickening smack.

"Hey!" a voice called. Feet pounded on asphalt.

I tried pulling myself up, but my ankle was on fire.

And then Paul Tuck was standing in front of me, eyes wide, mouth open. "You all right?"

I nodded, shaky all over. Talk about déjà vu. "I'm fine."

He sprinted over to the mangled SUV and peered through the closed passenger window. "There's no one inside. Someone must have forgot to set the brake."

I stared at the vehicle. It was one I had seen before, briefly, in my own driveway. It belonged to Clare Wells.

Before I could protest, Paul had his arm around my shoulder and was guiding me to a bench under the shade of a jacaranda tree. "That was close. You could have been killed."

Funny how that kept happening. I'd had three close calls, and each time, Rory Tuck had been nearby. Rory Tuck, the man who wanted to knock down my house so he could expand his housing development. The man who couldn't force me, but who wouldn't have to if an accident took me out instead.

"Yeah, I could have been." The pain in my ankle was making it hard to think straight.

"I'm beginning to think you're accident-prone." Paul crouched in front of me and lightly touched my swelling ankle. "Looks like you've sprained it."

"I didn't sprain it because I'm accident-prone. I sprained it because a car came at me and I jumped out of the way," I said through gritted teeth.

Paul tapped my bare knee. "Hey, hey. Just kidding. How about I go try to find a bag of ice and maybe a bandage to wrap that ankle?"

When I didn't answer, he placed both his hands around my calves and looked up at me.

"Stay right here, okay? I'll be right back. Don't move. And I'll bring some water too."

I stared after him, my thoughts muddled. From several yards away, a couple stared back at me. When they came into focus, I realized it was Stu and Clare. They must have been at Muertos Café because Stu was holding coffee cups.

He was dressed in a tan suit I had never seen before. My first thought was the color was all wrong. He looked much better in darker colors. The vertical lines around his mouth seemed more pronounced than usual, and his lips were pinched tight.

Clare hurried over to the SUV resting against the light pole. Stu was so focused on me that he didn't seem to notice it. He strode toward me.

"Who was that guy?"

Stu's suspicious tone was enough to make me wince.

"Him?" I shook my head. "He's just a guy who came to help after Clare's car nearly ran me down."

Stu glanced up at the hill and paled. "Her car came from up there? Are you okay?"

"I screwed up my ankle," I admitted.

Clare joined us, white-faced. "Dad. It's my fault! I could swear I pulled up the brake, but I guess I didn't." Her gazed shifted to me, stricken. "I'm so sorry, Maddy. I'm so sorry." Then she burst into tears.

Stu glanced over at the car against the pole, at me, then back again.

He tipped his head and scraped a hand through his brown hair. "I can't believe this. Goddammit, Clare."

"Stu, it was an accident," I said.

He exhaled loudly. "A careless one." Stu turned to his daughter and shook his head. "You're always in a hurry. How many times have I told you to slow down? Think about what you're doing?"

Clare cried harder. She clutched the pouch around her neck. "I know. I know."

Stu's expression softened. "Okay. Okay." He enveloped her in a hug and patted her back, avoiding my gaze.

I tried to stand up, testing my ankle gingerly. It hurt like hell and was probably sprained. But I'd had worse.

Paul came back with a bag of ice. He handed it to me with a curious look at Stu and Clare. "I'm guessing the runaway SUV belongs to you?"

Stu's face tightened. "That would be ours."

"And I'm guessing someone forgot to engage the brake?"

"Paul," I said in a warning voice. Before I could stop him, he was kneeling at my feet and wrapping a bandage around my ankle.

"What? I saw the whole thing happen. It nearly ran you over."

Stu crouched and took the bandage from Paul's hand. "I'll take care of this." He sounded friendly enough, but there was a subtle hint of warning in his tone.

Paul's mouth set in a thin line. He stood up, brushing off his knees.

Clare stopped crying and stood next to Paul, staring down at me with puffy, red-rimmed eyes. I took her hand and squeezed it.

"I'm fine, Clare. Lesson learned. Everything's okay."

Paul cleared his throat and shoved his hands in his pockets. Stu gave him a terse nod.

"I'm Stu Wells, and this is my daughter, Clare."

"Paul Tuck. Nice to meet you both." Paul gave a rueful smile. "All right. I'm out of here. It's back to work for me." Turning toward me, he added, "I'm glad I was here for yet another one of your mishaps." He winked and jogged toward his truck.

When he was out of earshot, Stu said to Clare, "Hey. Would you mind going back to the café and grabbing me a packet of sugar?"

Clare's eyes widened, but she nodded and walked away.

"What's this about *mishaps*?" Stu asked when we were alone.

"I've had a run of bad luck up at the construction site. A falling beam, then a massive tree limb. Paul's the manager up there."

Stu cleared his throat. "So, you were visiting him?"

"No. I was visiting Rory Tuck, the owner. I was snooping around. Trying to figure out why he might not want security cameras looking at his site."

"Is that all?" Stu sounded uncertain.

I snorted. "If you're worried about Paul, don't. He can come on a little strong, but I fend him off just fine."

Stu gave me a sheepish grin. "Sorry. My head goes to dark places sometimes. I don't like the sound of these mishaps."

"I don't like them either," I admitted. "Sometimes, it seems like someone is out to get me." I paused. "I have a question for you. Why did I have to hear from Clare that you're leaving town to join the Malena B show? You won't be here for our sleepover."

Stu sighed. "There's no excuse for that. I know how things are with your mom. I suspected you wouldn't be too happy with me, and I kept putting it off. I'm sorry."

"So am I," I replied stiffly. "Of all the people you could ditch me for, you chose my mother."

Stu sat next to me on the bench and slung an arm around my shoulder. His hand was warm, his grip firm but gentle. "It's not like that. Your mother isn't hiring me. The promoter is. And they're a big entertainment company. I couldn't very well say no."

"It's spelled n-o." I sounded and felt like a sulking child.

His fingers lightly brushed my collarbone. "You know that's not how this business works."

"You still should have told me."

Stu's mouth opened, then closed. "I *was* going to tell you."

I didn't know whether I wanted to cry or throw the ice pack at him. Stu was coming off a bad divorce. Maybe he wasn't ready for another relationship. If that was the case, there was nothing I could do.

I took a deep breath, trying to calm the storm raging within me. "Yeah, that would have been nice." I stood up. My ankle throbbed with pain. "Maybe I'll see you when you get back?"

Stu just stared. I picked up my phone and tapped out a message to Ron at the command center, asking him to send someone to pick me up. Stu looked confused. Or maybe helpless.

"Of course, you'll see me."

Stu grabbed my hand and squeezed it, but I couldn't look at him. I was being unreasonable, but I couldn't help it.

"I gotta use the ladies," I lied, pulling my hand away.

I could sense Stu staring after me while I limped toward the plaza.

"Maddy," he called out.

I pretended not to hear him.

Chapter 23

My ankle didn't hurt as much as my heart did. I was being unreasonable by not giving Stu a break, but I felt what I felt. There was no reasoning with the ache in my chest.

Sometimes, being a chingona had its downsides.

Rather than face the evening alone, I invited Julia to dinner. Then I asked Leo and Toby to join too, as insurance against the night turning into a therapy session. I needed to get my head straight about what had happened with Stu before I began blabbing about it to other people.

Ice packs had kept my ankle from swelling up too badly, and I had been able to limp my way through Palo Verde Market to buy ingredients for arroz con pollo and a salad. Julia said she would bring dessert, and the guys were coming with the fixings for G and Ts.

I received several messages from the command center and a few from Stu repeating his apology. My replies sounded as stiff as cardboard.

The evening air was still warm, so I poured myself a glass of chilled pinot grigio and sipped it while I diced the onion and green pepper, adding them to the cilantro sprigs sizzling in a pan of olive oil. When the onion was translucent, I stirred in the rice and watched it toast, trying to keep my mind on the dish and not Stu.

The rice was an even golden brown, so I added crushed garlic, chicken broth, and tomato sauce. In a separate pan, I added olive oil and seared the chicken, then turned it down to simmer and put on the lid. I would assemble the dish when we were ready to eat.

In a quick salad with hearts of palm, I threw in a can of crab and some capers. The dressing was easy too. Olive oil, fresh lemon juice, and black pepper.

Partway through setting the table, I stopped.

Cars didn't just go rolling down hills. Stu's SUV had an automatic transmission, so it should have stayed right where it was when Clare put it in park. It wouldn't matter if she had forgotten the hand brake. Cars in park didn't roll away. Someone tampered with the transmission, or someone who knew magic had set the SUV on its murderous journey.

So, what *had* Rory Tuck been doing at La Loma Plaza?

Julia swept in looking like a vision from the past, wearing a white spaghetti strap sundress and sandals. Her auburn hair was tied back in a single braid.

"It smells delicious in here!" She set down a covered tray on the counter. "I made Mexican wedding cookies."

Sam jumped on a chair and pushed his nose into Julia's side.

"Oh, you like me, don't you?" Julia scratched Sam behind the ears, and he purred loudly. "If only Ben Tomas would give me one quarter of the attention you do, my little man, I'd be a very, very happy girl."

Julia flopped into an empty chair and pulled the cat onto her lap. Sam's large, furry frame spilled over her legs. That didn't last long because Leo and Toby arrived, and Sam was all about Leo. Leo picked him up, slung him over his shoulder like a sack of potatoes, and proceeded to tell us about his day in court while Toby mixed gin and tonics.

As far as I knew, Leo was the only person alive Sam allowed to treat him like a baby.

And that's when I realized I'd had a very rough day.

First, I had allowed a man to make me feel like an insecure teenager, and then I fretted over a fifteen-pound furball who liked the guy next door better than he liked me. Maybe I needed to go back to therapy. By the time I had finished tossing the salad, the conversation had moved on without me.

"That asshole upped his offer," Toby was saying. "To everyone on the block, I hear. Well, not to Maddy because she's legacy. He can't."

"That doesn't mean he hasn't tried." I transferred the chicken to the pan of rice and drizzled some chicken broth over the top.

Leo gasped. "He's not supposed to do that! That's against the HOA rules! God, I hate that guy. Do you want me to write up a cease and desist for you?"

"Rory's cousin isn't so bad," Toby said. "He's actually pretty nice. I met him while on my morning run." He paused, shooting a sly look in his husband's direction. "Actually, he's pretty hot."

Leo snapped his head up. "Hey! I'm standing *right* here."

Toby blew him a kiss. "Just kidding. Seriously, Julia. Have you seen him? I know you've got that weird thing for Ben Tomas, but if he's not into you, then he's crazy. And you know what they say: A bird in hand is worth two in the bush." He wriggled his eyebrows suggestively.

"That doesn't mean what you think it means!" Leo laughed.

Toby swiped Leo's empty glass from the table and topped it up from the cocktail shaker. "And why are we sitting in the kitchen when there's a lovely patio out back?"

Leo sighed. "Because it always smells so good in here. And that's saying something because Toby is an awesome cook."

We took our plates outside, ate, and gossiped. I had almost forgotten about all my troubles when Julia asked if I was going to my mother's show.

"No," I said firmly.

"Why not?" All three asked in unison.

"I've had enough of Malena B's theatrics, thank you very much."

"Is there drama?" Leo asked. "She seems totally amazing, but if there's drama, I really want to know."

I crumpled a napkin and dropped it onto my plate. "It's just typical mother-daughter stuff. Nothing too exciting. She can just be…a little much."

Julia picked up my plate and headed for the kitchen. "Clare Wells said her dad is going to handle Malena's security. Didn't she, Maddy?"

I shot Julia a dark look.

Leo and Toby were all over that. "Is he?" Leo asked. "Like, her entire tour?"

"Yes." I sounded glum.

"How long will he be gone?"

I pressed a finger between my eyes and shrugged. If the conversation had been a car, it would have just plunged off a cliff.

"Not sure."

Leo and Toby exchanged looks. Toby shook his head slightly, and Leo gave a little grimace in response. I was about to get the "tread lightly" treatment.

Fine. The less said, the better.

The doorbell rang. Sam went racing for the front door.

"I didn't know cats did that," Toby said.

"He's not like most cats." I got up, heart fluttering. Maybe it was Stu coming to smooth things over.

It wasn't. It was Clare and a teenage girl.

Clare thrust a bunch of flowers at me. "I came over to say I'm sorry."

"That's sweet of you. Thank you." While I appreciated her thoughtfulness, I was afraid of the direction the conversation might go if she came inside. We chatted a few moments, but instead of leaving, Clare introduced her friend. "This is Iris. She's at school with me. Uh, I was hoping you could maybe help her?"

"Help her?"

Both girls stared at me hopefully.

Iris was taller than me by several inches, with long, straight black hair parted in the middle and Cupid's bow lips. She chewed on a ragged thumbnail. There was tension in her eyes, and her shoulders were curled slightly forward. The poor girl looked beaten down.

Clare nodded eagerly. "Yes. There's this girl on the basketball team who's really jealous of Iris, and she's always making up lies and shit about her. It's driving her crazy. I was hoping, maybe, that you could make something to help protect her? Like you did for me with the entities?"

And that's exactly the direction I was afraid of. I pulled them both into the entryway. Sam meowed and swirled around their legs.

I lowered my voice and said, "I have some guests. We don't have to tell them what we're talking about, okay?"

"Oh," Clare said. "Okay. So, you'll help?"

I didn't have the heart to refuse her. "Of course. But there's no guarantee it's going to work."

Iris blinked rapidly. "I'm kind of desperate, so anything you can do, I'd really appreciate it." She hesitated. "We have practice tomorrow morning."

Which was a nice way of saying she needed it immediately.

"Wait in the living room," I said, then went outside.

Leo was already yawning, and Julia and Toby were clearing the plates. It was going to be an early evening, thankfully.

"It's so cute Clare comes to you with her problems, yeah?" Julia whispered before heading out the door.

When the three of us were alone, I used my iron scissors to snip a lock of Iris's black hair from the underlayer. Her dark eyes widened.

"This is so weird."

"Yeah." Iris would get no argument from me. It *was* weird.

Lencha had grown up learning brujería on a ranch in Mexico before moving to Chavez Ravine. She had probably never questioned her right to practice the craft or her abilities.

On the other hand, I had a bad case of bruja imposter syndrome. But I was working on it.

I offered the girls the leftover Mexican wedding cookies Julia had made and suggested they mix up some chocolate milk. When they had disappeared into the kitchen, Sam on their heels, I went into my office and consulted Lencha's journal.

In the sunroom, Little Lencha glowed a soft yellow, as if lit from within. She hadn't done that in some time, so I took it as a good sign. I made a protection bracelet from purple ribbons, then laid it on the workbench.

The spell was simple, but it still required my full concentration. One just couldn't say the words. I had to *feel* them, imbue them with meaning. And I had to take the process very seriously. That was the most challenging part.

When I was finally done, a feeling of warmth and well-being spread through my chest.

The girls had decided to make hot chocolate and had poured a little milk into a saucer for Sam, who was staring at it suspiciously.

Clare chuckled. "He's so funny. Maybe he's lactose intolerant."

"He's the biggest cat I've ever seen," Iris said.

"He's special, all right," I replied.

Sam snapped his head up, and he meowed loudly.

"Weirdo." I sat across from Iris. "Can you hold out your wrist, please?"

Iris stared at the scissors in my hand, her face turning ashen. "Are you going to cut me?" Her voice was thin and high.

The poor girl. She probably thought the protection spell involved bloodletting.

"No, Iris. I'm not going to cut you." I pulled the bracelet I had just made from my pocket and dangled it in front of her. The satin ribbons were braided together, with the lock of hair woven throughout. I tied the bracelet around her pale left wrist and used the scissors to cut off the excess.

Iris studied it with large, solemn eyes. "Oh, it's pretty."

I supposed it was. Julia had chosen a beautiful shade of purple when we were at the botanica. The ribbon had cost more, but we hadn't been able to resist.

"Does she have to do anything special?" Clare asked.

Good question. Clare was a smart girl.

"No. But I do have a question for you, Iris. What is something you like to do? Something you're good at? Maybe even something you want to do as a job one of these days?"

Iris stared down at her bracelet, her nose wrinkling. "I like to write. Stories. My dad wants me to go to college to get a job that pays a lot of money, but I want to write books. Why?"

"Because *that's* who you are, Iris. A storyteller. That girl who's giving you a hard time? That's something she can't take away from you. It's who you are. Remember that. She's just an idiot with opinions that don't matter, but you're a storyteller. Okay?"

Iris nodded. "Okay," she whispered, holding up her wrist and inspecting the bracelet. "I love it. Thank you."

And then she hugged me.

I couldn't remember hugging anyone when I was her age. Maybe this generation was just more demonstrative, or maybe I had been the cold, hard teenager my mother accused me of being.

They said goodnight, calling their thanks all the way down the path to the car.

I watched them drive off into the night, wondering if some purple ribbon, a little hair, and my heartfelt words were enough to make a bully back off.

Chapter 24

The next day, the heatmap was quiet. No eruptions meant we could keep people in training sessions, so I was a happy camper, at least as far as work was concerned. When another day passed without a blip on the heatmap, I began to wonder if it was working, so I called Jo. The heatmap in Occult Affairs was also quiet. Which was weird but not unprecedented.

We weren't in unknown territory until a week had passed with no entity eruptions.

Their sudden absence was big news. The nerds at Occult Affairs were baffled. There had been lags between entity eruptions before, but never for this long. The news media were all over it, covering a range of theories.

All of this was bad news for my mother. Her tour depended on disoriented, newly arrived entities. Without them, there wasn't much of a show.

I knew things were bad when my mother texted me to get my advice. Which meant she was either desperate or in some kind of trouble.

This time, it was desperation.

Madeline, what do you think about bringing entities from the preserve to participate in the show? Who knows how long this dry spell will last, and the sponsor's getting antsy.

MOM. That does not sound like a good idea.

That surprises me. I thought you'd like the idea.

What does Stu say?

I wasn't about to ask him myself.

He's paid to worry, mija.

That was what I thought. She was looking for permission to ignore Stu's advice, but there was no way I was going to give it to her. The plan was incredibly risky: fetch an entity from the preserve and put it on stage with my mother for a "conversation." This wouldn't be a dazed new arrival stumbling over its own feet. Or paws, or whatever. It would be an inhabitant that might well have a chip on its shoulder and could have built up a tolerance to Smoke Bombs.

And the entity they had in mind made my skin crawl—an eastern Russian giant with pale skin and long, flowing hair.

He had been among the early wave of entities and had found his way into a theater, where he went on a rampage. After my mother communicated with him, he had calmed down, but that wasn't the end of the trouble. Turned out, women found him irresistible, and some alone time with a handler had resulted in the first and only entity-human offspring, which was still being studied at a secret location.

I could follow the sponsor's logic: since new entities weren't showing up, drag out the sexiest one available and have my mom chat with the eye candy. This was not a conversation for text, so I called her.

"I don't think these people are thinking this through, Mom," I said.

"What do you mean?" My mother sounded tired.

"Maybe you can keep this entity calm, and maybe it won't go on another rampage. Maybe it won't become angry and violent after being in the preserve. *Maybe.* But even so, there are people who don't like the way entities are treated. They think it's cruel to cart them off into the middle of nowhere and warehouse them, as nice as the preserve is. And now someone wants to bring out

155

the most notorious, most sympathetic entity and put him on stage in front of a paying public? For entertainment?

"Think about it, Mom. The tour—and you—are going to take some serious heat. You've already been accused of treating entities like some sort of circus act. This will really piss off a lot of people."

"Oh," my mother said faintly. "I hadn't thought of it that way." She hesitated. "What should I do?"

"Say no. The last time I looked, it was *your* name on the marquee. Make something up if you have to. Tell them you're getting bad vibes from the desert."

"But we're at the Hollywood Bowl on Saturday. It was specifically chosen because there were so many entity outbreaks in the area. But if they don't appear, we don't have a show!"

My mother was faced with a real quandary. She had built a small empire on unpredictable, sporadic entity eruptions. Everything from her TV appearances and her deal with Occult Affairs to her documentaries and her live tour depended on something nobody could control or predict. Which had always made me uncomfortable. I had told her so, but my mother thought my job as a daughter was to provide unconditional support. She had not wanted to hear it.

"Honestly, Mom, it's not all on you. There was no way you could have predicted this would happen. It's the promoter's job to figure out what to do. Postponements, ticket vouchers for future shows, whatever. But putting that seven-foot creature on stage in front of a live audience? What the hell are those people thinking? You know the weird effect he has on women. And there will be lots of those in the audience and backstage. God only knows what could happen."

"Ay, Dios mio." My mother gasped. "I hadn't thought of that either."

"That's the last thing you need. Entity-human sex live on stage."

My mother surprised me by laughing. "Some people already call me a demon lover. Can you imagine what they'd call me then?"

"A monster madam?"

We both laughed. I couldn't remember the last time that had happened.

Chapter 25

The entity dry spell continued. Which was great because I was incredibly busy finishing all the training and getting ready for the cactus festival.

I was proud of the way my team had pulled together to accomplish everything on our ambitious to-do list. Late Friday afternoon, I drove to North Hollywood, where the last Slingshot Academy training session was underway. The NoHo Axe Throwing Bar was packed with people. The chalkboard above the bar announced the day's special: slow-cooked brisket sandwiches. The smoky, meaty aroma made my stomach grumble.

I headed toward the back and found my group in the last lane. They were impossible to miss. For one thing, ammo hitting metal cans sounded a lot different than axes thudding against wooden targets. For another, my team was wearing a ridiculous amount of camo.

"You do know this is the Valley and not the woods, right?" I said to Ron Mendez.

He shrugged, unfazed by my teasing. "'Course. It's comfortable. But check this out." He proceeded to demonstrate his impressive command of the slingshot.

Bailey sniffed. "I hate to say this, but his aim is so good that if we ever have a serious problem, we may need to yank him out of the command center."

He spun around to face her. "Hey. I know what you're up to. Hands off my job." But I could tell he was pleased.

The owners of the academy, Chad and Tanner, were on their best, most professional behavior. They were doing a final evaluation, assessing each team member's skills and giving them a letter grade.

"I wish we had certificates or something." Chad shoved his hands into his pockets.

Tanner cracked his knuckles. "I told you we should! You said it was a stupid idea."

"I didn't say that!"

"Yes, you did. You said certificates were for middle school kids, not grown-ups."

So much for the professional facade. I quickly thanked them, then offered to buy my team a celebratory drink at the bar. Chad and Tanner excused themselves, mumbling something about needing to get to a gaming party, whatever that was.

A bartender with a thick black beard and a woolly chest peeking out of a black muscle T-shirt served our drinks at a large picnic table in the quietest corner of the main hall.

I stood up. "We've got a big day ahead. But first, I want to toast your new slingshot skills. Congratulations, and let's hope you don't need to use them at the cactus festival tomorrow." I raised my glass. "You are all amazing, and I'm grateful for your hard work."

"Tomorrow should be a snap without entities to worry about," Justin said.

"We've got plenty of other stuff to worry about. Chavez Ravine is opening its doors to the public for the first time. We've got the highest concentration of wealth in all of LA. Anything bad happens? It's on us. And when the festival is over, we need to make sure everyone who came in goes out. We've got procedures in place, so let's make sure we're following them. Plus, not everyone is leaving when the festival ends at five. Several hundred people bought the drinks-and-dinner package, so they'll be hanging out at various restaurants."

Liam shot his hand in the air. "I've got duty at Olga's."

Justin rubbed his palms together. "I'll be at Muertos. I heard they're doing al pastor with nopales tacos and mescal shooters."

"No shooters for you," I said.

Justin shook his head. "I wouldn't think of drinking on the job. But later, maybe."

"You're a dad now. You can't be doing things like that." Bailey smirked.

"Yeah, I'm definitely not the party animal I used to be." Justin ran a hand through his hair. "What about the construction site in La Loma? Are we responsible for that too?"

"Thanks for the reminder," I said, pleased Justin had brought that up. "No. The board asked the company to provide its own security."

That hadn't gone over too well, according to Charlie Perez. Rory had complained about the extra costs but eventually gave in.

"So that's that. Please review the contingency plans in case entities appear. It's not likely, but we need to be on our toes, just in case.

The idea sent a chill crawling up my spine.

My eyes flicked open. It was just after three o'clock in the morning. The Devil's Hour. The same time Hernan Frias had unleashed his monsters weeks before. The cat was awake too, moving around near my feet. When I flicked on the light, he was sitting up, as still as a statue, staring at me with his green eyes. He really was a beautiful animal. And a total weirdo.

I propped myself up on my elbows and returned his gaze. "What?"

He meowed loudly and began prowling around the bedroom. When he had done a complete circuit, he disappeared into the hallway. I knew better than to ignore his nighttime antics, so I climbed out of bed and found him in the sunroom. The Little Lencha figurine was glowing a strange shade of chartreuse.

Great. Now she was awake too.

"All right, you two." I flicked on a lamp. "Can someone please tell me what's going on?"

My great-aunt's spirit had only appeared to me once, at the beginning of my sporadic journey into brujería, but she had other ways of communicating. The clay statuette had no batteries, yet she managed to glow anyway. The greenish-yellow color was new, and it was garish.

Behind me, the cat hissed. When I spun around, he was flinging himself at the sunroom wall next to my workbench, where something fluttered. A moth—a big one with a wingspan that had to have been six inches. I had never seen such a large moth before.

Sam was in a frenzy, leaping and swiping at the insect with outstretched claws. If he caught it, he might have tried to eat it, and that would have been disgusting. I grabbed a dish towel from a hook above the workbench and caught the struggling moth within its folds, trying not to crush it.

After finding a large glass vase under the counter, I turned it upside down on the bundle and carefully slid the towel from under the vase. Sam leapt onto the workbench and stared intently at the moth. His fur was all puffed out.

The moth's wings were a deep shade of black, almost like velvet in the dim light of the sunroom. It threw itself against the glass, fluttering, as if pleading for its freedom.

A low hum filled the room, making the hairs on the back of my neck stand on end.

A feeling of unease settled into the pit of my stomach, and I wanted it out of my house. I grabbed my phone from the bedroom and took several photos of it, then slid the vase off the wooden counter, covering the opening with the towel, and carried it outside. When I released it into the darkness, it bumped into my head, fluttered around me for a moment, and disappeared into the night sky.

Back indoors, I opened the lid of my computer and typed a description of the moth. Within seconds, I was staring at a screen full of images of *Ascalapha adorata*, or the black witch moth.

Lovely.

A few clicks later, I learned that in Mexico it was known as *mariposa de la muerte*. The butterfly of death. Some people believed it was a harbinger of death or misfortune.

I really, really hated stuff like that. Even if my brain said it was nonsense, it was hard not to turn into a superstitious mess when I read creepy things like that.

Well, the moth can go screw itself. I rubbed my temples. What I really needed was sleep. I had a long day ahead of me, and I needed to be sharp.

After closing my laptop, I returned to the sunroom. Little Lencha gave one final sputter of greenish light, then went dark. I flicked off the lamp and stepped into my room to crawl into bed. The cat jumped up and settled behind my knees.

Eventually, I fell into a fitful sleep, with dreams about a long-haired giant chasing my mother, Clare growing black feathery wings, and Rory Tuck pursuing me with a bulldozer.

Chapter 26

I woke up early and got busy in the kitchen. Jo and Holly were due around nine, and at the last minute, I had invited Clare and her friend Iris, partly because I wanted to see whether my spell had solved Iris's bully problem.

While I made chilaquiles, I tried to keep focused on the cactus festival, but I couldn't shake the sense of unease lurking in the background of my thoughts. After the heat we had been having, it was wonderfully cool outside. I opened all the windows to let the fresh air in and the smell of frying tortillas out.

Sam was on patrol, padding through each room and hopping onto windowsills, tail flicking high.

I breathed in the aroma of garlicky tomato sauce and smoky dried pasilla chilis like it was an aromatherapy candle. The shredded chicken was placed into a bowl. I strained the broth and added it to the red sauce. When the guests were ten minutes away, I sliced a white onion and plucked fresh cilantro sprigs from my garden.

My phone chimed with another report from the command center. So far, so good. Extra guards were in place at the guardhouses. A long line of cars had already formed, visitors anxious to get good parking spots when the gates opened to the public at ten thirty.

I chopped the cilantro and dropped it into a decorative bowl.

Clare and Iris were first to arrive.

Clare was her newly buoyant self, but the tall, black-haired teenager who walked through the door with her had been transformed, shoulders pushed back and a ready smile on her face. She looked a lot more relaxed than the last time I had seen her.

"Good morning, ladies. It's a lovely day for a cactus festival. Clare, would you mind helping me set the table for six? Placemats and dishes are in the hutch."

"Sure thing." Clare expertly laid out the place settings, silverware on the proper side and in the right order. Somebody had taught her well.

I took a carton of eggs out of the refrigerator. "Iris, how are things going with that…friend of yours?"

"Ava is totally leaving me alone," Iris said. "It's the weirdest thing, right, Clare?"

Clare smiled. "Honestly, whatever you did? It's magical. Ava suddenly started acting all funny around Iris, almost like she was scared of her. And remember that time she ran into you on the field and she practically freaked out?"

That was much better than I had dared to hope. *Damn.* Maybe my brujería skills weren't as lame as I had thought. Or maybe my little pep talk had done the girl some good. She seemed to radiate a confidence she had not had before. I supposed it didn't matter. The bully had backed off, and that was enough to put a spring in Iris's step.

From the table, Clare glanced at me briefly. "Some of our friends were curious about Iris's bracelet, and we might have told them you made it. Now, they're wondering if they can see you too. We're meeting up with them at the cactus garden, so maybe they could talk to you?"

I wondered what sort of trouble I could get into if word got out I was making amulets for miserable teenagers. While I wanted to help, I really wasn't sure I should. What if a parent objected to a stranger making allegedly magical bracelets for their teen daughters? Plus, I was busy at work. I didn't really have time to start a brujería side hustle.

"Let me get through this festival and we'll talk," I said noncommittally.

"Okay, we'll talk Monday!" Clare said. She wasn't going to let me off easily.

"What smells so amazing?" Iris closed her eyes and sniffed.

"Chilaquiles, and you have big decisions to make. Fried egg: yes or no? One or two?"

"Yes!" they said in unison. Then, "One, please."

I was frying the eggs when Jo, Holly, and Julia arrived, and suddenly, the kitchen was filled with women laughing and talking. The sun had come out, and soft light was streaming in through the windows.

Jo sported a glamorous pair of white glasses that darkened in the sun. Holly was wearing a loose gray romper, her platinum hair newly trimmed into a pixie cut. But it was Julia who had our full attention. Always a flamboyant dresser, she had taken it to a whole new level with flowy, hot-pink pants and a cropped tank top in a bright cactus print.

"Aw, you're even wearing cactus earrings!" Clare said.

Julia laughed and tilted her head so the dangling earrings tinkled. "They're cute, yeah?"

I loaded up the girls' plates and set them down on the table. "There are two kinds of cheese. Help yourself!"

I turned back to the stove to fix the other plates, and the conversation turned to the cactus festival. No one talked about entities, but Clare did say she had spoken to her father first thing in the morning. Something had happened on Malena B's tour. He had said not to worry and he would tell her more after the story made the news.

I glanced down at my phone. My mother hadn't messaged me. Surely, I would have heard from her if something bad had happened.

If I hadn't frozen out Stu, I wouldn't have been in the dark.

I handed out the remaining plates and took my place at the table. The room was bright and cheery, and I took a moment to marvel at the big changes in my life since I had moved to Chavez Ravine. I now had a lovely, comfortable home and a cat. A weird one, but he had my back. And I invited people over instead of pushing them away.

My attention returned to the conversation. Clare and Iris were offering to help Julia at her booth, and she accepted eagerly. Jo and Holly were plotting out what they wanted to see, consulting the festival schedule between their plates.

"What's this cactus demonstration garden?" Jo asked.

Julia glanced up from spooning crema onto her second helping of chilaquiles. "Our master landscaper, Ben Tomas, created it years ago. It's a garden in Palo Verde with all the cactus species that are native to our area. It's really awesome. You should definitely go. Ben will be there, giving some short talks on the hour."

"Oh, is that what it is?" Clare said. "I've always wondered. I thought maybe it was a nursery or something, where they sell cactus. I'm excited to see it!"

"Me too!" Iris added.

"Maybe we can meet up," Holly said. "Late this afternoon? Jo and I have tickets for dinner at Olga's Cantina. We're super excited. Maddy's always talking about it."

"And we're grabbing pan dulce at Muertos Café. We're walking there from here." Jo glanced over at me. "We can still leave our car here, right?"

"Of course. There are shuttles running in a loop, so if you get tired of walking, you can always catch one."

By ten o'clock, the kitchen was clean, and my guests were headed out the door.

Jo stopped midway down the path and called, "Good luck today." She tried to smile, but it ended up more like a grimace. She knew exactly what kind of security challenges we faced today, and the uncertainty on her face showed it.

Chapter 27

Except for Ron Mendez in the Palo Verde command center and the guards stationed at the two entry gates in Bishop and La Loma, all my people were on patrol. I had convinced the board to let us buy e-bikes because they were more maneuverable than SUVs in traffic and crowds.

Bailey had signed up for bike duty and so had Liam. All the guards wore backpacks containing slingshots, ammo, and Smoke Bombs. Just in case.

I had asked Cora to be on Hernan Frias duty. If he took an unexpected turn for the worse or if anything out of the ordinary happened, I needed to know about it. My biggest fear was that Hernan would have a relapse and his protection spell would falter. I called her to let her know things were going smoothly so far and to ask after her charge.

"He's fine. Annoying as ever," Cora said. "And you were right about bringing him pan dulce from Muertos Café. It got me in the door, no problem."

The gates opened at ten thirty sharp. Judging by the long line of cars coming slowly through, the festival was a hit. My unease intensified as the day progressed, with cars clogging the roads and thousands of people milling about. I couldn't wait for it to be over.

By noon, we had to implement a one-in, one-out rule for crowd control. It made me a little nervous to have so many cars lining the roads where entities had emerged several days before, but people knew to stay inside their vehicles if that happened.

It was amazing to watch the cactus festival unfold. Julia and many others had worked hard to put together a fun, interesting event, and it was paying off. I headed to the command center, where I found Ron and Brandon tipped back in their chairs, staring intently at the heatmap.

"You guys want to take a break and grab something to eat?" I asked. "There are some awesome-looking food booths out there."

Brandon shook his head. "Nah, we're good. My girlfriend and her family are selling nopales burritos, and she said she'd drop some by."

"Those sound good." I was still stuffed with chilaquiles, but I made a mental note to grab one later. "You should still take a break, though. It's not good for you to stare at that screen for hours on end."

"We're fine," Ron said. "If you don't mind, I'd rather stay here. My grandmother said she woke up with a bad feeling. She told me to keep a close eye on everything."

That got my attention.

"Is there something I should know about your grandma? Like, she's a bruja or something?"

Ron snorted. "Nothing like that, but she's one of those people who gets malas vibras."

"Bad vibes?"

"And when she gets them, we all hear about it." Ron sighed.

Brandon shrugged his shoulder. "You left out the bit where she ran outside, screaming her head off, and woke you up."

I stared at Ron. "Did that happen?"

Ron cleared his throat. "Oh yeah. She found a moth in her bedroom. You'd think she'd never seen one before. So I had to go over and shoo it outside. She wanted me to kill it, but it was kind of pretty, so I couldn't bring myself to do it."

My mouth went dry. "Was it big and black?"

"Yeah. She called it a witch moth, and she said it was a bad omen or something, so I didn't want to take any chances. Sometimes, my grandmother is right about stuff."

A black witch moth had paid a visit to Ron's grandmother too. How many others had been called on by the black-winged insects? Julia hadn't mentioned anything, and neither had Cora.

Brandon kept going. "Justin's wife found one in their bathroom. He said she screamed so loud she woke up the baby. And Liam found some flying around inside his garage."

Every nerve in my body began to jangle. If the insects were trying to freak me out, they were doing a very good job. I left the guys to it and went back to the Palo Verde Plaza.

While standing in line at a booth selling iced coffees, I ran into Ben Tomas.

"Do we have lots of black witch moths around here?" I asked.

His serious brown eyes flared. "Not usually, no. But I had my crew out this morning real early for a final tidy-up before the festival got started, and they said they saw a bunch flying around just before sunup. And I had one in a storage shed too. My grandmother grew up in Mexico, and if she ever saw one, she'd get hysterical because she was certain something bad was going to happen to someone in the family." He grimaced.

I didn't like the sound of that. *Any* of it.

Ben lifted his iced coffee into the air. "I gotta go. I'm doing some talks at the demonstration garden soon."

"I heard. My friends are planning on going."

"Julia?" Ben sounded downright hopeful.

"I'm sure she'd love to, but she's manning her own booth."

Ben's shoulders slumped the slightest bit. "Oh."

"Why don't you stop by and say hello?" I suggested. There was no harm playing matchmaker, especially knowing how Julia felt about him.

He nodded eagerly. "That's a good idea. She's such a talented artist."

And smart and funny and beautiful, I wanted to add. But instead, I wished him luck, then headed to my Jeep. All the talk about black witch moths had given me an adrenaline rush, so caffeine was no longer necessary.

I walked through the throngs in the plaza and up and down some of the side streets. It seemed like a great crowd. People were having a good time looking at the homes and landscaping, and everyone seemed to be on their best behavior.

I needed to know what was going on in the other areas, so I drove toward Bishop, scanning the smaller streets, and headed up the hill. After taking a back road toward Palo Verde, I continued on to La Loma, eventually finding myself at the construction site at the top of my block. Rory's crew was at work inside the gates. Perhaps he had decided it was cheaper than hiring security guards for the day. And it kept him on schedule.

I headed down the hill. Might as well run by the house and let Sam out for a potty break, I figured.

I pulled into the driveway and was just getting out of the Jeep when my phone rang. Not one call, but two. Ron *and* Jo.

My heart skipped a beat. I accepted Ron's call first.

"The entities have come back," he said breathlessly. "Not here, don't worry. Some mermaids at the waterfall in Eaton Canyon."

Eaton Canyon was a popular nature area in Pasadena. This wasn't the first time creatures had shown up there.

"The pretty kind or the scary kind?" I asked.

"The scary kind with teeth," Ron said. "There's also some other activity beginning to show in Hollywood, but the spots keep moving around. I'll text you when I know more."

Hollywood. My mother was supposed to be at the Hollywood Bowl that evening. That was good news for her, then.

"Thanks, Ron. I gotta go. I have Jo on the other line."

We hung up, and I answered Jo's call.

"Took you long enough," she snapped. "I called to tell you our entity drought was over, and then I remembered you've got your own damn heatmap." Jo still couldn't get over the board agreeing to pay for its own system.

"I heard about the mermaid with teeth." Those presented a special challenge. Smoke Bombs were less effective around water or steam. A lot had to be used in those situations. And the teeth required steel mesh gloves.

Jo sighed. "It's enough to make me glad we don't live anywhere near water. We're off to that cactus garden. I'll let you know if I hear anything more from my guys."

"I'd appreciate that," I said, and we hung up.

I gave Sam a treat for not scratching any of our breakfast guests before I left and drove to the La Loma gate. The line outside was down to just half a dozen cars waiting their turn to enter.

We only had a couple of hours to go, and we'd had a good day so far. When things went well, I never knew why. One could argue security wasn't necessary because everybody behaved themselves. I preferred to believe people behaved themselves because they knew there was security. And that's the story I would tell the board.

Back at Palo Verde Plaza, I ran into Bailey cruising around on her bike. Her green eye shadow matched the festival T-shirts all the guards were wearing.

"How's it going?" I asked.

Bailey exhaled loudly. With a thumb and index finger, she pulled her shirt away from her skin. "Good, but my butt hurts. I don't know how people can stand being on a bike for so long in this heat. My cheeks are numb."

I couldn't help but laugh. "Sounds like the board should have popped for extra padded seats."

"For sure. Liam says he's going to have to take an ice bath after this."

I laughed but only for about two seconds. Both our phones blasted to life with a high-pitched ring tone. The one Ron had chosen to signal an entity outbreak in Chavez Ravine.

My stomach dropped. There was an outbreak at the cactus demonstration garden.

"Go!" I yelled at Bailey. "I'm right behind you."

I only hoped Clare and Iris weren't there to witness Chavez Ravine's first entity outbreak in person.

Chapter 28

I drove like a mad woman up the hill toward the cactus garden. While at Occult Affairs, I had responded to hundreds of outbreaks, but this one was different. It was on my home turf.

I felt shaky all over. And I was afraid. Scared of the scene that might be waiting for me.

How the hell had this happened? The spell protecting Chavez Ravine must have failed. It was the only explanation, but finding out why would have to wait. I called Cora and asked her to check on Hernan again, but I didn't spell out why.

While I parked my Jeep on the sidewalk outside the cactus garden, my job—*our* jobs—had gone from prevention to response and containment. That was a transition I had hoped we would never have to make.

When I reached the garden, three security bikes stood next to a tall hedge. The wooden gate was wide open. Even from the sidewalk, I could hear shouting.

Stay there.

Don't move

Get back.

I said stay there.

And then screaming. Clare and Iris.

I grabbed my front pack from the passenger seat and ran, pulled out my slingshot and ammo, and stuffed them in a pocket where I could easily grab them.

Through the gate, I emerged between a break in the wall of cactus. Chaos unfolded before me.

Ben Tomas was frantically swinging a rake at a chupacabra lunging toward him, mouth open, razor-sharp teeth glistening. Jo and Holly were several yards away, huddled together, trying to fend off another creature circling them. Three more chupacabras had cornered Clare and Iris against a wall of silver cactus covered in spines.

"What are you waiting for?" I shouted. "Hit them with a Smoke Bomb."

And then I saw them.

Deflated pouches. The faint cloud in the air.

"We did!" Justin called. "It didn't work!"

Maybe we had received a bad batch. While Clare and Iris continued shrieking, I fumbled for my pouch and hurled it between the chupacabras menacing the girls. It exploded when it hit the ground, and a cloud of purple smoke engulfed the creatures.

When it cleared moments later, all three chupacabras were still on their feet. They whipped their heads in my direction. There was no disorientation in their eyes. The two closest to Jo and Holly were inching toward the women with slow but calculated precision.

This was far from the typical newly emerged entity behavior. The things were fully and terrifyingly alert, eyes gleaming with a malevolent intelligence that sent shivers down my spine.

Damn.

"Slingshots," I yelled.

Bailey, Justin, and Liam sprang into action. So did I. We loaded our slingshots with steel ammo and started firing.

The creatures screeched in pain when the pellets hit them. They backed away from their prey, but still, they didn't go down.

175

Obviously, the protection pouch I had made for Clare wasn't working. And then I noticed she wasn't wearing it around her neck. Had she lost it or forgotten it?

Iris was wearing her protection bracelet, but it worked on bullies, not entities.

Ben was making a valiant effort with the rake, but he was also facing off against the largest chupacabra. He took a powerful swing, and the steel tines connected with the creature's wrinkled, scaly back. They stuck there for a moment before Ben pulled the rake away and, with it, a chunk of skin. The creature howled.

I was desperate, but I yelled, "Keep going," because that was our only option.

Voices came from the road. Girls' voices.

"Clare?" someone shouted.

Oh, no. Clare's friends had arrived to meet up with her and Iris, and they were showing up at exactly the wrong moment.

"Don't come in here," I shouted. "It's not safe."

They didn't listen.

Instead, they charged in, only to start shrieking when they witnessed what we were up against. I faced the girls to order them away. The girl standing closest to me was petite, with thick blond hair and round blue eyes. Around her neck hung one of my handmade white cloth bags, which she gripped tightly with both hands.

The girls were all wearing their sachets. *Time to put those to the test.*

I held out a hand to the blond girl. "Give me your pouch. Hurry. Just throw it."

I managed to snag the sachet and quickly made my way toward Clare, careful not to get too close to the monsters. When I tossed the sachet to her, she caught it effortlessly.

"Hold it out in front of you and wave it around," I instructed.

Clare did as I asked, and to my amazement, the chupacabras hissed and backed away. *Hallelujah.*

Clare had smart friends. And brave ones. No one needed me to tell them what to do. They immediately sent their white pouches flying, all ending up where they needed to go.

Within moments, Jo, Holly, Ben, and Iris were waving sachets out in front of themselves. The chupacabras didn't fall over or scatter, but they put some distance between them and my friends.

That bought us a few seconds. I needed to use that time to come up with something.

"Aim your slingshots at their heads," I called.

I had no idea if that would work, but it sure couldn't hurt.

As it turned out, it made all the difference.

A creature turned toward me with a snarl. I loaded a ball and pulled back the rubber strap, nailing it between the eyes. The sound—a gross blend of cracking and squishing—almost made me lose my chilaquiles, but the creature immediately fell to the ground.

Within a couple of minutes, the other chupacabras were prostrate, and we finished them off with our batons. They were still alive, but they would be out of it until we could crate them up.

Moments later, more guards pounded up the gravel path. Bailey took my Jeep and got some crates from the command center storage room. Soon, we had safely loaded the creatures into the large containers.

Clare threw her arms around my neck and began to sob. "I forgot to put on my necklace this morning."

I patted her back, which was damp with perspiration. The poor thing smelled of sweat and fear. "It's fine. *You're* fine."

Her friends ran over. "Did you see that? Those pouches really worked!"

Jo stared at me, frowning. Her glasses were askew, and her hair was messy, but she was as observant as ever. "What was in those pouches?" Her tone was as sharp as a knife's edge. It almost felt like an accusation.

I shrugged. "It's a long story. I'll tell you later."

Holly led Ben Tomas to a bench. He was clutching his hand. Blood seeped through his fingers from where the chupacabra had managed to sink its teeth into him during the scuffle.

One of the guards hurried over with a first aid kit and wrapped the wound tightly.

"Ben, we need to get you to the clinic," I said. "Entity bites are nothing to mess around with."

His face was pale, and sweat beaded on his forehead.

Jo came over. "How about we take him? Better than sending one of your folks. You'll need them here."

I nodded. Jo and Holly each took one of Ben's arms and walked him to a shuttle stop.

I sat on a bench in the cactus garden and tried to process what had just happened. Entities in Chavez Ravine. I could hardly believe it. These hadn't been the usual semi-harmless entities. They had been alert and vicious. And worst of all, immune from Smoke Bombs.

My whole approach to security would have to change. I wasn't sure how yet, but I was very thankful the board had approved the heatmap and staff increases. We would need them…and maybe more.

Clare and her friends babbled nervously, sharing pictures they had taken of the fallen creatures.

"Clare, do you have a key to your dad's house?"

She nodded slowly and patted a pocket in her jeans.

"Good. Bailey will go with you to the house. I want you to go inside, lock the doors, and stay there until I say it's all clear."

Bailey corralled the girls and led them out of the sun-drenched garden.

When they had gone, Justin said, "How the hell did the Smoke Bombs not work?"

"No idea. I need to figure out why these entities were so different. They weren't normal, and the resistance to Smoke Bombs may just be the tip of the iceberg." I called Ron at the command center. "Please tell me you're not seeing anything else?"

"Not yet, boss."

We had been lucky. The chupacabras had appeared in the middle of a walled garden far from the biggest, densest crowds. And none had escaped. No telling what would happen next time.

I had to make a tough call. One the board might not like.

"I want this festival shut down," I said into my phone. "Now. Follow the entity emergence protocol. Start by sending messages to all the vendors, telling them to close up. Use the patrols to start moving people to their cars and out of here."

"Got it, boss. Um, I'm already getting questions about what to tell the public."

"We tell them the truth, but we keep it simple. We had an entity emergence, and everything is under control, but as a precaution, we're closing the festival."

When we hung up, I sent a brief message to the board, asking them to refrain from calling me so I could give my full attention to the situation. Then I sent an emergency alert asking all residents to return home as quickly as possible and remain indoors until further notice. Images of Eileen Simpson going into hysterics flashed in my head.

179

I called Cora. She answered right away, out of breath. People were talking in loud, panicked voices in the background.

"Tell me this isn't happening!" she cried.

"It is. Have you checked on Hernan yet? I've got my hands full, Cora, but I need to know if something happened to him and, therefore, to his spell."

"Oh. You don't think…" Her voice drifted off.

"That's *exactly* what I think." I probably sounded angry and resentful because that was how I felt.

If Hernan had taken ill and his protection spell collapsed, he had put the entire community at risk. All because he was a stubborn, egotistical old man who had refused to let me help him.

Chapter 29

I drove back to Palo Verde. An orderly evacuation was underway. The main road was crowded with cars heading toward the exits, windows rolled up, children's faces pressed against glass.

My phone buzzed. It was Eileen Simpson. I ignored it. After all, I had asked the board not to call me, but as usual, she thought she was special.

I headed straight for the command center. If more entities were going to show up, I wanted to be there. Ron and Brandon were standing in front of the heatmap, arms crossed against their chests.

"Nothing yet, boss," Ron said.

Brandon pointed at a lit-up area far from Chavez Ravine. "Looks like there's some coming up in Runyon Canyon."

"That's near the Hollywood Bowl, right?" I settled in behind a desk and logged into a computer.

"Sure is."

My mother had lucked out. The entity drought had ended, and they were showing up not far from the Hollywood Bowl. If Occult Affairs didn't sedate them with Smoke Bombs and cart them off, they would sense my mother and begin making their way toward her, just in time for her show. At least, that's what would happen if they were normal entities.

Would she have been able to calm the chupacabras? Or were they immune to her powers like they were immune to Smoke Bombs?

181

I called Jo. She was still at the hospital with Ben. He was doing okay, but the doctor was planning to keep him overnight.

"Are you going to tell me what was in those pouches you made?" she asked.

"I will, Jo, I promise. It's kind of a long story. But I need you to find out something for me. Are the entities that are appearing outside Chavez Ravine showing the typical signs of emergence?"

Jo sighed. "I'm all over that. I was wondering the same thing myself, and I was about to call you. Yes, they are. And the Smoke Bombs are working just fine. In fact, it works on your chupacabras too. They started coming around, so my guys hit them with Smoke Bombs, and they worked just fine. I hate to think you got a bum batch, but that may be the case. I've got a new shipment headed your way." She hesitated. "Mads, I'm worried about what's going on up there."

I sighed. "That makes two of us."

Jo wasn't finished. "Chavez Ravine has been immune from entities from the start, but the moment that immunity ends, your entities have a whole new set of behaviors? That emergence was one for the books, and we still haven't done any analysis. Who knows what else we'll discover? So my question is this: Even with the heatmap, are you sure this is something you still want to handle alone?" She paused. "Maybe the better question is, *can* you even handle it?"

I had been wondering the same things myself. "I don't know."

"You want me to put people on standby?"

It wouldn't hurt. We couldn't afford to be overrun. But if I allowed Occult Affairs officers inside the gate, the board would have my head. Unless the incidents of the day caused them to have a change of heart. I had no good options.

"Thank you. Yes." My voice sounded distant. "Let's hope it doesn't come to that."

"You're doing the right thing. It's out of your control," Jo said, then hung up.

But was it? The sachets I had created for the girls to help them overcome their fright had worked on entities, at least to a degree. Before that, the only things that had worked were Smoke Bombs and batons. Whatever I had made using rudimentary magic had been enough to get the chupacabras to back off until we could take them out with slingshots.

What if I could come up with something better, something stronger?

There was another what-if I really didn't want to consider.

What if my attempts at magic had attracted the entities? My mother seemed to think that was a possibility. It depended on my having inherited her psychic abilities, which I seriously doubted, but maybe there was some truth to it.

My phone rang again. It was Cora.

"You were right."

A siren wailed in the background.

"Hernan had a stroke. A bad one. They're just taking him to the hospital now. Poor Marta was all alone when it happened. She said he'd insisted on going out to his shed. She followed him out there because he was so unsteady on his feet, and when he went inside, he had a bad susto. She thinks that's what caused the stroke."

I pressed a finger between my eyes. "Any chance it was a big black moth?"

"It was," Cora said, voice rising. "Marta called it a black witch moth. It sounded a bit dramatic to me. How did you know?"

"There have been a few sightings today." I changed the subject. "There's something I need to tell you." My eyes were locked on the heatmap, imagining hints of red where there were none. "Those entities that showed up at the cactus garden were chupacabras. And they weren't normal."

I explained what had happened at the cactus garden. Cora gasped several times while I spoke.

"But what does it mean?"

"I have no idea. Maybe it was a one-off. If we have another outbreak, we'll have to see if it's the same." I didn't sound hopeful.

"Oh, my. Maddy, what can we do?"

"Be prepared. We're going to need to keep everyone on lockdown for the next twenty-four hours. Maybe forty-eight, I don't know. I know that's a lot to ask of people, but we can't take a chance. If we were to get a full-strength ghoul or troll, the results could be disastrous."

"Valgame Dios," Cora murmured. "Eileen's already up in arms. She's furious about you ending the festival early and sending out that alert."

I was in no mood for Eileen's nonsense. "Cora, we nearly lost some lives today. I realize that may not be as important to her as her next sale, but I'm not going to put my neighbors at risk. Do you want to send the lockdown message, or do you want me to do it?"

I drummed my fingers on the desk while I waited for a response.

"It'll be better coming from you." Cora seemed to have regained her composure. "You have a lot of goodwill in the community after the Bad Pete video. People trust you."

The Bad Pete video had been a godsend. Pop star Pete "Bad Pete" Drury had captured video of me taking out monster birds with my slingshot. He said I was his hero, which was a little over the top, but I didn't complain. Since he had millions of followers, the video had gone viral. It had also saved me from an idiotic performance improvement plan engineered by Eileen Simpson.

Cora promised to update the other board members, and we hung up.

I sent the community-wide alert and braced for another call from Eileen, which I would gleefully decline.

And I didn't have to wait long.

My phone buzzed, and I reached for the hell-no-I'm-not-answering button. Until I saw who it was. Stu Wells.

"Thank you for saving my daughter," he said without preamble.

"You're welcome," I replied stiffly. "She's at your place with her friends. When I get a break, I'll go check on them."

"Thank you. I won't be able to get to her until the morning." He sounded worried.

I cleared my throat. "She'll be fine. They're smart girls."

Bailey had messaged me already. Clare and her friends had come up with the idea of hanging their sachets in the windows around the house to ward off entities. Probably not a bad idea.

An awkward silence followed.

"Your mom is really something," Stu finally said.

That's what he had to say? "That she is."

"It's been fun getting to know her. My mom was, like, exactly the opposite. She was sweet and all, don't get me wrong, but she was totally passive. No ambition. Malena's story is quite incredible."

The way to my heart was *not* through my mother. "That's nice." Like a robot.

Stu must have registered the tone in my voice. "I can't believe we had entities in Chavez Ravine. It's a game changer. I

185

can hardly wrap my head around it." He paused. "Well, all good things come to an end, right?"

My breath hitched in my throat. Was he talking about entities or us?

"I guess so."

When we hung up a few moments later, I felt flatter than a pancake. Of course, I could call Stu back and talk things out like an adult, but that would require more maturity than I had at the moment.

Justin and Liam returned, and after a quick logistics meeting, all the guards went out on patrol. The double shift would be tough, but I needed people in all three neighborhoods. If there was another outbreak, I wanted someone to be close by.

Hours dragged by while Ron, Brandon, and I stared at an unmoving heatmap. The sun went down, and I started to sense cold all over my skin, as if I had just entered a walk-in refrigerator. My chest felt funny too—like I was wearing a weighted vest.

"Boss?" Ron's tone said it all.

I looked up.

A small red dot on the heatmap was rapidly expanding.

Chapter 30

"Where is it?" I yelled, getting up from my chair and walking closer to the heatmap.

Brandon checked the coordinates on the console and shouted a street address in Palo Verde. "Hold on a minute. Looks like it's Ben Tomas's equipment yard."

That was the first I had heard about an equipment yard, but it made sense. All that landscaping equipment had to be stashed somewhere.

"Have Bailey, Justin, and Liam me meet there," I said. "Keep the rest where they are, in case we need to respond somewhere else. If we need backup, we'll let you know."

Without waiting for a response, I ran for my Jeep and sped toward the northern end of Palo Verde, closest to Elysian Park. There was no traffic, and I found the equipment yard easily enough. Three patrol vehicles were already parked outside the wooden gate. A tall, solid hedge obscured the chain link fence surrounding the yard. I paused long enough to strap on my front pack, then went through the gate.

The equipment yard was huge, filled with trucks, a couple of trailers, and a large, covered area with mowers, shovels, rakes, and shears. Beyond the shed was a nursery with rows of plants and flowers. There was a good-sized greenhouse and a potting shed along the back perimeter. It all looked well-organized and tidy, but there was no sign of an entity. Or my team.

Blood whooshed in my ears while I looked around. Every muscle in my body was tense. If someone had walked up behind

187

me and said, "Boo," I would have done bad things to them before I could bring my instincts under control.

There was a sudden explosion of sound from the far end of the yard, and my body gave an involuntary jerk.

Justin and Liam were calling to each other. Bailey shrieked. I ran.

The group was hidden behind a potting shed. Justin and Liam were frantically trying to deploy the purple pouches on a giant bat which had a tight grip on Bailey's long hair. Its massive wings flapped wildly. The creature was horrifying. Its nose was shaped like a diamond but glistened like obsidian. Its red eyes glowed with an otherworldly intensity.

"Get it off me!" Bailey's screams echoed through the yard. She struggled against the bat's hold.

The bat's body was enormous—about the size of a small child. I had never heard of an entity like this one.

Smoke Bombs exploded into the air. The bat released its hold on Bailey's thick mane. In one swift move, Bailey unclipped the baton from her belt and began swinging at the creature, which flitted away from her, then turned and rushed back, claws outstretched.

"It's not working!" Justin shouted.

The bat was immune to the tranquilizer and, like the chupacabras earlier in the day, was alarmingly alert. We readied our slingshots. By the time we had loaded the steel ammo into the rubber bands and taken aim, the bat was making another run at Bailey's skull.

The creature's movements were erratic, so the ammo whizzed past its head. The thing missed Bailey but turned around to make another pass. It hardly seemed to register that there was anyone else there. Bailey's copper hair shimmered under the lights.

I grabbed a tarp from the potting shed and threw it over her. "Keep this on and stay down," I yelled.

Bailey dropped to her knees. The bat wheeled in the air and let out an angry shriek.

While Justin and Liam continued to go at it with their slingshots, I grabbed a long-handled shovel and darted forward.

"Hold your fire!" I began swinging, aiming for the bat's nose. After a few near misses, the shovel connected with its head. In a sweeping arc, I dragged the creature to the ground and stood on the blade to hold it there.

And I had thought the chaneques were ugly. This thing was hideous.

Justin and Liam ran up, holding their slingshots. I shook my head.

"Better not. The ammo might ricochet if it hits the shovel."

The bat was putting up a mighty fight to free itself. Justin gave it a few kicks, while Liam fetched another shovel. It took a while, but eventually, it went still.

Bailey had thrown off the tarp and was running for the truck. That girl recovered quickly.

"I'll help her with the crate." Liam sprinted away.

Justin called in the all-clear to the command center. I took a few photos of the thing with my phone, then sent them to Jo with a request to identify it.

Did the new Smoke Bombs work?

Negative.

Fuck.

Yeah. Not sure what's going on.

Bailey, Justin, and Liam pulled on metal mesh gloves and loaded the bat into the crate. I took a few calming breaths.

Jo messaged back.

Prelim analysis: Camazotz. Death bat of Mayan origin. Some kind of sacred vampire thing.

I had never heard of it. Why had it appeared here in Chavez Ravine? And why was it also immune to the tranquilizer? The whole situation was deeply unsettling.

I met the others at the truck. Bailey was pale but composed. Her hand shook slightly while she tucked a loose strand of copper hair behind her ear.

"We need to get this thing to the Dump as soon as possible. Jo's expecting it. She's sending some of the nerds to meet you."

"Sure thing," Justin said. The tailgate of the truck slammed shut with a clang. "I don't think I'll be telling my wife about this guy. She was freaked out enough by that black moth."

My early morning encounter with the black witch moth seemed like an eternity ago.

I climbed into my Jeep, exhausted, but I couldn't shake the feeling that the camazotz was just the beginning of a new and disturbing chapter in the supernatural history of Chavez Ravine.

Chapter 31

After a quick stop at the command center, I headed home. I left Ron and Brandon with strict instructions to call me in the event of another entity emergence.

On the way, I stopped to check in on Clare. She and her friends were eating ramen and watching a romcom. They were still on edge, but otherwise, they were fine.

I had not been inside Stu's house before. It was bigger than it looked from the outside. The great room gave off lodge vibes, with leather furniture and lots of brown and gold plaid. Somehow, it was very Stu.

"Under no circumstances do you go outside," I warned. "And if you hear or see anything, call me. Okay?"

While I looked around the room, a horrible thought struck me: the entities we had seen in Chavez Ravine behaved differently than the others, so what if they could open doors or come up through kitchen sinks? For half a second, I considered inviting the girls over to my place, but there was a good chance I would need to leave to deal with another outbreak, so they were probably better off where they were.

Clare saw me to the door, where she gave me another hug. "Thank you so much again. I don't know what we would have done if you weren't there."

She was a very huggy girl. And sweet. The irony of the timing did not escape me. Clare had warmed up just as my relationship with her father had frozen over.

I patted her back. "No biggie. I'm serious, Clare. I want you to call me or the emergency number at the first sign something's not right."

She gave me a sassy salute, then went back inside. The right thing to do would be to text Stu and tell him all was well with Clare, but I was too annoyed with him to bring myself to do it. Besides, when he checked in with his daughter, she would tell him I had been by.

When I pulled into the driveway, the beam from my headlights illuminated a small group of people sitting on the Adirondack chairs on my porch.

Why was it so freakin' hard for some people to follow directions?

"What part of 'lockdown' did you not understand?" I called.

Julia came running toward me. "I'm sorry, I'm sorry, but I didn't want to be home alone, so I came here. Leo and Toby saw me and came over, and I was just telling them about everything that happened."

I took Julia's elbow and gave it a none-too-gentle squeeze. "Outside? When the emergency orders *clearly* said everyone needed to stay *inside*?"

"We were just trying to get her to come to our place until you got home," Leo called from the porch. "Don't be too harsh."

Harsh was exactly how I was feeling.

Toby jumped to his feet. "Tell her Leo! Tell her!"

I'd had enough surprises for the day.

"Everyone inside! I have a cat to feed."

Sam greeted me with a deadly glare, fur bristling. If looks could kill, I would be ten feet under. Dinner time had come and gone, and Sam was not about to let me forget it. He let out a dramatic meow, raced for the kitchen, and paced in front of his bowl.

"All right, all right. I'm sorry, Sam, but I had a really crazy day."

That was a first for me. Not only was I talking to my cat, but I was apologizing to it.

I opened a can of his favorite—Salmon Delite—then added some dry treats on top.

The others remained in the living room, talking in uncharacteristically quiet voices. Something was up. It seemed like forever ago that I had made chilaquiles for breakfast. Now I just wanted to take a shower and crawl into bed. I really, really did not want to get wrapped up in more drama.

After taking my time changing the water in Sam's bowl, I went into the living room. Leo held the screen of his phone toward me, lips pursed. Julia and Toby flanked him, holding onto his arms.

I sighed and stared at the screen. Leo turned up the audio, and my heart quickened while I watched cell phone footage of the chaos at the cactus garden. Then confusion and panic as people ran for their cars. Then interviews with festival goers about the abrupt ending of the cactus festival.

"This marked the first known incident of entities emerging in the exclusive enclave," the female reporter with a shiny black bob said into the camera.

They ended the story with a mention of Ben Tomas, a legacy stakeholder of Chavez Ravine and the genius behind the beautiful landscaping, being mauled by a chupacabra. One that had also threatened the head of Occult Affairs's command center. Jo was going to love that.

"Shit," I said.

"It's all over the news." Leo scrolled through more videos. "But that's not all."

"Want me to get some wine?" Julia asked hopefully. "I could use a drink myself." She shuddered.

I nodded. "How's Ben?"

"Higher than a kite. They gave him some meds. That chupacabra toxin is very painful, the doctor said."

Julia went into the kitchen. I flicked on a lamp and flopped down on the couch. At least I was coming home to a nice house with stylish furnishings in lots of bright colors to cheer me up.

Toby sat next to me. Leo lowered himself onto the striped ottoman usually reserved for Sam. He held out the phone.

"That was just the warm-up act. You're not going to believe the main event."

I clasped my knees together and leaned forward. "All right. Hit me."

That's exactly what it felt like too—getting sucker punched. I gasped, watching the video in disbelief.

Leo and Toby exchanged looks. Julia shoved a glass of chilled white wine into my hands.

The video showed a crowded amphitheater, the stage brightly lit. My mother walked across it wearing a gold caftan, talking into a microphone about the entities now headed their way. The audience erupted into excited applause.

In the distance, shouting. The camera swung wildly, capturing a dough-faced man rushing down an aisle with alarming speed.

Someone burst out from the wings. It was Stu leaping in front of Malena just as the man threw something at her. It was a bucket, and as it spun, purple liquid sprayed through the air. But instead of hitting my mother, it splashed Stu, coating his head and torso. Moments later, security guards appeared and dragged the assailant away. Two women in black pantsuits came out of nowhere and whisked my mother off stage.

Toby scrolled through his phone again and held it out. Apparently, there was no end to the onslaught of things I didn't want to see. I drank the rest of my white wine and watched. The news clip was from a live report outside The Hollywood Bowl.

The reporter was a serious young woman with a high forehead and wide-set dark eyes.

'Thank you, Hal. We've just received the following statement from the LAPD, saying the man who threw paint at Malena B, the famous psychic currently on her sold-out Entity Whisperer Tour, is now under arrest. They say he'll face charges of disorderly conduct, vandalism, and assault. Malena B was taken to the hospital with minor injuries. Police are crediting her personal security detail for foiling the attempt. As for motivation, the thirty-six-year-old suspect is believed to be associated with an entity rights group. According to their website, the group believes shows like this one prioritize entertainment and profit over—quote—the well-being of our otherworldly visitors.'

Toby swiped away the video and sat back on the couch. "Your boyfriend saved the day."

"He's *not* my boyfriend." I stared straight ahead at nothing in particular.

"Let's just give her some space, yeah?" Julia suggested quietly.

Leo jumped to his feet and yawned. "Sounds like we can all use a little rest. Care to walk us to our door to ensure we make it inside without being attacked by one of the scary chupie things?"

I looked at him and rolled my eyes. But he was serious.

I grabbed the slingshot out of my front pack and stuffed some steel pellets in a pocket.

"Vamonos." At the front door, I grabbed a flashlight from the skinny table in the entryway and ordered Julia to stay inside. "March," I said.

"Hey, I'm not a prisoner!" Leo wailed.

195

The idea of a jail cell for non-compliant residents was awfully tempting.

Still, I was on high alert. I swung the beam of my flashlight around. But all was quiet, and when the two had crossed the threshold, they turned with sheepish expressions and waved.

"Are we on lockdown tomorrow too?" Leo called.

He wasn't the only one who wanted to know. Cora had sent several messages conveying the board's concern about an extended lockdown.

"Not sure yet. Keep an eye on your phone for updates," I said. "Goodnight."

Back at home, Julia had washed the wine glasses and was rummaging through an overnight bag in the living room. She pulled out a slinky nightgown and held it against her chest.

"You never got an extra bed, yeah? I can sleep on the couch." She blinked at me hopefully.

"No, I still just have the one bed. Couch it is."

I was past the age for sleepovers and way too old for sharing my bed with anyone other than my cat. Or maybe Stu, though the chances of that happening were slim to none.

I went to the room that served as my office, rummaged around in a closet, and returned with a set of fresh sheets and a cotton blanket.

While we made up the couch, Julia said, "Thank you for letting me stay over. I know I'm being a baby, but those chupacabras really freaked me out, especially seeing what one of them did to poor Ben."

This from the woman who had beaten one of Hernan's supernatural creations with a rolling pin until it crumbled to dust.

"Not a problem. It was a weird day," I said between yawns.

"I'll probably feel better about things in the morning after a good night's sleep. All the racket from those trucks on my street keeps waking me up."

I straightened and stared at Julia. She lived a few blocks away in La Loma, near an open space.

"You mean, trucks from the construction project? Why would they be way over there? There's only one entrance, and that's from my street."

Julia shrugged. "I don't know. By the time I get home from the studio, there's usually one or two parked across the road, and they don't move until the middle of the night. They make a lot of noise starting up. It's really annoying."

"Well, it's pretty quiet here, so I hope you sleep better tonight. See you in the morning."

Never had I felt so tired. I barely made it through my evening routine, turned off the light on the nightstand, and climbed into bed. Sam jumped up and nuzzled my legs, and I closed my eyes.

For about five seconds.

My eyes popped back open, and my brain went into overdrive. Why would the construction company deliver supplies after hours? There wouldn't even be anyone there to receive them. And why park the trucks in Julia's neighborhood?

I remembered what Stu had said when he discovered someone had put black tape over our security cameras. That he thought something shady might be going on at the site, but he couldn't prove it. Since then, I had met the owner of the construction company, a man who was such an asshole that his own cat ran away.

What was Rory Tuck doing, and why was he doing it in the middle of the night?

Chapter 32

If snoring were an Olympic sport, Julia Suarez would have had a gold medal. With my pillow over my head, I finally fell asleep and, by some miracle, made it until morning without an entity eruption.

I brewed coffee and went into my home office. Once there, I logged into Chavez Ravine's surveillance camera feed, found the archives I needed, and checked the footage for the last week.

Yep. Just as Julia had said. One truck, sometimes two, parked on her street. A little after midnight, they rumbled off. Minutes later, they went by my house and up the hill to the construction site.

How about that? The trucks came through the La Loma gate during business hours, but they didn't unload until the crews were long gone. In the daylight, the guardhouse cameras caught the name on the sides: DLN Transport.

I did a quick search. DLN was a small trucking company based in Santa Cruz.

I tried to see if there was some kind of connection between DLN and Tuck Family Construction. Nothing obvious popped up, but there was a link to a public filing by the construction company. They were in the process of changing their name to Tuck and Tuck Construction. And Paul Tuck was listed as one of the owners.

That was interesting. Paul had said he was just helping his cousin out, but apparently, he had bought into the business.

If I hadn't had an urgent entity problem, I might have tried to figure out what was going on.

But I *did* have an urgent entity problem.

And, apparently, an HOA board problem.

When I checked my email, I noticed just how big that problem had become. Dan Berman had forwarded me a sampling of messages from residents expressing their concerns about a protracted lockdown. Eileen Simpson had sent both emails and texts indicating the lockdown was unacceptable. So did Rory Tuck, who said he had scheduled important work for Sunday and demanded it be allowed to continue. If I didn't comply, he would file a complaint with the board.

Even Charlie Perez had left a carefully worded note expressing his appreciation for all the hard work my team and I had done but ended it by saying life and business had to continue in Chavez Ravine. He had a point. Even if I extended the lockdown, there was no guarantee I could figure out how to banish or sedate these new, more aggressive entities anytime soon.

On the other hand, I had a well-trained security team. We were not without resources. If things got really bad, we could call in Occult Affairs for help. Jo would love that.

And one other thought had been nagging at me: the board could easily override my decision at any time. So far, even Eileen Simpson was acting as though I had the authority to make everyone stay in their homes. I honestly didn't think that was true, but the board assumed it was, and I loved that. Better to give in and keep that authority than force the board's hand and lose it.

It was time to end the lockdown.

I called Cora and let her know. She seemed relieved, so she must have been taking some heat for not pressuring me. I drafted a carefully worded note to the community, acknowledging their concerns and letting them know what to do if they saw an entity emergence.

Then I messaged my team to give everyone a heads-up.

I chatted with Julia for a few minutes over coffee. She was happy to hear the lockdown was ending. Julia needed to open her shop, so as soon as she finished her coffee, off she went.

I took my coffee to the sunroom and sat on the wicker couch to think. The protective pouches I had made for Clare and her friends had worked enough to get the chupacabras to back off. Maybe I was on to something. Perhaps I could figure out a way to enhance the sachet or the spell that activated it. Ideally, I could create something to immobilize the entities in the same way the Smoke Bombs did.

My knowledge of brujería was basic at best, so that was a tall order, but it was worth a try. I flipped through Lencha's notebooks on remedies, cleansings, amulets, talismans, and everything else she thought I needed to know about Mexican witchcraft.

Sam joined me on the couch in the sunroom while I pored through Lencha's notes. Nothing obvious jumped out at me. If I doubled the ingredients, would that double the power? Maybe the solution was simpler. Perhaps I could come up with more powerful words or say them with more conviction.

I flipped through the pages, and a passage caught my eye. "…to make protection stronger…" I stopped and read through that chapter.

It seemed like exactly what I needed. It was a ritual that amplified the protective power of any charm, including sachets. Nothing too challenging, but it did require bright moonlight. For someone who was supposed to be a fledgling witch, my knowledge of lunar cycles was embarrassing. Thankfully, there was the internet.

I was in luck. We'd had a full moon two nights prior. There would be plenty of moonlight, as long as clouds or fog didn't block it.

I read through the list of ingredients I would need for the ritual and began gathering them up. Sam watched me from the couch. Little Lencha's clay eyes seemed to follow me while I went about my task at the workbench.

The ritual called for fresh herbs and chilis. Luckily, I had the herbs growing in my backyard, but I would have to hit the market for the chilis.

I grabbed my scissors and went outside. As I stepped out into the cool morning sun, a gentle breeze rustled the leaves of the trees. The air was filled with the earthy aroma of damp soil and the sweet scent of jasmine growing under the palm trees. I was making my way to the pots of herbs when I noticed a new plant nestled among a bed of golden poppies. Its leaves were lush and bright green, and small red and orange peppers hung under its branches.

I froze.

I hadn't planted it, and I was pretty sure Ben hadn't either. He had shown me every single flower and plant he had put in.

"Did you do this?" I didn't really expect an answer from Little Lencha, but hey, maybe someday.

The ritual hadn't called for a specific type of chili. The new plant looked like a habanero, which was very hot. There was no reason not to use it. Time was short, and it would save me a trip to the store. I cut off a few chilis, then went over to the herbs and snipped away. All sorts of fresh goodness was dropped into my basket.

I laid everything out on the workbench, ready for some moonlit spell casting later.

After taking a quick shower, I wolfed down a piece of toast with peanut butter and drove to Clare's house to see how she and her friends were doing.

Fine, as it turned out. They were eating French toast and bacon and watching a movie with dragons. Nests of blankets and pillows were strewn across the living room. Every flat surface was covered with smudged glasses, half-empty bowls, and soda cans from the night before. The girls lolled about in tiny shorts and tops and waved at me in a friendly, distracted way. The room smelled of scented vanilla candles and burned microwave popcorn.

In that moment, I couldn't help but feel empathy for every parent of a teenager.

Clare wasn't my kid, but I didn't want her to get into trouble when Stu returned. "Clare Wells, if your father gets home and sees this, he is going to be seriously displeased."

Clare giggled. "You make him sound like that old grouchy lady from *Pride and Prejudice*."

Suddenly, I was laughing too. I knew I'd heard that line somewhere.

The front door creaked open, and Stu walked in. His mouth opened and closed when he saw me, then his lips pressed into a straight line while he took in the chaos. He scraped a hand through his hair, exhaled loudly, and pulled his daughter into an embrace.

"I'm so glad you're all right," he said, kissing her temple.

"You should have seen Maddy." Clare's voice was muffled against his shoulder. "She was amazing."

"I'm sure she was," Stu said briskly, releasing Clare and shoving his hands into his pockets. "Sweetheart, why don't you and your friends start cleaning up. I've got to get you to your mother's on my way to work."

Clare frowned. "I don't want to go to Mom's. I told you." She turned to me, brightening. "I can stay here, and Maddy can check on me. Or maybe I can stay with her. There's no safer place to be!"

At first, I was flattered, but I really did not need a teenager hanging around while I cast magic spells and argued with my cat. Some things were best done alone.

Stu shook his head. "Absolutely not. Maddy's got better things to do than to babysit you. How could you even ask such a thing?"

"Because she's nicer than you and Mom at the moment, that's why."

I snorted. "I'm an awfully cranky person, Clare. You've just caught me on a couple of good days."

Clare groaned, turned on her heel, and went stomping off toward her friends.

"Sorry about that." Stu dipped his head, cheeks flushed. "And thank you for rescuing my daughter."

"Thank you for rescuing my mother," I replied stiffly.

Then came the inevitable awkward silence. I was trying to think of something to say when I recalled the delivery trucks.

"Remember when you found the tape on the cameras near the construction site? And you said you'd heard some things about the contractor? Well, I definitely think something sketchy is going on." I told him about what Julia had said and what I had confirmed with the security camera footage. And that I thought Rory Tuck was a jerk.

Stu's eyes flicked upward, and he bit his lip. "Something's definitely going on, then. The secret deliveries prove it. I just wish I knew what it was." Stu stared at his shoes for a moment, then said quietly, "I've got something to tell you."

Uh oh. I wasn't ready for this.

203

He cleared his throat. "After I saw you with that Paul guy, I may have been a little jealous, and then I got to wondering who he was. That's kind of where my mind goes. So, I did some digging. He's got a criminal record. He got into some trouble up in Santa Cruz. Some kind of fraud involving a trucking company called DLN. And he lost his construction job. I think that's why he came down here to work for his cousin."

Okay, that wasn't what I had feared.

My thoughts went skittering off in two different directions. First, Stu had been jealous enough to do some homework on Paul, which meant he still cared about our relationship. And second, Paul Tuck wasn't the horny choir boy he pretended to be.

Chapter 33

When I got to the office, the first thing I did was revise the schedule so my folks could catch up on their sleep. About half of them had done a double shift, and the rest had pulled lots of OT, and yet, not a single one of them complained. Which just made me even more determined to do right by them.

Then I put a map of Chavez Ravine up on my giant-ass TV screen and stared at it, thinking. Both entity eruptions had happened in places connected to landscaper Ben Tomas: his cactus garden and his storage yard. Maybe that was a coincidence, but I needed to know if there were other areas which fit the profile.

I asked Brandon to come up with a list of places in Chavez Ravine where Ben spent a lot of time. Turned out, there were lots of them: parks, the running path at the top of the hill that went through Phantom's Pass, tiny parklets, a few vista points up near Elysian Park, and a half dozen empty lots where Ben grew native plants. For such an unassuming guy, Ben had his fingerprints all over the community.

With Brandon's report in hand, I walked over to the command center to talk with him and Ron.

Both seemed to own a never-ending supply of camo. Ron sported the traditional green and brown, but Brandon wore orange, yellow, brown, and black. It made my eyes hurt.

"You think the entities are connected to Ben Tomas?" Brandon asked, his voice rising.

"Oh, Brandon! I didn't see you there, with your camo blending into the background so perfectly."

He rolled his eyes.

"Entities mostly emerge in areas with vegetation. We've only had two appearances, but we're looking for commonalities. Both the cactus garden and the equipment yard have lots of vegetation. How about you two go through that list, pick the biggest areas, then route some patrols by them on a regular basis. Make sure they're looking for the early signs of an eruption. It can't hurt."

Ron's eyes widened. "Hey, boss, this might be nothing, but I was checking in with the guard over at the La Loma gate, and he said some trucks just came in a little while ago with a bunch of landscaping for the construction site. Trees and bushes and flowers and stuff. They've got a crew coming in to plant them."

So that's what Rory had scheduled. It seemed a little early to begin landscaping, but he was about to start doing tours for prospective buyers, so it made some sense.

"Boss, is that an area we should be concerned about? The construction site?"

Hell, yes. But not for the reasons he was suggesting.

The site was in Chavez Ravine, but it didn't have any dues-paying owners yet. Also, I wasn't much inclined to help Rory Tuck.

"No. If there's an outbreak up there, we'll deal with it, but I wouldn't make it part of our patrols. We've got our hands full."

Ron and Brandon exchanged looks. One less area for them to worry about.

At lunch, I grabbed a quick bite at Muertos Café. Even without the lockdown, it wasn't very crowded. While I waited for my cappuccino, I asked the barista why he thought it was so quiet. His name tag read: "Malik."

"I think people are still a little nervous. It's kind of freaky we're getting entities here, especially that whole chupacabra thing. Man, I would *not* want to run into one of those. I mean, the regular shit is bad enough."

He made a skull design with the foamed milk in my coffee and tossed his head to clear the bangs nearly covering one eye.

"I live in Hollywood, and it's like entity central over there." Malik leaned across the counter and lowered his voice. "To be honest, I think people around here are a little entitled, you know? It's like, 'Welcome to our world, suckers.'"

I wondered what Hernan Frias would think of that.

It was time to put my skills to the test.

If my guards were going to repel entities immune to Smoke Bombs, each would need two pouches, and I wanted a few spares, just in case. Every black pouch got a selection of herbs, bits of chili, a pinch of minerals, and a small tin medal.

Nearly an hour later, I stared at thirty-six black cloth pouches lined up on the counter. Each was tied with a black string I had cut with my iron scissors.

Little Lencha looked on, her ever-shifting expression radiating approval.

With moonlight streaming into the sunroom, I began the amplification ritual. As soon as I started saying the words out loud, my impostor syndrome kicked into high gear. It didn't help that Hernan Frias's words played on repeat in my head.

I was a pretender. A nobody.

I closed my eyes and pictured my grandmother standing at the same workbench, conjuring cures for her neighbors. Then I imagined my great-aunt Lencha casting a spell so powerful, it had banished fierce supernatural beings from Chavez Ravine for decades. The strength and power of these women flowed through my veins, and it helped me to squeeze Hernan Frias's ugliness from my thoughts.

With a voice I had never found before, I began my incantation. I was being swept up in the sound. The words were mine, and I was saying them, but it was as if someone else was moving my lips.

When I was done, I took a deep breath and scanned the black pouches arrayed on the workbench. They looked exactly the same as they had a few moments before.

I was hoping there would be some sign the incantation had worked, some indication they were charged and ready for action. But there was nothing. I would have to find out the hard way if the pouches were useful.

Early the next morning, before the overnight team left, I called an all-hands meeting and handed out the pouches. Predictably, that kicked off a discussion about the white brocade bags Clare's friends had used at the cactus garden.

I explained I had made the pouches for Clare and her friends based on an old family tradition and had been surprised by how effective the ingredients were against the entities.

Ron studied me with a mixture of respect and amusement. I hoped he hadn't mentioned the sweeping ritual to his co-workers.

"Is it some sort of new Smoke Bomb?" Brandon asked.

I shrugged. "In a way. I've been doing a little experimenting. No guarantees these are going to work, but we might as well give them a try."

Bailey fingered the black cloth. "These aren't meant to explode, right?"

"I was getting to that. No. These are different. All you need to do is get them close to the entity. You can wave them around or try throwing them directly at the entities. We'll learn together what works best."

Justin and Liam exchanged looks. "You're saying these should work better than the white ones did against the chupacabras? Will it drop those fuckers?"

I sighed. "That would be the best-case scenario. Please remember, these are in the experimental stage. They might not work at all, so don't rely on them. Have a backup plan in case. But do give them a try. See what happens. If they neutralize the entity, great. Move fast and crate them. But if nothing happens, then move to your slingshot or use whatever else you have to contain them. Any questions?"

Bailey shot her hand up. "Those chupacabras didn't behave like the newly emerged entities we see down in the city. Anyone else notice that?"

Justin gave an exaggerated shudder. "Hell yeah, I did. Those things were wide awake. And vicious. I can't figure out what could account for that. Can you?"

Everyone turned to me.

"No, not yet. But we've never had entities here before, and it's possible they behave differently in different geographical areas."

Liam frowned. "But, boss, entities have been showing up in all sorts of terrain since the beginning. Why would things suddenly change?"

"I don't know. Maybe the nerds will be able to tell us once they've taken a look. What I do know is that we all need to be extra careful if any more entities show up here. Got that?"

There were nods all around. Brandon lifted the black pouch to his nose and sniffed.

"What's in them?"

"A bunch of stuff. It's not toxic, so don't worry."

Ron raised his chin. "My grandma says our boss is a bruja, related to Chavez Ravine's most famous bruja, Lencha Bantacorte."

Wonderful. Thank you, Ron. That's exactly what I was hoping you wouldn't say.

"What's a bruja?" Liam asked.

Ron smiled smugly. "A witch."

The room erupted in whispers.

Justin's eyes widened. "Is it true? Are you really a bruja?"

I shot Ron an annoyed glare, and he quickly backtracked. "Oops. Sorry, boss."

I was stuck. A quick internet search would confirm everything.

"Well, there are brujas in my family, but I'm no Lencha Bantacorte. Let's stay focused on the task at hand, shall we?"

On the wall, the heatmap came to life. It was a timely distraction, if not a welcome one.

Ron noticed it first. "Boss, you need to see this."

I clapped my hands. "Okay, meeting adjourned. Night shift, go get some sleep. Dayside folks, we've got an eruption to tend to."

I walked up to the screen for a closer look. Faint red spots formed, but instead of growing bolder and more defined as they usually did, they abruptly vanished. A moment later, they reappeared but in a different place.

The HOA board was going to freak out when they heard about this.

"What's up with the heatmap?" Bailey asked.

Ron and Brandon were on their feet, noses inches away from the screen, shoulders up around their necks.

"Gnomes," I said.

"Uh," Bailey wailed. "I hate those things. They're so annoying."

Justin and Liam were already grabbing their gear. "Where is it this time?"

"La Loma," Ron said over his shoulder. "On the runner's trail next to Elysian Park. Looks like a couple hundred yards from the construction site."

I sighed. "I'll meet you guys up there. You're more than capable of handling some gnomes, but the guy who owns the construction company might need some special attention if he's around. Also, try the pouches. Gnomes can be immune to Smoke Bombs, so see if the pouches do anything."

The guys took off in a security vehicle, and I followed in my Jeep.

At the top of the hill, I parked on the street. An enormous truck was backed halfway into the entrance of the construction site. A group of men had been unloading small trees and plants, but they stopped to stare up at the trail where the action was. I quickly scanned the area for any sign of Rory. So far, so good.

"Chavez Ravine security," I called. "We've got it under control."

They stared after me while I ran past and climbed up the hill to the trail.

Justin, Liam, and Bailey were barely visible through a haze of purple dust. They had surrounded five gnomes, their gnarled faces contorted in fury. Liam and Bailey had deployed Smoke Bombs, but Justin was waving a black pouch in front of the gnomes.

The little creatures weren't backing down. Their pointed hats quivered on their heads, and their diminutive bodies shook in anger. The gnome closest to Justin stumbled and fell to its knees. The other four veered off the trail and headed down the hill. The rocky terrain didn't slow them in the slightest. Within minutes, they had vanished into the labyrinth of the construction site.

Dammit.

My team stared at the immobilized gnome. Justin had put his pouch on the creature's chest, and it struggled as if the bag were an elephant.

I smiled. *How about that?* My pouches worked, at least on gnomes. That was progress.

"I told you to skip the Smoke Bombs," Justin said smugly.

I didn't blame either of the guards. They had acted on instinct. But they should have course-corrected more quickly.

"Sorry, Maddy," Bailey said.

"Yeah." Liam grimaced. "We messed up."

"Don't sweat it. We just learned something." I crouched and studied the gnome.

Its round black eyes followed my every move.

I lifted the pouch off the gnome and held my breath. It got to its feet, eyes flashing with a mix of confusion and anger. Instead of running off to join its pals, it swayed slightly, trying to regain its bearings.

I moved the black pouch closer. Its knees knocked together, and the gnome toppled sideways.

When I tossed the pouch to Bailey and told her to back up, the gnome again got to his feet.

"Whoa!" Liam said.

Justin wrestled the gnome to the ground and placed a pouch on its chest.

I felt light as air. The moonlight ritual had worked. Not quite as well as I had hoped, but it was progress. The pouch had required very close or direct contact, which one could manage with a gnome. It would be tougher with something big and scary, like a chupacabra or a camazotz.

I picked up my phone and called Ron. "We have one gnome under control and are about to search for four others. Send someone up here with crates. Tell them they'll find one ready to be boxed up on the trail just west of the construction site." I waved to Bailey and Justin. "Leave that one there and let's go down and find the runaways."

We headed for the entrance to the site. I would have to figure out what I could do to make the pouches stronger. And come up with a protocol for using them with dangerous entities.

Justin must have been thinking along similar lines. "What if we put something incredibly sticky on the pouches so we can throw them and have them attach to the entities?"

"Good one!" Bailey bounced on her toes. "That way, we wouldn't have to get too close. And maybe Maddy can make them bigger? With more of that stuff inside?"

My team, if anything, was smart and adaptable. I had work to do, but I had a great team to help me do it. Because annoying gnomes were one thing. A fully alert ghoul was another, and we had to be ready.

My phone went off. I glanced down at the screen and winced. It was Rory Tuck.

Chapter 34

Rory Tuck was charming as usual. "You need to get here right now. Some weird fucking creatures are pestering my men."

There were many things I wanted to say. All but one involved profanity.

I went with the nice one. "We're here now."

Seconds later, we met Rory at the gate.

"They're stealing our plants and doing who knows what with them," Rory exploded. "I can't have these things interfering with our work. Get them out of here now!"

I really, really hated being yelled at, no matter who was doing it. But when Rory Tuck raised his voice to me, it made my blood boil. I had to keep my cool. There would come a time for me to chat with Rory about his middle-of-the-night activities, but this was not it.

"Yes, that's what we do. We get rid of entities. Did you see where they went?"

Rory gritted his teeth and motioned for me to follow. He stomped down the main road of the construction site, kicking pebbles out of his way. For a short, stocky man, he could move fast. I followed, preparing myself for whatever chaos awaited us around the corner.

The gnomes scurried about, their tiny hands clutching plants and shrubs. They darted from one spot to another. The gnomes had picked a lovely spot for their work—a wide, shaded area at the end of a cul-de-sac.

The landscaping crew was keeping a safe distance from the gnomes. One of the men stepped away from the group and walked toward the clearing. He was rewarded with a dirt clod to the head.

Rory pointed furiously at the small, bearded beings. "There! Look at what they're doing! Get them out of here!" He was yelling again. That was really getting old.

The gnomes seemed oblivious to our presence. They were focused on the plants and, apparently, on putting them into the ground. There was a lot of squinting up at the sun, pinching dirt between their fingers, and muttering.

Rory stomped a foot. "Are you just going to stand there?"

"I'm assessing the situation," I said through clenched teeth.

Rory glowered. "Well, assess faster, then. I need to get my crew back to work!"

There were some people I would bend over backward to help. Rory was *not* one of them.

"If I may please ask for your patience. I have some people coming. We'll get to it as soon as they arrive."

He grumbled something under his breath but stepped away.

I'd had two near-fatal accidents at that site and only had one suspect, but I figured I was safe as long as I was helping keep things on schedule.

Bailey, Liam, and Justin ran up, carrying two crates. I cleared my throat and turned to Rory.

"It might be better if you all left and let us handle it."

Rory shook his head. "No, thank you. I plan on making sure you do your job."

I could have made a scene and ordered him away, but there was no guarantee he would comply. It was his property, after all. And we couldn't wait forever. We needed to round up the gnomes before they scattered again.

"All right, fine. I can't make you leave, but please stay out of our way. And we'd appreciate it if you kept quiet and didn't distract the gnomes."

Rory made a zip-my-mouth-shut gesture, but he managed to do it in a surly way. I turned my back and rolled my eyes. My team smirked as we huddled together.

"What an asshole," Bailey muttered. "What's the plan?"

Gnomes were notoriously fast. They were also oblivious to their surroundings when they were engaged in a task. There were four of them and four of us.

"Do you have four black pouches between you?"

They nodded.

"Good. Which one of you wants to try to tackle two? The rest of us will take one."

Liam held up his hands. They were the size of dinner plates. "I'll do it. These might actually come in handy for once."

I was not thrilled about having an audience. Rory Tuck, grandson of Irish witch Spencer Tuck, might be able to sense the magic in the pouches, and that would certainly put him on guard. I didn't need him knowing I had skills too.

"If Rory asks what's in the pouches, just say it's a new form of Smoke Bomb." I kept my voice low. "And do not mention the 'B' word."

Bailey raised her eyebrows.

I clarified. "Bruja, not that other 'B' word. You can say that one all you want."

We approached the gnomes from different angles, holding the black pouches and trying to corner the gnomes without startling them. Luckily, they were busy digging holes, presumably for the plants they had stolen from the truck. As we closed in, they finally seemed to sense our presence.

They turned toward us, their small faces twisting into scowls. One of them hurled a clump of dirt in my direction.

I dodged it and lunged forward, tackling the gnome and, in a totally improvised move, rubbing the black pouch across its face. It gagged and sputtered, going still beneath my hands.

While Bailey struggled to subdue her gnome, Justin's captive broke free and kicked him in the shin. Liam grabbed it before it could get away, grappling with two gnomes at once. His enormous hands pinned them to the ground, but I saw the problem immediately. He didn't have an extra hand to use the pouch, so after placing one on my captive's chest, I scrambled over to help. Within seconds, we had four gnomes laid out flat on their backs, pouches on their chests, panicked expressions on their wizened faces.

Rory came pounding up. Questions formed in his eyes. He looked from me to my team and finally to the black pouches. I had to admit, it was a weird sight.

"What in fuck's name just happened here?" Rory's voice was filled with disbelief.

The gnomes twitched.

I stood up slowly, brushing dirt off my knees, and met Rory's gaze steadily. "It's a new form of Smoke Bomb," I lied, watching for any hint of suspicion in his eyes.

Oh, there was a hint, all right. "Is that so?"

The gears turned in his head while he tried to make sense of the situation. He sniffed. A chill ran down my spine. What was he sensing?

I pushed back my shoulders. "Okay, guys. Let's get our visitors crated up and ready for the Dump."

Rory stared at me for a long moment, frowning. "I'm still not a happy camper about this entity situation. Yeah, sure, you handled *these*. But they were gnomes. What if we get those

217

chupacabras here, right in the middle of one of my home tours? What are you going to do about *that*? Chavez Ravine isn't supposed to have entities. That's why we're building this development here in the first place!"

I plastered a professional smile on my face. It actually hurt. "We have a heatmap and are responding in a timely manner to all incidents. You also have our hotline number. And I'm not sure if you read the disclosures when you bought this property, but Chavez Ravine does not guarantee, nor has it ever guaranteed, an entity-free zone."

Rory's face grew red, and his hands were tight fists. I wasn't sure if the man was angry there were entities on his property or because he needed me to take care of them.

As unfortunate as it was that Chavez Ravine had its first ever entity outbreak, it might have been the best life insurance policy I could have asked for.

Chapter 35

The weird feeling started the instant I stepped out of my Jeep in the parking lot behind La Loma Plaza. I tried to ignore it because I desperately needed coffee and some pan dulce from Muertos Café to get me through the rest of the afternoon.

When I passed the spot where Clare's car had nearly run over me, the hairs on the nape of my neck lifted. It was as if something was begging me to pay attention. I stopped and looked around.

Just off to my left was a large hole in the grass. *Damn.* It had the telltale signs of an entity emergence.

My phone blasted to life, making me jump.

It was Ron at the command center. "Boss, we've got another one. At La Loma Plaza."

I cursed under my breath. With the lockdown lifted, people had ventured out of their homes. The shopping center was busy.

"I'm here now." I turned around in a complete circle, scanning the foliage, the roofs, the spaces in between buildings, but noticed nothing unusual.

No one was screaming. Yet. Maybe we would get lucky, and it would just be a couple of industrious gnomes, but I wasn't counting on it. There was too much at risk with so many people milling around.

"Ron, send everyone you've got and tell them to bring the new pouches. Tell them to park in the back and keep it low-key. No need to freak everyone out if we don't have to."

"No problem, boss. Let me know when you figure out what it is."

The emerging entity hadn't left any footprints. Sometimes they did; sometimes they didn't. So that wasn't especially worrying. But the size of the hole was.

Too big for chaneques, gnomes, or goblins. Not big enough for trolls. About the size of something like a camazotz.

Justin had said the one that got Bailey came swooping out of a tree at the storage yard, so I scanned the ones nearby. Just the idea of razor-sharp bat claws tangled in my hair made me shiver.

I was still getting used to smart entities. When I was with Occult Affairs, the entities I dealt with had been so whacked out by their emergence, they had been easy to find. But in Chavez Ravine, the entities had enough presence of mind to hide or launch a surprise attack. That made me nervous.

"Come out, come out, wherever you are," I whispered.

A blood-curdling scream pierced the air, and I began running. It was coming from the direction of Muertos Café. When I reached the covered breezeway, I looked in both directions. People were pressed against the walls, too afraid to move.

Another scream, this one long enough for me to determine it came from an open window at the café. Heart pounding, I rushed inside.

A dozen or so customers and a couple of baristas were in the middle of the dining room, staring out onto the patio. It was empty except for a tall, spindly figure standing very still in the shade of a wide palm tree.

A ghoul. A particularly horrific specimen of murderous monster with an insatiable craving for human flesh. Narrow, pale face. Black holes for eyes. A dark, tattered cape covering a misshapen, lumpy torso.

Whoever screamed decided she had been quiet long enough and screamed again. It was a fiftyish woman with a ruddy complexion. Her bob hairdo had lots of sharp angles and brassy highlights. I hurried over and took her arm.

"Ma'am. Please stop. We don't want to agitate it."

She turned to me slowly, blinking. "What the hell *is* that thing?"

I quickly locked the patio door. Sometimes, the less said, the better. There was no need for people to know that thing on the patio was a vicious, flesh-eating beast. That would just cause a panic.

I raised my voice so they could all hear. "All right, everyone. My name is Maddy Madrigal, and I'm head of security. Obviously, we're dealing with a fairly serious entity here. I have a team headed our way. If you can all take your seats, please, and remain calm and quiet."

"But we've never had them here before," the lady with the bob cried.

I gritted my teeth and led her to a table away from the windows facing the patio. "I really need you to keep your voice down. If that isn't something you can do, I'm going to ask you to go to the bathroom and stay there." The bathroom was down a long hallway, far from the patio.

Everyone took a seat, including bob lady, who muttered all the way. I texted Ron to let him know about the ghoul, then sent a carefully worded emergency alert. People outside were asked to go indoors. Anyone at La Loma Plaza needed to seek shelter immediately.

Ron texted me back. I was just about to read it when there was a collective gasp.

The ghoul was pressed against the window, its mouth open wide, tongue licking the glass. Its twisted form seemed to contort and elongate while it clawed at the window, desperate to reach the terrified people inside.

Justin, Bailey, and Liam burst through the doors of Muertos Café. They came to an abrupt stop when their eyes fell on the ghoul making a spectacle of itself in the window.

Liam eyed it nervously. "I don't think the new pouches are going to work on that thing."

"We'll just have to use them all," Justin said. "You know. Strength in numbers."

Bailey snorted. "Yeah, like anyone wants to get close enough to *that* thing. Look at those teeth."

My team knew to speak in low voices. Not that anyone in the café was paying attention to us. All eyes remained fixed on the ghoul, which was turned sideways, sliding back and forth across the glass.

"I think we need to use everything we've got," I said. "Hit it with Smoke Bombs and then the pouches. All of them. Justin, you mentioned we should coat the pouches in something sticky. Any ideas?"

He frowned. "Something like a super glue would work. It only takes a second to bond. It might work."

"It's worth a try," Liam agreed, frowning. "But where are we going to get super glue?"

The barista I had met earlier had been following our conversation. He went behind the counter, reached into a drawer, and pulled out a tube. "Here you go. I use this stuff to fix busted table legs. Works like a charm."

Music to my ears.

Malik cleared a space on the counter for the team to prepare the pouches. He spread a sheet of waxed paper to protect the countertop. "Don't get that shit on your fingers," he warned. "Not unless you want your skin to come off."

We carefully squirted super glue on both sides of the pouches. It occurred to me only three guards had responded.

222

"Where's everyone else?"

Bailey snapped her head up. Her eyeshadow was a dark, shimmery gray. "Didn't Ron mention? We've got two other incidents. Some more gnomes and a lone chupacabra. Both in Bishop."

Ron had sent me a text, but I hadn't had a chance to check it.

We carefully picked up the pouches by their dry edges. The next part was going to be tricky. We needed to throw them at the ghoul without getting them stuck to anything else, especially ourselves.

"Is there a way out through the kitchen?" I asked the barista.

He nodded. "Yeah. I'll show you." Malik paused. "You need any help?"

Before I had a chance to respond, Bailey said, "Thank you, but no. We've been trained to do this." Her tone was withering and her message clear—she had no time for amateurs.

Malik's lip curled. "Whatever. I've got an application into Occult Affairs."

I made a mental note to mention him to Jo. Occult Affairs was woefully understaffed, and he seemed like a capable guy.

We needed to move before the ghoul figured out it could break the windows. We followed Malik through the kitchen and filed out into a courtyard. Just as the barista was closing the door, I thought of something.

"Do you have a ladder?"

Malik stuck his foot in the door to prop it open, reached back inside, and pulled a metal ladder from a closet. "If you guys are going to use that, I can hold it steady."

"That would be helpful." I turned to the others. "The roof is flat. We can go at him from up there. Hopefully, he won't see us coming if we're low and quiet."

223

They nodded.

My heart was like a jackhammer in my chest by the time we made it up to the roof. Justin carefully handed his pouches to Liam, crawled combat-style to the edge over the patio, then beckoned us over. We tiptoed to join him, delicately holding the pouches.

I peered down onto the patio. The ghoul had its back to us and was pounding the glass with his fists, moaning loudly.

"On my count," I whispered. "One…two…three!"

We carefully threw the pouches at the ghoul. They flew across the patio and hit their marks. Bailey even managed to get one on its head.

The ghoul screeched and spun around.

"Hit him again," I ordered.

More black pouches went flying, all landing on the ghoul. It seemed to realize it was covered in lumpy things and tried scraping them off, but when his skeletal fingers came into contact with the cloth, he shrieked.

The pouches were having an effect, and my heart did a happy dance. But that came to an abrupt end.

The ground shook, sending vibrations all the way up the roof. Cracks spiderwebbed across the patio. The ghoul was pounding the concrete, and a hole was beginning to form. Was it trying to escape by going back where it had come from? If it could do that, it could pop up again anywhere.

We could not let that happen.

Before I could stop him, Justin dropped off the roof and hurled a Smoke Bomb. Unaffected, the ghoul kept widening the hole. There was no choice but to follow Justin. Liam went over next, then Bailey.

My ankle was still recovering from dodging the runaway SUV, so I lay on my stomach and dangled my legs off the edge. I gripped the rain gutter with both hands and eased myself over the side. Even that short fall sent a shooting pain up my ankle. When I turned, the ghoul was gnashing its teeth at Justin, who stood between the creature and the hole, swinging his baton.

Liam, Bailey, and I pulled out our slingshots, loaded steel pellets into the rubber bands, and aimed. Justin jumped aside, and we took our shots. The ghoul howled when the pellets hit its flesh. Everything we had done had slowed it down, but nothing had completely stopped it. It continued to dig at the edges of the hole.

The patio door banged open, and Malik burst through. "Want me to try this?"

He held up a handheld torch, the kind restaurants used to melt sugar and toast meringue. It was small, but it would burn hot.

I waved him over. "Go!"

The barista charged the ghoul. A long flame erupted from the torch like a fiery blade. The ghoul let out an ear-splitting scream when its flesh singed. The monster staggered to its feet, its open mouth revealing rows of terrifying teeth, then collapsed in a heap.

I rummaged around in my front pack and pulled out a wide roll of duct tape. Until we could get a large crate there, we would have to secure the ghoul. Duct taping its entire head would be our first step. Bailey and Liam used the metal mesh gloves to get that done while Liam and I began taping the pouches to its arms and legs, binding them to its torso in the process.

I sighed. We had never had to worry about stuff like this when I worked for Occult Affairs. Hit them with Smoke Bombs and down they went.

The barista wiped his brow with the back of his hand. "That was…intense."

All the adrenaline pumping through my body was making me very alive and very jittery. "Yes. It was. Thanks to all of you." I turned to Malik. "And thank you for coming through for us today. I really appreciate it."

Bailey punched his arm. "Yeah. You were actually pretty great." She stuck out her hand. "I'm Bailey, and this is Liam, Justin, and Maddy."

"I'm Malik. It's nice meeting you. Maybe one of you can put in a good word for me at Occult Affairs?"

Justin grinned. "I can do that."

"Me too." Liam shot his hand up.

Malik tucked a loose strand of hair behind an ear. "Awesome. Can anyone use some coffee?"

"Maybe an espresso shot?" Bailey asked.

Malik chuckled. "Oh yeah. I can whip up cafecitos that wake the dead. And I've got some sugar skull pastries in the back."

After the day we had just had, that was the least my team deserved.

Everyone trooped inside, leaving me alone with the shivering ghoul and my dark thoughts. I texted Ron to send someone with a large crate. He responded he would and also that the other entities had been contained, thanks to the pouches. I smiled. The new, upgraded pouches were better, but they still couldn't defeat a creature as powerful as a ghoul.

I needed stronger magic. Unfortunately, I didn't think I had the time to learn it.

Chapter 36

The moon—a bright white disc in an inky sky—seemed to taunt me.

Go ahead. Try another ritual. See where that gets you.

I poured a glass of pinot noir and plopped down on the wicker couch, too tired to do anything but sit there and think about how inadequate my magic had been. Half-measures weren't enough. Not when it came to protecting people and places like Chavez Ravine. My great-aunt Lencha had probably never had this problem. Maybe if I had started learning brujería back when I was a kid, I wouldn't be so lame.

I was up a creek without a magic paddle. My aunt's spirit had tried to help me out, but from beyond the grave, there was only so much she could do. The truth was, I wasn't much good at the whole witchy thing.

Sam paced at my feet, his tail flicking back and forth high in the air.

I sighed. "What? You've already had your dinner. And treats."

He meowed loudly.

"I've had a really bad day, Sam. Seriously. My ego is very fragile at the moment. And I jumped off a roof, and my ankle hurts. So please, give it a rest."

The cat surprised me by jumping up on the couch and settling in next to me. I patted the top of his head, like I had seen Julia and Leo do dozens of times. He swatted my hand with a paw. At least he had retracted his claws.

"You really know how to make a girl feel wanted." I barked out a bitter laugh. "I should have named you Stu."

Sam kneaded the cushions and then pushed his big head into my hip. I grabbed a muslin throw and pulled it over us. It was nice just sitting there, staring out into the moonlit garden.

At least until unwanted thoughts started pushing their way into my brain.

What if another ghoul showed up? What if the Chavez Ravine variety of entity could figure out how to open doors or windows? What if Rory Tuck managed to kill me before I could realize my potential as a bruja?

Eventually, I must have drifted off to sleep. When my eyes snapped open, the clock on my phone showed it was just after three a.m. Sam was prowling around the sunroom, batting something around in the dark. Something soft. I hoped he hadn't killed a giant black moth. That would have been gross.

I flicked on the lamp. Sam was playing with something in the shadows, but I couldn't make it out. I drew closer, squinting, trying to figure out what it was.

Sam whacked it, and it skittered across the floor.

A bright red habanero chili. A long vine with shiny green leaves had snaked under the French doors. It was covered in orange and red habaneros dangling like ominous ornaments.

With the agility of a soccer player, Sam batted the chili across the room, sending it skittering along the tile floor. It came to rest beneath my workbench. On the counter, Little Lencha glowed purple.

My breath caught in my throat.

The air seemed to tingle with electricity. The vine almost writhed and twisted, as if it was reaching out toward me. Was Lencha trying to tell me something? If so, what?

228

I closed my eyes to focus on the figurine, but I was overcome with a powerful craving for Chili Colorado. The thought of the spicy, rich stew made my stomach growl. The craving was so powerful, I couldn't get to the kitchen fast enough. Of course, there was no such thing as chili Colorado without chilis, so I plucked a few from the vine on my way by.

Sam followed closely behind, his tail fluffed. He watched while I gathered the ingredients from the fridge and pantry. It was weird to make spicy beef stew at three o'clock in the morning, but I was so hungry I didn't give it a second thought.

After preparing a cup of Yerba Buena tea, I chopped the onions and garlic. The seeds and stems were removed from a handful of dried Guajillo chilis. Then I scraped them into a pot of water along with two whole tomatoes. I brought the concoction to a quick boil on the stove and turned off the flame.

Sam weaved between my legs while I browned slices of beef and sprinkled them with spices.

The warm, familiar aroma of cumin and frying meat filled the room. After the chilis and tomato had softened in the hot water, I added all the ingredients—including some chopped habaneros—into the blender. When I had a smooth red sauce, I poured it over the meat and stirred, focusing on the scent of spices and the sensation of the cool night breeze on my skin.

I put the pot over a low flame to simmer. Then, to kill some time, I toasted several white corn tortillas until the edges were slightly crispy. Because I was so hungry, I spread some salted butter on one and ate it.

While the stew simmered, I took my time setting the table. From the hutch, I pulled out a Mexican Talavera bowl. The blue, yellow, red, and green pottery was perfect for this strange occasion. I set out a colorful, striped placemat on the table with a cloth napkin, a spoon, and a fork.

When the dish had simmered long enough, I ladled the Chili Colorado into the bowl and garnished it with a dollop of crema and a sprinkle of queso fresco.

The aroma was intoxicating. Sam sat on the table, his eyes fixed on the steaming bowl in front of me. I tore off a strip of warm tortilla and scooped up some chili. The flavors exploded on my tongue. A second later, so did the heat.

Those habaneros were hotter than any chili I had ever tasted. Tears welled in my eyes, and my nose began to run. I poured myself a tall glass of water and continued eating. My entire body grew so warm I began to sweat.

My hunger could not be satisfied. Despite the heat from the chilis, I ate quickly, then served myself another bowl, thankful no one was around to witness my gluttony.

Except for the cat.

Sam's green eyes were focused on me intently, as if he knew something I didn't. His tail swished back and forth.

"What?" I asked between bites. My mouth was on fire from the habaneros.

Sam meowed, jumped off the table, and began pacing in front of the stove.

While I sat back in my chair, a tingling in my stomach spread up my chest, to my arms, and down to my fingers. I glanced at my hands. Just beneath the skin, a faint red light pulsed, illuminating a strange network of green filaments. I stared in disbelief, unsure if the habaneros were playing tricks with my head. Was there such a thing as a hallucinogenic chili?

I went into the sunroom. Lencha glowed the same reddish hue as my hands.

The magic of Lencha was coursing through me, a gift bestowed through the power of the habaneros.

I felt something I had not experienced before—a knowledge, a confidence, a certainty I had the raw power of magic at my command. It just needed me to shape it.

Was this the new me? Or was this just a temporary gift? A little boost to help a girl out?

Use it or lose it, the saying went.

I stepped through the French doors and into the garden. My skin tingled where the moonlight touched it. My brain didn't know what to do next, but my arms did.

They reached toward the moon. I closed my eyes and pictured entities trapped behind a barrier thin as a veil but impenetrable as a fortress. When I imagined the shimmering green strands beneath my skin shooting upward in all directions, the tendrils expanded and reached across Chavez Ravine until they wound together above me.

Once the vines united, I made a gesture with my hand, and the red glow intensified at my fingertips. The vines began to twist and dance, creating an intricate pattern in the night sky. A low hum filled the air, vibrating through my bones. The moonlight washed over the restless tendrils, strengthening them.

It took every ounce of my will to complete the shield that would keep the entities away. When the green filaments had become a dense canopy of vines nearly blocking out the night sky, a bright red chili appeared and fell to earth. It landed at my feet.

And then it was over. It had been a gloriously simple process.

When I opened my eyes, the vine had retracted back into the garden. A half dozen or so habaneros remained scattered on the tiles. I scooped them up and placed them in a small bowl on the counter, just in case I needed a boost.

All energy seemed to drain out of me. I stumbled into my bedroom and crawled into bed. My eyes were so heavy, and I couldn't keep them open a moment longer. The last thing I saw before succumbing to sleep was Sam's big head on the pillow next to mine.

Chapter 37

I awoke to my alarm, just as I did most mornings. My thoughts immediately turned to my nocturnal feast and the protection spell which had followed it. I remembered the feeling of creating a protection canopy of vines over the three neighborhoods of Chavez Ravine. And I wondered if it had worked.

Could I have cast a spell as powerful as Hernan's? Or as long-lasting as Lencha's? It didn't seem likely, but time would tell. As usual, I checked my phone to make sure I hadn't missed any calls or alerts from the command center.

Nothing.

Despite my crazy night, I was rested and ready to go to work. In fact, I felt…normal. And hungry for breakfast, weirdly. I started coffee, then called the command center.

"Looks like we're getting a bit of a break," Ron said. "I came in early, just in case, but everything's been quiet."

That was good news, but it was hardly proof my spell was working.

I fed Sam, then waited for the coffee to brew. Sitting at the kitchen table, I stared at my hands. There was nothing magical about them. They needed some lotion, just like every morning, but that was it. My muscles were a little sore, but it had nothing to do with magic. It was what I had expected after all the excitement at Muertos Café, and it reminded me I was overdue for a workout.

After I drank some coffee, I pulled on my workout clothes and did a forty-five-minute upper body session, then showered and fixed my makeup and hair.

For a change, my eyeliner went on smoothly, but other than that, I didn't feel very magical. In fact, my chili fest and spell casting were starting to seem like a strange but happy dream.

My thoughts circled back to Rory Tuck. Nobody had ever tried to kill me before, and I wasn't quite sure what to do about it. I didn't have any actual evidence, and my suspicions were based only on an assumption: that Rory had inherited magic skills from Spencer Tuck.

It wasn't exactly something I could take to a judge. But I couldn't just hope for the best either.

I needed to confront him, to let him know I knew. And that I wasn't going to go quietly. That might be risky with a man like him, but after the night I'd had, I was feeling confident I could handle anything he threw at me.

I dressed in tan pants and a top, pulled on my gold trench coat, and checked the results in the mirror. Had Lencha's magic given my skin a golden glow? I moved in for a closer look. It was probably just the light reflecting off my coat.

My caramel-colored hair was having a good day too. Of course, one good camazotz would take care of that. Though, if entities broke through my protection circle, I would be too depressed to care.

After I had restocked my front pack, I said goodbye to Sam, opened the front door, and nearly fell over Stu. He was placing a vase of flowers on the doormat.

Stu straightened. The vertical lines around his mouth deepened as he grimaced. "Hi."

I glanced down at the flowers. A whimsical arrangement of deep red and bouncy sprays of green and silver foliage that looked very expensive.

"What's this?"

"Flowers." Stu flushed. He also looked like he was trying hard not to roll his eyes at the question.

"I know that. What are they for?" Yes. I was going to make him say it.

Stu cleared his throat. "Well, a better apology, for one thing…" His voice drifted off.

There was something stuck in the flowers. An envelope. And not the small kind the florist would give you, but the size that holds a card. This was turning out to be a very different morning than the one I had prepared myself for. When I reached down for it, Stu snatched it away.

I laughed and held out my hand. "I'm pretty sure that has my name on it."

"Yeah. I was trying to take the easy way out. You know. With a note. But now that you've caught me…" His eyes seemed to register my outfit and that I was on my way out the door. "This is maybe a longer conversation than you have time for?"

I scooped up the flowers, set them on the little table in the entryway, locked the door, and sat in an Adirondack chair. "That note couldn't have been very long. Try me."

Stu exhaled loudly, then dropped into the other chair. "I'm sorry for being such a jackass. My therapist says I'm conflict-averse after that whole thing with my ex. Not that that's an excuse. I should have told you about the job with your mother's tour and not let you find out about it from someone else. Obviously, I gave you the impression I didn't care about…you know, us, when that's pretty much all I've been thinking about. You and me. That was shitty, and I'm really and truly sorry."

235

"The note said all that?" I felt light all over.

"Not all of it." Stu smiled grimly. "It didn't say Clare likes you better than me now." He looked away, frowning.

I reached over and tapped his knee. "Get over yourself. It's not an either-or situation. Your very smart kid is totally capable of feeling affection for two people at once. I'm just thrilled to be on her good side."

Since Stu had fessed up, it was only fair I did too.

"Honestly, I should have just called you when I found out, instead of making assumptions, but I don't always think clearly when my mother is involved. She really, really gets in my head."

Stu moved closer so his knees touched mine. "You said you two had issues, but I didn't know it was that bad."

"Oh, it's *bad*." I stared down at my hands. "The years'-worth-of-therapy kind of bad. I'm not making excuses. As they say, I can't control my mother, but I can control my reactions to her." I sighed and took a deep breath. "My turn to say sorry. Sorry."

Stu tilted his head while he studied me. "Mmm. Is there something different about you?"

Was I glowing with magic? Now, that would be an unexpected benefit.

"Not that I know of." I shrugged. "Thank you for the flowers. And for the apology. I appreciate it."

"What do we do now?" Stu couldn't have sounded more awkward if he had tried.

"For starters, don't be afraid to be honest with me in the future. I'm not that scary." I paused. "Am I?

He smiled, leaned forward, and cupped the back of my calves, like Paul had done when Stu saw us in the La Loma Plaza parking lot. It was much sexier when Stu did it.

236

"Of course not. Here's what I'd like to do—work on that honesty thing and pick up where we left off." He tipped his head back. "Except…Clare is with me until my ex gets back to town."

I smiled. "Maybe we can all watch a movie together and I can cop a feel under the blanket."

Stu rewarded me with a heartfelt laugh. "Actually, that sounds pretty damn good to me." He got to his feet. "I heard about that ghoul at Muertos. Great work. Where're you headed?"

"To see Rory Tuck."

Stu frowned. "What do you want to see him for?"

If I told him the truth, Stu wouldn't rest until he had talked me out of it.

"Just some business I need to clear up."

Stu squeezed my hand. "Good luck with that, then. And I sure hope the entities give you a break."

I did too, but for different reasons. If more entities appeared in Chavez Ravine, it would mean my protection circle hadn't worked and my magic had failed. And if that was the case, going to see Rory Tuck was very risky indeed.

When I pulled up to the construction site, I still had no idea exactly what I was going to say to Rory Tuck. I could only hope the right words would appear in the correct order when I needed them.

As usual, the site was humming and clanging with activity. I had almost reached Rory's man cave of a trailer when someone called my name.

When I turned around, it was Paul.

"Hey," he said, running up. "Here to see me, by any chance?" He winked.

Here we go again.

But something was different.

Was I imagining it, or was there something off about the guy? His smile wasn't quite right, and he seemed to radiate a dark, nervous energy.

"No, I'm here for your cousin." I didn't owe Paul any more explanation than that.

"Bummer." He smiled. "Is there anything I can help you with?"

I shook my head. "Not really. Is Rory around?"

"Depends on what you want to see him about. You know how moody he is. Just trying to spare you, if you get my drift."

The muscles in my jaw tightened. Was Paul trying to prevent me from seeing his cousin? Why would that be? I cleared my throat.

"Paul, I have to get to work soon. Is Rory around or not?"

Paul's goatee quivered at my sharp tone. "Not. But he should be back in literally minutes. Why don't I show you the really awesome water feature we just put in? You'll love it."

I sincerely doubted it, but I wasn't going to leave until I had spoken to Rory.

Paul led me down a narrow path toward the back of the property. It was quieter there, away from all the workers and the constant noise of their tools.

"Ta da!" Paul gestured toward a large pond with a fountain in the middle. There were even some wooden benches around the bank.

"Nice." I couldn't have sounded less interested.

Paul shifted from one foot to the other. "Is everything okay? You're acting kind of funny."

Something about the guy was putting me on edge. "Nothing funny going on here. Just got a busy day ahead of me."

"So, what was it you wanted to talk to Rory about?"

"I'd prefer not to say."

"You can tell me. I can keep a secret." Paul's smile faltered. "Is it anything to do with the deal that Rory's trying to pull off? If so, that's not anything you want to get mixed up in, trust me."

"What deal is that?"

But he was lying. There was no deal. Paul was trying to delay me. But why?

"I shouldn't have said anything." Paul gave me a rueful grin.

I studied him. The boyish charm had faded, and his body language was threatening. I hadn't noticed before, but he bore an uncanny resemblance to the photo I had seen of Spencer Tuck. Younger, of course, and better-looking, but the features were strikingly similar.

My brain went *click, click, click*.

I had been so focused on Rory I hadn't paid much attention to Paul. The guy who had lost his last job because of shady dealings involving the same trucking company parking their vehicles on Julia's street in the middle of the night.

The guy who owned one-third of Tuck and Tuck Construction had as much motive to get me out of the way as Rory did.

The pieces of the puzzle fell into place, and I recognized his deceit clearly.

His sudden appearance after each of my "accidents." Playing good cop against Rory's rough demeanor to throw me off-balance. And steering me to a secluded part of the construction project, where we were alone and far from anyone who could help.

I'd had the wrong guy. It had been Paul all along. The asshole.

Paul's grin faded when he noted the suspicion in my eyes. I needed to get out of there, so I turned on my heel and began walking quickly away from the pond.

Paul called after me, but he was yelling in a foreign language. It had to be Irish. I couldn't understand what he was saying, but the urgency in his voice was unmistakable.

And then, a low growl.

My blood ran cold. I spun around. A monstrous creature came through the trees. A chupacabra had emerged while Paul and I had been talking.

But the shape and size were all wrong. It was unlike any dog I had ever seen: enormous, with a rough, shaggy coat and strange yellow eyes.

The monstrous dog glanced at Paul, who pointed at me. His face was a cold, blank mask. Paul was commanding this beast of nightmares.

"Go on," he said. "What are you waiting for?"

Obviously, he was talking to the dog, but his words broke through the icy fear that had taken hold of me. I had a strong urge to run as fast as I could.

But I wasn't without power. Lencha had given me the gift of magic. I just hoped I could figure out how to use it against the monster.

The thing's lips peeled back, revealing a row of nasty, yellow, very sharp teeth. I didn't want to think about what those massive jaws could do to me.

It crouched and slowly began to advance.

When I was working for the LAPD, we had run into the occasional aggressive dog. Sometimes, a stern command was enough to get them to back off.

I planted my feet wide, held out a hand, and shouted, "Stop!"

It froze. Drool dribbled from its mouth, and it locked its gaze on me. Then it lunged.

I dropped to the ground, and the thing flew over me. The stench of filthy dog filled my nose, and a hind leg scraped across my back. I quickly rose, turning around in time for it to lunge at me again.

Even though I leapt to my right, the beast smashed into my shoulder, spinning me around. I lost my footing and tumbled to the ground.

The creature was already above me before I could scramble to get back up. Strings of drool hit my face and neck. It panted in anticipation.

The monster dog slowly lowered its head, jaws opening. Its hot breath smelled like rotting meat.

My fear rose, threatening to overwhelm and immobilize me.

A rush of heat surged through my body, and a faint red glowed under the skin of my hands. Green filaments pulsed just under the flesh.

"You stop right there, mister. Don't you dare move."

The surprised look on its face was almost comical. I had spoken to the monster like an errant chihuahua. But it seemed to be working.

The dog rose and turned to Paul, who was clenching his fists, his nostrils flaring. Paul thundered something in Irish.

Before the dog could attack again, I focused all my energy on the creature. With a swift flick of my wrist and a brief whispered incantation, I sent the tendrils through the air toward the beast. Paul seemed startled by my movements, but neither he nor the dog appeared to notice the glowing strands stretching in their direction.

But I could see them just fine. They wrapped themselves around the creature and began to tighten. The beast gave a grunt of surprise, then yelped. It tried to shake itself free from the threads, but it began to shrink.

"What the hell?" Paul spoke in English.

The beast's body continued to diminish until it was the size of a small dog. After shooting a frightened look in my direction, it gave a high-pitched yelp and ran off. I got to my feet.

Paul glared. If looks could kill…*Oh, that's right.* He had already tried to do that three times. After flirting with me. The pinche cabron.

Somewhere in the distance, someone was shouting. And then Rory was there, clutching his side, face red.

"What the hell is going on?"

Paul was too focused on me to respond.

Rory grabbed his cousin's elbow and nearly pulled him off his feet. "What the fuck are you up to? Did you use your magic against Maddy, Paul?"

I rubbed my hands. They felt itchy and slightly hot. "He just tried to kill me. Again."

Rory's eyes blazed with fury. He took a step toward his cousin. "How many times have we talked about this, Paul? We don't do this. Not here. Not ever. That's not what this family is about. Not anymore."

Paul curled his lips into a sneer. "Come on. She's going to fuck everything up. She won't sell. And if she doesn't, none of the others will either. I had to do something to protect us."

"Protect us?" Rory's voice cracked with disbelief. "From what, exactly?"

Paul scoffed. "Don't act like you're better than me, Rory. You've done that ever since we were kids, and I'm sick of it. You're just as desperate to buy up that land as I am."

"Not like this, Paul. Not by hurting people. And not by hurting a woman who's done a pretty damn good job protecting this community."

I didn't know what surprised me more: the fact the two cousins were having it out in front of me or that Rory had just paid me a compliment.

But Rory wasn't done. "I really thought you'd change after your problems in Santa Cruz. I sincerely hoped you would. But you didn't. You didn't change one little bit. And Paul, I don't think you ever will."

Rory's eyes hardened, and he raised a hand in the air.

A sudden commotion broke out in the sky. The air was filled with the harsh cawing of crows, and a dark cloud of them descended. I stared at Rory, who commanded the flock and directed them to their prey.

The black birds swooped down, diving toward Paul. He threw up his hands and cried out, but the birds pecked and clawed at him. Paul turned and ran. The crows followed, wings beating furiously.

Rory spoke softly while Paul disappeared into the woods. "He's always hated crows."

Well, I had been right. The Tucks *were* hereditary witches, and I had just witnessed the proof. I found myself laughing uncontrollably at the absurdity of it all.

Chapter 38

Hernan Frias summoned me. He had issued the command through Cora, possibly because I couldn't tell her no.

I was making breakfast burritos for my crew, so I wrapped up two more—one for him and one for Marta—and drove to Bishop, muttering all the way. When I walked into his sunlit room at the back of his gloomy house, he was propped up in bed, looking suspiciously well for a man who had just had a stroke.

"No pan dulce?" Hernan's speech was slightly slurred, but he had no problem conveying his annoyance.

I set the foil-wrapped burrito down on the tray in his lap. "Hey, this is a breakfast burrito, señor. No complaining."

Hernan lifted the burrito and sniffed it. "What kind?"

"Chorizo. Chorizo con huevos." I lowered myself into the leather easy chair and braced for the conversation that was to come.

Hernan frowned. "Where did you get the chorizo?"

"The Palo Verde Market butcher counter."

"Good. They know how to make it there." Hernan peeled back the foil. "Con papas?"

I rolled my eyes. "Yes, with potatoes. What kind of horrible person do you think I am that I'd make a chorizo burrito without papas?"

"You're a Bantacorte, aren't you? God only knows what you get up to in the kitchen."

I froze. Hernan was wearing a distinctly sly expression. He unwrapped the top half of the burrito. Did he know about the magic chili?

Hernan sniffed. "I'm not an idiot. I knew the moment I got back to Chavez Ravine that something had changed. That's what the cards told me too. That's why I asked you to come. To see it for myself."

I sat up straighter in my chair. "And do you? See it for yourself?"

Hernan's craggy face seemed to sag. He gave a dejected sigh. "I do. You know, it's not really fair. I've devoted my adult life to learning brujería. Then you just show up one day and start throwing your weight around. And then good ole Lencha takes pity on you and gives you some magic."

He licked a greasy finger and wagged it in my direction.

"I don't know how she did it, but don't you deny it because I can see—no, *feel*—for myself that you're different. Tengo razon?"

"Yes, you're right. That's what happened. Just don't ask me how."

Hernan grunted. "I didn't plan on it. It's more interesting to you than to me." He gave the burrito a poke as if to test how well I had rolled it. "You created your own protection circle around Chavez Ravine, didn't you?"

"I figured it out. No thanks to you."

"Let's just hope it works," Hernan said. "Mine's no good anymore. Not with the condition I'm in. My spell was always a little fragile. When I started getting sick, it seemed to take more and more of my energy to keep it going. I knew it was just a matter of time before it failed."

I got up and cut the burrito in half, then sat back down again. The room was suddenly filled with the savory, spicy aroma of chorizo sausage. Hernan gave an appreciative sniff.

"And yet, knowing your spell would fail, you still refused to help me," I said.

Hernan took a bite of burrito. He chewed slowly, then swallowed. "A real Bantacorte wouldn't need my help."

Ouch. The man might have been ailing, but he could still deliver a jab. It was time to ask the question that had brought me there.

"Hernan, I'd like your thoughts on something, if you could please just be straight with me for once. I don't think this is anything you or I can know for sure, but I'm still curious to know what you think."

Hernan raised his eyebrows. The brujo wasn't above a little flattery, after all. "What about?"

"The entities that appeared here before I put up the protection spell...They didn't suffer the usual disorientation and confusion as the others. These were alert, calculating even, and a lot more dangerous. Why do you think that is?"

Hernan took another bite of burrito and chewed thoughtfully, staring out the window into the garden. "The protection I created was weakened, but it wasn't completely gone. That meant only the strongest and most powerful of them could break through. I think that's why they were different. They were the elite. But like you said, I can't be sure."

I had been thinking along the same lines. "Makes sense. It's possible they even got a little supercharged pushing through the magic."

Hernan shrugged. "Anything is possible with magic. It's not precise. That's what you need to watch out for, Madeline. Cuidate."

Wow. The big man himself had just warned me to be careful. Could that mean he secretly cared? Just a little?

Hernan pushed away the tray and leaned back against the pillows. His eyes fluttered closed. "That was delicious." His voice was hoarse. "Muchas gracias. Come see me another time. Tell me how it's going. And next time, I'll have al pastor."

Yes, Hernan cared. About his stomach.

When I pulled the door shut behind me, he was snoring softly.

Minutes later, I parked the Jeep outside the construction site. I had one more bit of business with Rory Tuck.

He was huddled with a small group of men, going over what looked like blueprints. As I approached, Rory left the group and walked toward me.

"I'm kind of busy right now. If you need something, let's schedule a time to meet later."

"I'm sorry for dropping by without warning, but there's something you need to know. Can we step into your office for just a moment?"

A brief flash of irritation showed the old Rory wasn't too far beneath the surface, but he jerked his head in the direction of the trailer.

Once inside, I didn't waste time. "When you built that new fence to hide the entities in Elysian Park, who decided how tall it would be?"

"I gave that project to Paul, so he decided. What does that matter?"

"One more question: Are you aware we have security cameras along the fence with Elysian Park? And that the cameras are capable of seeing the entrance to this site?"

His eyes narrowed, but his answer came quickly. "No. I don't pay much attention to anything outside my property. I don't get it. What does it matter?"

I took a deep breath. "It matters because someone put tape over the lenses of those cameras. There was something happening they didn't want those cameras to record. And when we removed the tape and got the cameras working again, the fence went up and blocked their view of the project. In other words, someone worked hard to make sure our cameras wouldn't be able to see anything happening on your site."

I paused to let that sink in.

"So, help me out here," he said. "Who would care about the cameras, and what did they have to hide?"

"I can only answer your first question, but when I do, I think you'll be able to answer the second one. I believe your cousin was accepting deliveries in the middle of the night. Several times, trucks came through our gates but didn't come directly to the site. Instead, they'd park on a neighborhood street a few blocks away until after midnight, when they'd come up and empty their cargo. I have security camera footage that shows the movement of the trucks, but thanks to Paul, I don't have footage showing what they were carrying."

Rory's expression went from concerned to confused to angry in about three seconds.

"If I hadn't sent him back to Ireland, I'd wring his skinny little neck. You're right. Now that you've told me that, I *do* know the rest of this story." Rory sat heavily in his chair and slowly shook his head. "As you may know, the Chavez Ravine Association requires us to build using a certain grade of materials. They want to be sure the homes we make are up to a certain standard. It's more expensive for me, but it's worth it to do business in these neighborhoods. So, we order top quality materials and store them in the yard.

"Well, a couple of my guys started noticing that the supplies they unloaded one day would be gone the next. But they didn't just disappear. They'd be replaced by sub-standard versions. Same products, lower quality. Construction sites can have all kinds of theft problems, but I'd never seen anything like that before. And it kept happening. We'd re-order the high-quality materials, and they'd disappear again. We couldn't figure it out, but it was driving up our costs and hurting the schedule."

"And Paul was behind it," I said. "I'm sure you know he got into trouble up in Santa Cruz. Was it the same kind of scheme?"

Rory drummed his fingers on his desk. "Close enough. And it should have been a warning sign for me. I never should have brought him down here. If he ever comes back to this country, he's going to regret it."

He stood up and gestured toward the door.

"Family. You expect the best from them, but you're so often disappointed."

I heard that loud and clear.

Chapter 39

We had gone more than a week without an entity appearing in Chavez Ravine. The rest of Los Angeles had returned to normal, if one could call it that. Entities popped up a few times a day, but Occult Affairs managed to keep it under control.

My team had been through a trial by fire, and they had done beautifully. Morale was high, and the residents were grateful. It wasn't unusual for guards to get high fives while they rode their bikes on patrol. The calm was unlikely to last, but I was determined to savor it as long as I could.

One evening, as I was arriving home, Leo came bounding across the yard. "We won!"

"Hi, Leo. What did you win?"

"No, *we* won, all of us! The rules proposal failed!"

"Oh! That's good news!" And it was, for everyone except Hernan Frias. His proposal to make it harder for non-Latinos to buy property in Chavez Ravine had gone to a vote of the residents, and I was relieved they had done the right thing.

After I fed the cat, I poured a glass of pinot noir and went outside to enjoy the late afternoon sun. I had not checked email for hours, and when I finally did, there was the note from Cora announcing the results of the vote. It turned out well, but it had been close.

Hernan's attempt to increase the Latino population in Chavez Ravine felt like discrimination—the very thing our families had fought against. He would not be happy, but I wondered if he ever was.

Another email from Cora. She was throwing a tamale party at her house, and my team was invited. She had said it was her way of thanking them for keeping the community safe.

I had told Cora about the magic chili and the new protection circle. Naturally, she had been elated, but she couldn't go around telling everyone the HOA's head of security had officially achieved bruja status. It had to stay between us.

And I still wasn't sure what my bruja status entailed. Would the magic just come to me when I needed it? Under what circumstances? Only in life and death situations? Or would it work in less dire cases too? The two times I had used magic, it had required intense mental focus. Most of what happened in life was fairly mundane. Was there such a thing as mundane magic?

There was only one person I could think of who might have the answers, and that was my mother.

She picked up the phone on the first ring. "Hello, mija. I can only talk for a moment because my massage therapist will be here any minute."

That was okay by me.

I gave her the condensed version of my magic chili story. Her reaction was disappointing but not surprising.

"Really? Lencha did that? For you? Aren't you a lucky girl. Now, in my day, we called that skipping the line. I wish she would have done that for me. There was a point in my life when I really could have used it."

I let it go, as I had so many things over the years. "So, Mom, how do you think this is supposed to work? Because it's not like I feel any different. How…magical do you think I am?"

My mother scoffed. "How am I supposed to know?"

"Because you're psychic?"

"Madeline, don't be smart. If you would like to come see me, I would be happy to do a reading. But this is between you and your great-aunt. Unfortunately, I've been left out of it entirely."

I didn't know why I had expected more from her. She was incapable of giving it, but her words still echoed in my head long after we hung up. *Skip the line.* Was that what Lencha had done for me? It did feel like cheating, and it only made my imposter syndrome worse. I had also allowed my mother to make me feel guilty, again, over something that was not my fault.

Now I was a bruja with baggage.

At home, I was the lady who fed the cat and took out the trash. At work, I was the boss who managed a staff, prepared for the unknown, and worried about what would happen to my people if my magic succeeded. The board and the budget wouldn't allow us to continue at the level we were currently operating if there were no entities. Just the idea of layoffs gave me a sense of dread I couldn't shake.

The evening of the tamale party, I wore a new outfit Julia had talked me into: a V-neck wraparound in teal, and silver two-inch heels. When I arrived at Cora's house, the party was in full swing. Much to my surprise and Ron's disappointment, Bailey had invited Malik as her plus one.

My team—except for those currently on shift—gathered in the backyard, drinking Mexican beer and eating chips, ceviche, and guacamole.

When the sun set, string lights flicked on in the backyard. I went inside to see if Cora needed help in the kitchen. It turned out she did, so we chatted while I chopped onions and Cora doled out cheeses and salsas into serving bowls.

"Stu's coming," she said. "And his daughter. I hope you don't mind that I invited them." She shot me a sly look from the kitchen island.

"If I didn't know better, I'd think you were playing matchmaker."

She chuckled. "My kids say I'm better than those silly dating apps." She lowered her voice. "Caitlin is actually the one who told me about you two. She says her uncle really, really likes you." This last bit was said in a sing-song voice.

"Did she?" Note to self. Caitlin, the HOA's redheaded executive assistant, wasn't above gossiping about Uncle Stu.

"She did." Cora crossed to the door, poked her head out, and grabbed a pair of tongs from a drawer on her way back. She lowered her voice. "And apparently, his daughter, Clare, told his ex-wife about his new girlfriend—meaning you—and that upset her."

"That's interesting," I said flatly. "Considering she cheated on him."

"She doesn't sound like a very nice person."

It was time to serve the tamales. I helped Cora round everyone up and steer them into the dining room, where we had set up a buffet. The tamales were keeping warm in several large chafing dishes. Next to them were bowls of rice, beans, salsas, cheeses, and spicy pickled vegetables.

"I've never been to a tamale party that wasn't around Christmas," Ron said, loading up his plate.

"Me neither," Justin replied. "But hey, I'm not complaining. I can't believe I'm eating Cora's famous tamales in Cora's house! My wife was so mad that she and the baby both have colds."

"How's that guy who got bit by the chupacabra?" Liam asked. "Is he out of the hospital yet?"

I nodded. "Ben Tomas. He's much better. He's been home for a few days now." Under the attentive care of Julia, who was thrilled to play nurse.

Bailey and Malik were still outside, huddled together on a wicker loveseat under a string of twinkling lights.

Liam followed my gaze. "Wow. You know how many guys have been after Bailey since I've met her? I lost count. And then that guy shows up with a kitchen torch."

I was about to reply when someone tapped my shoulder. Before I could fully turn around, Clare was throwing her arms around me in a bear hug. She was surprisingly strong. I still wasn't used to so much teenage affection, and I patted her back like I was burping a baby.

Over her shoulder, Stu was grinning at us. When Clare finally released me, his eyes lit up in approval as he took in my dress. His gaze lingered on the V-neck showing just enough without revealing too much. A rush of heat flushed my cheeks, and my heart skipped a beat.

"Wow. You look great." His voice was low and husky.

Clare rolled her eyes. "Yuck. Stop. Children are present."

While we ate, I helped them both remove the corn husks from their tamales. They clearly had no idea what they were doing.

"Have you never had tamales before?" I asked.

"Dad is the most boring eater ever. To be honest, he's not much of a cook, and neither is my mom."

I had no idea how people survived without knowing how to cook.

Clare continued. "Seriously, it's kind of pathetic. I want to learn. You're such a great cook, Maddy. Would you teach me?"

Stu leaned in closer. "Watch yourself. The next thing you know, she'll have talked you into holding cooking classes for her and her friends." His lips brushed my ear, and my knees went a bit weak.

We were interrupted by a clinking of glass. Cora called for everyone's attention so she could make a toast. We all gathered in the living room, holding our plates of tamales and drinks while she raised her glass.

"I just want to say how grateful I am for each and every one of you," she began. "You've gone above and beyond these past few weeks. I think I can speak for all the residents of Chavez Ravine when I say we feel safer because you're here. So, thank you. Now, get back to the food. And save room for dessert!"

As people dispersed, Stu lingered at my side.

"Not to be a downer," he said in a low voice. "But has the board said anything about your new staffing level if we don't have any more entities?" Stu's blue eyes looked troubled.

"Not yet. I won't lie. It's been keeping me up at night."

He winced. "I'd be worried about that too. Eileen Simpson is all about controlling costs."

The same Eileen who had made my early days of employment with the HOA a nightmare.

Stu shook his head. "Enough of that. We're at a party. We should party. Want to find a dark corner and do things?"

I couldn't help but laugh. "That would be the height of professionalism."

"And I'm sure that would win me Father of the Year," Stu joked. His warm hand slid down my back.

We spent the next hour outside, drinking beers with my team. Cora broke out a bottle of Mescal. Her husband, Mateo, a jovial man of around seventy, entertained us with stories of Cora's early ventures in the tamale business.

Toward the end of the evening, I was back in the kitchen to help Cora serve dessert. She had ordered a Mexican sheet cake spiced with cinnamon and topped with chocolate icing. We were sliding squares onto plates when Ron appeared, eyes as wide as saucers.

"Boss, I just got a call from the command center."

A plate slipped from Cora's hand and shattered on the tile floor.

My mind started firing off random thoughts. The protection circle was down. My magic had failed. Another ghoul—or something worse—was on the loose somewhere.

"What is it, Ron? Entities?" My voice sounded faint.

Ron shook his head. "No, boss. Nothing on the heatmap. But we got a call from La Loma. Someone found a body."

And then, just like that, it struck me.

The bad feeling I had been having wasn't due to my newfound magic or my worries about the future of my team. It was something else—something I had been ignoring for the last several days. A sort of dark energy had been gathering and building, and it had just made its presence known.

I quickly said goodbye to Stu and Clare and slipped into a waiting security car. My hands started to emit a faint glow. Whatever was coming, I was ready.

Author's Note

My grandmother had a friend named Lencha, a middle-aged single woman from Mexico who supplemented her income by offering her healing services in Boyle Heights, a neighborhood in East L.A. She was a curandera, a healer, not a bruja.

In my eyes, this quiet woman with the long black braid and simple cotton dresses was magical.

Lencha made a red string bracelet to protect me against La Llorona (the weeping woman of Mexican folklore) and the terrifying boogeyman known as El Cucuy. Thanks to my grandmother's scary stories, I was convinced the only thing that stood between me and those monsters was Lencha's bracelet.

My grandmother's friend was the inspiration for Maddy's great aunt, Lencha Bantacorte. The witchcraft she practiced and passed down to Maddy is rooted in traditions that are a combination of indigenous and spiritual practices from around the world.

As the story evolves, so do Maddy's skills. Of course, my version of brujeria is fiction, but at its heart it's based on this rich history.

Keep Reading for a Preview of

Chapter 1

There's a reason I never considered a career as a homicide detective, and it was lying on the floor of a beautiful Spanish-style home.

Throw any kind of shrieking, spitting, hairy entity at me and I'll be fine, but a body? Yuck.

When I first took the job as head of security for the Chavez Ravine Homeowners Association, murder had been the least of my worries. Entity eruptions and board politics were the things that kept me up at night.

But the unthinkable had happened, and according to the people who found the body, the victim had met a brutal and horrific end.

I was at a party when I got the call. One of my security officers, Ron Mendez, whisked me to the scene in his marked vehicle. I thanked him for the ride, got out, and stared at the house.

Ornamental streetlamps broke the darkness of the summer night. The landscaping was lush, the palm trees majestic. Crickets and a few birds provided a soundtrack for the peaceful setting.

But there had been no peace for the home's owner. Brandon, a sturdy young security officer who had encountered his fair share of terrifying creatures in his short career, stood on the lawn, pale as a sheet of paper.

And then there was Becca Tey. The actress paced back and forth on the driveway, trembling as though it were freezing, not a warm, still evening.

"I can't believe it," she kept repeating. "Who would do that? What would do that? It had to be some sort of animal."

Or entity, I thought. A chill ran up my spine. Chavez Ravine had been entity free ever since I managed to cast a protection spell over the community.

I walked over to Brandon, staying on the pavement due to my heels. "Any sign of a break in?"

He shook his head and pointed to the side yard. A tall hedge separated the victim's house from the Craftsman-style home next door.

"No forced entry as far as I can tell, but there's an open window around back."

The house was situated on a cul-de-sac with three other homes. A hill loomed above the dead-end street. At the summit of the tree-lined ridge stood Elysian Park—a favorite entity hangout. The proximity of the park to the murder scene made me nervous for a whole bunch of reasons.

Several neighbors were outside on their front porches, but for now, they were staying there thanks to Ron. He spoke with them in hushed tones, trying to gather as much information as he could before we ceded control to the LAPD.

"You didn't touch the window, did you?" I asked Brandon.

He scraped a hand through his hair. "Course not. I touched the lady's neck to see if she had a pulse, but I was real careful not to touch anything else."

"You wouldn't happen to have any plastic bags in your vehicle, would you?"

Brandon's eyebrows shot up. The guy was smart. He knew exactly what I had in mind. "As a matter of fact, I do." He jutted his chin out at the neighbors. "Those people will see what you're doing."

I thought for a moment. "Not if you go over there and tell everyone we're calling the police, and they need to wait inside. Tell them it's going to be a long night and there won't be anything to see anyway."

Technically, I had no business going inside. I might be head of security for the gated community in the hills above Los Angeles, but my job had its limits. Homicide was the exclusive domain of the LAPD.

Which was going to be a problem. The police and the residents of Chavez Ravine went through a major rough patch many years ago when the cops enforced the city's eviction order. The passage of time hadn't even put a dent in the resentment that seethed just below the surface. The board—my bosses—had instructed me to keep the cops out of the three neighborhoods that make up Chavez Ravine, no matter what.

Which is a fine policy for the occasional car break-in, but not when you find a dead body. I was going to have to call the police and deal with the board later.

But first, I had a little business to conduct. I headed for the front door.

I was, after all, the head of security. And the board would have questions, so I'd better have answers. Plus, I'm an ex-cop, so investigating comes naturally.

And that's how I rationalized my decision to enter a crime scene I knew was off limits.

Brandon fetched a box of latex gloves and a roll of black plastic bags from the back of his vehicle.

While he sauntered over to deal with the neighbors, I tugged on the gloves and pulled the bags over my heels, securing them around my ankles with rubber bands.

Becca hurried over. "You don't want to go in there."

"Maybe not, but I need to see this for myself." I paused. "How did you happen to find her, Becca?"

Becca was around fifty and the plastic surgery she'd had over the years wasn't aging gracefully. Still, with her flashing dark eyes and long black hair, she was a striking woman.

She sniffed loudly. "We've known each other forever. Her name is Misty Denner. She's a character actor. A really good one. Unlike me, she gets lots of work." There was no trace of bitterness in Becca's voice, just admiration. "She broke her ankle last week on a shoot, so I came over with a bottle of wine and some snacks to keep her company. We were going to watch a movie together."

Misty Denner. I vaguely recognized the name. "Okay. I'm going to take a quick look around, then I'll be right back."

She gave a curt nod, then looked away. I first met Becca when I was fresh on the job, and we were dealing with some scary supernatural creatures. Becca was quirky and had a few bad habits, but she was honest and thoughtful, and I liked her.

"I think I'll go throw up in the bushes again," she said in a small voice. I thought she was joking, but as I walked across the wide porch, the sounds coming from the hedge told me she was not.

The front door was open. Brandon had used the emergency code on the pin pad next to the mailbox.

The moment I crossed the threshold, a pungent odor invaded my nostrils. At first, I thought something in the kitchen had gone bad, but after a few more sniffs, I decided it smelled more like wet, stinky dog.

The house was more than twice as big as mine, but still smaller than many of the others in Chavez Ravine. Misty had leaned into Bohemian decor, with teal painted walls, a mish mash of furniture, an enormous zebra striped rug, and a smattering of brightly colored floor pillows. Two table lamps lit the room.

I took it all in. Very artsy, very much like the woman in the framed photos on the wall. Misty Denner had played quirky, oddball roles on TV and in the movies for years.

Vases of fresh flowers crowded a tile-topped sofa table, along with get-well cards, probably for the broken ankle.

I peered into the kitchen. The lamp light didn't reach quite that far but from what I could make out, it was clean. No lingering cooking odors. A pizza box sitting on top of a trash can suggested Misty had chosen well. Agostino's at La Loma Plaza made a mean pie.

The hall was long and dim with a faint light coming from a room toward the end.

I swallowed hard, dreading what came next. I would just take a quick look and get the hell out. Just a peek to see what we were dealing with, thirty seconds, max, then I would call the police like a good girl.

I mean, if I could deal with entities and monsters, there was no need to freak out about a body, right?

Forcing my shoulders back, I took a deep breath. The plastic bags on my feet crinkled as I walked toward the light.

Within seconds, I was standing outside the murder room trying to take it all in.

A bedside table lit the scene.

Misty Denner was crumpled on the floor at the foot of the bed, head bent at an unnatural angle, her small face bruised. She was wearing shorts and a loose shirt, her thin arms and legs covered in what appeared to be bite marks. Her flesh was smeared with blood.

She was a tiny thing with shoulder-length brown hair that looked dyed. If I hadn't known she was around fifty, I would have guessed I was looking at a teenager.

The foul musty odor I'd noticed when I first entered the house became a thick stench in the bedroom, and it made me gag.

Covering my nose, I dragged my eyes away from the body.

The casement window was large and wide open. Of course, it was open—we hadn't had an entity in Chavez Ravine for some time, and violent crime was unheard of in our community.

Was.

An attacker could have climbed through the window easily. A book on the floor near the nightstand suggested Misty had been reading in bed when he did. Or when it did.

Probably it. This was no ordinary homicide.

My heart sank. The protection spell I had cast to keep Chavez Ravine safe from entities must have failed, letting in whatever monster had done this to poor Misty Denner.

Reluctantly, I picked up my phone and called 911.

Books by Debra Castaneda

Maddy Madrigal Mysteries
Monsters, mayhem, and Mexican food

Barely Magic
Maddy lands a cushy security job in a gated community but must confront a supernatural threat and come to terms with her magical heritage.

Somewhat Magic
In the heart of Los Angeles, Maddy Madrigal battles legendary creatures and unscrupulous developers as an old protective spell begins to fail.

Desperate Magic
Maddy Madrigal must unravel a web of supernatural clues and confront ancient predators to stop a string of brutal murders.

Mortal Magic
Something ancient and deadly is roosting outside Chavez Ravine, and Maddy's weapons, magic, and extremely agitated cat aren't enough to fight it off.

Dark Earth Rising

Themed novels that can be read in any order

A Dark and Rising Tide

When a massive storm surge hits the central coast of California, the ferocious surf destroys buildings, floods streets, and washes up something sinister from the depths of the Monterey Bay.

The Devil's Shallows

Eight miles of mystery. One night of terror. Residents trapped in a remote neighborhood confront the unimaginable.

The Copper Man

Haunted tunnels. Unexplained deaths. Eerie sightings. Decades after The Copper Man killed her brother, Leah Shaw returns to the remote mining town of Tribulation Gulch where a lethal mystery awaits.

The Root Witch

A beautiful forest. A terrifying legend. It's 1986. Two strangers, hundreds of miles apart, grapple with disturbing incidents in a one-of-a-kind quaking aspen forest.

Circus at Devil's Landing

Creatures that howl in the night, a mysterious circus, and a clash between a ringmaster and a woman determined to rescue her captured lover.

The Spore Queen
A charming reporter, an ailing tech mogul, and two strangers hiding secrets are brought together by a mysterious fungus, one that will either save them or destroy them.

Chavez Ravine Novels
Stand-alone novels set in Chavez Ravine, Los Angeles during turbulent times

The Monsters of Chavez Ravine
A 2021 International Latino Book Awards Gold Medal Winner! Before Dodger Stadium, dark forces terrorized Chavez Ravine.

The Night Lady
A rebel curandera, a plucky seamstress, and a young reporter are pulled into the investigation of a killer terrorizing Chavez Ravine.

The Haunting of Chavez Ravine
La Llorona is terrorizing people in the hills of Chavez Ravine, and a sassy curandera and her clever young niece must stop her.

The Christmas Cucuy
It's Christmas Eve, 1949, and Kiki's dreams are about to come true: she'll be singing at Palladium with her old bandmates. But when she threatens her rambunctious son with El Cucuy, her plans change.